IN THE REINS

Carly Kade

In the Reins
A Novel by Carly Kade
Copyright © 2016 by Carly Kade

Author Photograph by Melanie Elise Photography
Cover Photograph vlastas/Shutterstock
Edited by Ann Luu
ISBN: 0996887903
ISBN: 9780996887908
LCCN: 2015917795
Carly Kade Creative, Phoenix, AZ

Carly Kade Creative
Phoenix, Arizona
http://www.carlykadecreative.com

For DD,
I followed my dream.

McKennon Kelly.

He was good with his hands – working on his truck, tucked neatly beneath the hood, shirtless, glistening beads of sweat reflecting the sun.

McKennon Kelly.

He was good with his hands – controlling his horses, thin leather straps looped between gloved fingers, easing tension with a touch to their sweaty, strained necks, a beast's calm inside the width of his palm.

McKennon Kelly.

He was good with his hands – gracefully whisking a fly away from his lemonade, putting his dusty boots up and turning his cowboy hat down.

McKennon Kelly.

I appreciated that he was good with his hands when I imagined, dreamed, thought of him touching my body bare.

McKennon Kelly.

He startled me when I realized I was the object of his long, lingering, heartbreakingly blue electric stare.

PROLOGUE

The anger came later as I drove wildly, blindly, furiously down the expressway going 90 in a 70. My hot tears pooled at the corner of my eyes before overflowing into rivers streaming out and across my mascara-stained cheeks. The painted pavement lines streaked and blurred across the road before me. It wasn't Michael that had me in a rage. It was my life.

I found myself assessing the last 28 years of it, and I couldn't remember a time when I felt happy ... complete. I strained my aching mind, searching its recesses for something that could make me feel whole. It wasn't men; it certainly wasn't being engaged to a dream man (as my friends had called him); it wasn't my career although I'd always wanted to be a writer; it wasn't moving away from home; it wasn't living in another state or being in the big city. I scoured my mind for some trace of anything that really ... *really* made me happy. Blank.

Was I having a pre-midlife crisis? I nodded to myself. *Probably.*

The researcher in me temporarily cast aside, I didn't even know where I was wildly driving to, just far away from there and from him. That was all I knew. The turn of events replayed in my mind. I gripped the wheel tighter and pressed the pedal harder.

CHAPTER ONE

"I'm through, and I'm leaving," I said flatly.

"Where do you think you're going?" Michael countered, catching me by the crook of my arm, eyeing the pulled-out empty drawers of my dresser.

"I found this," I replied, emotionless, wiggling myself out of his grasp, and tossing the piece of crumpled paper I had been clutching onto the hardwood floor beside his shiny Prada-wielding feet.

I delivered this discourse with certain calm, more so than I imagined I would have, after pacing our studio apartment waiting for him to come home. I always knew something wasn't quite right between us. There never was that fire in our relationship that lit me up and made it impossible for me to live without his touch. I believed that sort of burning desire between a man and a woman was possible all of my life. I was disappointed to the point of paralysis to not have found that with the man I intended to marry. All this time, and I never did anything about it ... until now.

"What is this?" he retorted with a grunt, bending down to retrieve the ball of shame from the floor.

I watched his eyebrows crease and form a 'V' as he reread the delicate handwriting that wasn't my own. He didn't look at me. I didn't want him to.

"We weren't meant to be," I said, glazing my embarrassment at finally acknowledging it. I placed my two carat pillow-cut engagement ring, reflecting brilliance in the overhead lighting, on the nightstand.

Without remorse, I turned my back to him and lifted my bags off the plush king-size bed that we'd never share again.

Luckily, I didn't have much to pack. I'd made a habit of living life light. I decided in college that I didn't want material things to weigh me down. I was committed to investing in the expansion of my mind rather than my possessions. Never did I think that, in the end, it would be a person who kept me tied down. In this moment though, I felt surprisingly free, surprisingly not angry, and surprisingly glad that fate found a way for me to get out of this lackluster relationship.

Fate always did that for me. It always extracted something from my life and replaced it with another choice to make before I allowed myself to circle the ring, prepared for the emotional beat up. I'd known that I didn't want to be with Michael for a long time. I just kept hoping that something or someone would change.

It became glaringly obvious. I had to be that change.

"Devon, let's talk about this," he said, his lovely brown eyes showing only a hint of conscience.

I'd always hated that about him. He could never fully admit that he was in the wrong. He was able to justify his actions every single time, at least in his own mind, and I'd forgive him every time. He always took my breath away, looking at me, seducing me with those lovely brown eyes.

Mud. His eyes are the color of mud.

"Michael … Don't. Neither of us wants this. I feel it. I know you do too. Let's not fight. Not tonight. Not anymore. Just let me go."

I didn't beg or plea. This was a matter of fact.

"Where will you go, Devon?" he sneered.

"I don't know."

I shut the door behind me gently, knowing it was the last time I would walk through it. I sighed and took my first step toward change.

CHAPTER TWO

Wake up!
Lost in thought, I failed to acknowledge the sea of red lights in front of me because I was reliving the past, pedal forced flat, physically going forward fast but mentally going backwards, excelling my mind in rewind.

Brake lights flashed from every direction, and in the distance, an 18-wheeler veered across all three lanes of the expressway. I snapped out of my head, into action, just in time to jerk the steering wheel to the right, right off the blacktop, and into the dirt patch on the side of the road. I missed the car ahead of me by millimeters. I threw my whole self against the steering wheel, my shoulders slumped, tears burning the corners of my eyes, searching for breath, my stomach a nervous knot.

What the heck, Devon! You have a breakup on your hands, not a death wish.

Finding the will to gather myself, I wiped my puffy eyes with the heel of my hand, staining the cuffs of my white shirt with mascara and looked up.

There it was … fate … again. It was knocking on my door, ringing my doorbell.

Ding, ding, ding.

There I sat, black streaked down my face, spun out on the side of the road, dust still settling around my car, focusing on what sprawled out in front of me. Shock and awe took hold as I let my vision adjust through the dirty windshield. There before me, several horses were grazing in a lush meadow speckled with lavender clover, just a yard or two from the fence in front of me. A few of them took notice and picked up their heads, ears pricked forward, contemplating my little car idle on the side of the road.

My mind burst awake in an instant. I felt alive in a way that I hadn't felt in years, having run my car off the road, avoiding a freak accident and now staring out into a field of horses.

Suddenly, I was aware. I was back in my apartment in the city, rereading my brainstorming journals, taking note of the millionth time I'd scrawled, '*I will have a horse again!!!*' across the top of one of my writing projects. I was conscious of all the times I'd aimlessly doodled a horse on pieces of scrap paper while I was on the phone with a friend from back home, sipping red wine in the wee summer night hours. I was a child again, five, six, seven … 10 years old, playing with model horses in the bathtub, taking riding lessons at the local farm, joining a 4-H horse club, begging my parents for a horse for years and then shockingly receiving one for my birthday. Yes, my parents provided the perfect childhood mount.

It was fate. The universe, my universe, had spoken and heaved me in front of this random horse pasture in my desperate, frantic, altered, life re-evaluation state. I reflected back to being a teenager, lost among my peers, and, in the midst of my parent's divorce, feeling completely incomplete until I was out at the barn riding my horse. My childhood horse silenced my doubt, that inner nagging voice, and lifted me out of the darkness for so many of my adolescent years. She taught me how to succeed and gave me my first taste of success in our small town show ring.

It occurred to me that when I sold Cricket to move to the city, I lost part of myself, a part of me that I desperately missed, but locked deep down inside of me. I thought I wanted a career, a career in the city writing fabulous articles for fabulous magazines. In the end, I had chosen to live where horses could not have a place in the feature story.

In preparation for my new life, I had boxed up every trophy, ribbon and picture, leaving Cricket packed away from my heart in a basement back home. I walked with a blind eye past the horses for hire in the park. I refused to watch movies about horses. I found myself welling with tears when I watched the pegasus leap out and unfold its wings at the beginning of the DVDs I rented. I cried when I went to the Belmont Stakes and heard the roar of hooves down the racetrack.

Horses … Horses made me happy, complete.

Then and there, in the middle of some state, in a wild state of being, I vowed I would own a horse again. With a new sense of direction, I steered my car back on the highway, gingerly maneuvered gaps in the traffic jam, boldly crossed the grassy median, and took the first exit south.

CHAPTER THREE

The choice to steer south set off a whirlwind of activity when I crossed the state line two months ago. First, I rented a small apartment and set up my office in the spare room.

Being a writer afforded me great freedom. I cherished that I could write from anywhere and whenever inspiration struck me. My editor was only a speed dial away. I felt fortunate that I had a modest savings account that I hadn't told Michael about to fall back on as my last project had been a moderate success. I had written a vegetarian diet cookbook, a companion piece to an article of mine that had been published in Organic Lifestyle magazine. I knew I could sustain my dream horse and myself for a decent amount of time until my next assignment came in. Once I was settled into a space of my own, I did what I do best. A writer knows how to research. So I researched.

I researched horse breeds and bloodlines on every equine website I could find. I watched lessons from top horse trainers and read every horse magazine under the sun. I frequented local tack shops then I bought everything I knew I would need for my future horse online. You name it, I did it. I discovered a favorite website, www.HeavenSentHorse.com, and scoured through the sale ads, looking for something that would strike me.

Time and time again, I found myself returning to the breed of my youth, the western pleasure prospect. I sorted through what felt like thousands upon thousands of online ads for Quarter Horses, but, in the end, it was the flare of the color breeds that I really loved. I found myself typing '*Palomino*' and '*Paint*' into the equine search engines. I knew fate would guide me again. I knew it was just a matter of time before fate would lead me to the right horse at the right time.

I researched incessantly that second month, soaking every-thing in, putting everything I had out there, and nothing spoke to me. I did this for hours upon hours, day after day, staying up way too late, and waking up way too early. I was a woman obsessed. I was so consumed that I didn't have time to think of Michael or the male species in general, and I was grateful for that.

One particular morning, I swore off the whole empty search and sat down at my laptop with a steaming cup of aromatic coffee to work on an article I had been assigned for a woman's magazine about eating organic. I was typing midsentence when one of my search engine alerts popped up, telling me new horses had been added to HeavenSentHorse.com that matched my criteria. I mini-mized the bubble and sat back.

It had been a few days since any new horse ads had been posted to the site. I had browsed every horse within a three-state radius, and nothing had appealed to me. I took a long sip from my over-sized coffee mug, swallowed, and inhaled deeply.

Could this be it?

I had plunged myself into the world of horses for the past two months and nothing had inspired me, especially not the fact that the value of a finished, well-trained horse had almost doubled in price since the days of my childhood.

So much had changed.

My mind went into overdrive, and I started to reason with myself, debating the pros and cons of being in the market for a horse right now. It was all so different, and my research told me that I had so much to learn. This business of horses seemed foreign to me now that I was an adult, from the price range of a good horse to the way I noticed people were riding. Things had evolved while I'd been busy building my life in the city.

With a roll of my eyes and a defiant grunt, I shoved those thoughts into the back of my head and told the negative voices to quiet down. I knew what I wanted, and I wasn't going to talk myself out of this. I gulped the last of my light roast, a nice caffeine buzz settling in, and leaned forward, directing the mouse to the link in my inbox.

The click took me to a single result. I'd had better days with nearly 50 overpriced horse pictures staring back at me, but today, this one ad took me by surprise. It didn't feature a picture and only had a solitary line of text.

It read, '*Cute Paint with a Great Personality. $1,800. Must Sell.*'

No way.

The horses I had been looking at were all priced well over $7,500. For a mere $1,800, my assumption was that this horse must be scary looking or ill or half dead or worse.

Then I looked at the address. It was stabled only 20 minutes from my apartment. Intrigued, I read further and, below the ad, it listed bloodlines. Because of my diligent research, I recognized the quality immediately. I was astonished at the beyond reasonable price on this animal.

There had to be something wrong with it, I tilted my head in contemplation and looked out the window, *or could this be fate calling?*

I picked up my cell and dialed the number.

CHAPTER FOUR

Two and a half months after leaving Michael and the big city, I found myself walking into a stranger's barn and paying for a horse sight unseen. Most horse people would call me crazy.

Invitation's Sealed with a Kiss was her registered name, but they called her Faith. She was a bright, spirited, young Paint mare, and I fell in love with her instantly.

She was incredibly pretty with bay and brown patches over white puzzled across her body. Her coloring was referred to as tobiano so they told me. She had an abstract heart-shaped spot on her neck.

These days, I was all about connection. I had it with Faith, the moment she put her muzzle on my shoulder and blew warm breath into my ear. I knew I would never be in a relationship with human or animal that lacked connection again. I wasted three years of my life living a connectionless lie with Michael. With 30 lingering around the corner and a broken engagement on my resume, I realized, maybe for the first time, how clear it was that I only had this one wild, precious life. I intended to live it fully from here on out.

Bring on the fear, bring on fully living. Devon Brooke, this is your time! Your chance to change your ways! I want it all.

All at once, I was a horse owner. I knew Faith was young and needed a lot of conditioning before I would have myself a finished show horse, but it was a journey I looked forward to, relished in. I knew that with hard work came great reward, and I knew that I had found the horse that would take me where I wanted to go. It had always been my dream for as long as I could remember to own a horse that had the talent to compete at a world-level horse competition. Fate whispered to me that Faith was just that horse.

I trusted my instincts. They hadn't abandoned me during those years I had been away from the equine scene; I still knew a good one when I saw one. It came from a place innate in me.

Or call it fate.

As luck would have it, Faith's previous owners also agreed that we were a perfect fit. They even offered to continue to stable her until I was able to find a suitable facility. They kept the price tag on her board low, happy that she was going to a good home, not to mention the fact that I was reducing the size of their costly herd. Relieved that I had Faith safely stored for another month, I settled in at doing what a writer does best.

Again, I researched.

I asked everyone from tack shop clerks to feed store managers if they knew of any private barns in my area. I was in search of a peaceful environment, one without the chaos that comes with multiple horse owners boarding their horses under one roof.

I needed a quiet place, off the beaten trail, almost a sanctuary, where I would have a chance to process, to think, to let the grudge of the city and Michael fall away from me. I needed to let the frenzy of a fast-forward life slip away. I wanted the slick the city left on my skin, my life, my soul to melt away under the silence of a country horse farm. I wanted to experience lack of expectation and judgment as I bonded with my new mare, to see what I really remembered about being a horse owner (if anything at all), to be free of the scrutiny of other riders and the herds of gossipers that claimed to be riders at upscale boarding facilities.

In my search for the isolated space I craved, only one was brought to my attention, and I pulled into the driveway nervous.

What if I were rejected by the owner for the thing I wanted most? What if I were turned away for the very same reason I sought this barn out? All I wanted was to be alone with my thoughts and my animal. Maybe they wanted that too and that would make me the intruder.

I knew I wanted to care for Faith myself. I wasn't expecting someone to do those chores for me. I wanted – *no*, needed – to get dirty, not city-slick dirty, but earth dirty, hard-work dirty. I wanted to know Faith, inside and out. I wanted to know how much water she drank during the day, how much feed it would require to put weight lost from training back on her, the nutritional content of the hay she received. I wanted to clean her stall and have the satisfaction of sweat running down my back, leaving salty, damp trails along my spine. I didn't want anyone else to know her needs better than I did. I wanted to reconnect with my roots. I wanted to be a bona fide cowgirl this time around.

I walked sheepishly from my car toward the establishment, passing up the temptation to drag my feet through the dirt. Once I crossed the threshold of the barn doors and moved into the cool shadows, I had to adjust my eyes, the transition from bright sunlight threw me off. In adjusted focus and upon first impression, the barn was quiet, almost lonely, and I knew it was exactly what I needed.

I looked from left to right. The grand 20-stall barn stood almost empty, the lush pastures uninhabited, not a person in sight. As I pushed down the cement aisle, I heard a rustling in one of the box stalls and noticed a lone worker tending to the bedding.

I asked him if the owner was available. He didn't lift his head to look at me as he motioned his pitchfork.

"Over there," he said under his breath.

I looked in the direction of his tines and saw in the distance, at the top of a lush hill of green grass, a woman perched at a picnic table under the shade of a large tree wearing a big floppy hat.

I said nothing more to the stable hand as I turned and glanced again around the stable. The space gave me the lingering sense that something good had happened here, but was since long gone. As staff emerged from the shadows, their soft half smiles were those of the ones who were left to tend the ghostly premises, their eyes seemed all knowing, but their voices I knew would not be telling. I felt like they might be protecting something, afraid of something, longing for something. I didn't need to know their story.

If I could bring Faith here, I would respect them and their silences as somehow I knew they would do the same for me. Whatever happened here, I would leave them to their secrets and their silences to mind myself and occupy only my small space.

I even felt compelled to share in the sadness of the place. I would linger between the rustle from the stalls and the billow of the breeze. I would become a part of this silence. I would enjoy the quiet peace here that only nature dares breach. I wanted to disappear, to be nobody, even though I once had a life where I thought I was somebody. I felt strongly that this feeling somehow linked me to the people still staying on here.

I took a deep, steadying breath in the shadows of the barn, turned to the sunlight, and walked toward the woman. As I approached, she did not stir. She seemed locked in place, entranced by something. Once I reached the crest of the hill, I saw that she was looking down on an arena where, amidst a whirl of dust clouds, a man was working with what looked like a young colt.

"Excuse me," I said, breaking her trance.

She turned to me, and, under the brim of her considerable hat, she wore a smile. This woman was much older than I would have expected for someone who owned a horse farm.

Much too old to ride without breaking a fragile bone.

She was delicate. Her skin was paper thin, peach and luminescent, so transparent that I could see the blue blood working through the veins in her hands. Her clothing was exquisite, and each skinny finger bore a glimmering bauble. She was the perfect Southern belle. Her gossamer white sheath of a dress clung to her slight, frail body, spilling over the edge of the picnic table, fluttering on the light humid breeze.

I couldn't help but think that I might break her if I spoke too loudly. When she finally addressed me, it was in a sweet, low, musical voice.

"I just love it when he starts working with the young ones."

She met my eyes. Hers were cloudy blue sapphires cloaked by the soft wrinkles that accompanied well-cared-for elder skin. I was taken aback by her beauty. Age had been good to her.

Straining to see, I squinted down into the arena. I was shocked that she could see what the man was doing down there until I noticed the pocket-sized pair of binoculars hidden under the palm of her right hand.

I offered my hand to her and introduced myself.

"I am Devon Brooke, ma'am."

She reached out to me with her dainty, crooked fingers and gave me a squeeze.

"I am Sophia Matilda Washington-Clark. Please just call me Sophia. Why don't you tell me a little about yourself, dear? Maybe you can start with why you're here," she said, inquisitively.

Here it is! My window of opportunity. It's now or never, Devon.

I felt ready. The clerk at the local tack store warned me that I'd only have one chance to convince her to take on a boarder. I practiced what I would say at this moment over and over. It began with Cricket, skipped over Michael, covered the moment of enlightenment in front of the horse pasture, and ended with finding Faith.

This is it.

I crossed my fingers behind my back and silently prayed I'd deliver a good pitch.

CHAPTER FIVE

"...So that's how I came to learn about Green Briar, Sophia," I said, nervously, wiping my brow.

Sophia pursed her time-lined lips and cocked her head in thought. She considered me for quite some time.

Please say yes ... please say yes ...

Finally she spoke. "You can keep your horse here," she said, nodding. "You seem like a very nice girl. I'm intrigued by your story."

Devon, you can stop holding your breath now!

She looked me up and down, narrowing her eyes as she surveyed me.

She spoke sweetly again but had a slight sound of hurt in her voice as she continued. "Just mind your p's and q's. Don't mean we aren't a friendly bunch, but we are a pretty private group out here. I take it that is what you are looking for though."

"Oh, yes, ma'am," I said, trying not to sound desperate.

I wanted this place. I wanted to suck in all of its secrecy and make it my own. I didn't want to have to explain my life, my breakup, my breakdown, my missed years of horse knowledge. I wanted to be a part of the private bunch, yet separate, alone.

"And don't bother with him either." She jutted her chin toward the arena. I was shocked. I didn't want to bother with any "hims."

"You don't have to worry about that, ma'am. I will be sure to keep to myself out here."

"Well, I believe you, dear, but just so you know," she paused to emphasize her point. "He is a cowboy through and through. He breaks his horses and then breaks hearts six ways sideways. Done it to everyone out here, and he'll do it to someone new, too."

Sophia sighed. It was a breathy, heavy sigh. I wanted to bottle it and sell it; it sounded so pretty.

"I have a soft spot for him so I let him keep on here, but he takes a little piece of my heart every time he goes. I can't help adoring him, but I've learned after all these years not to count on the cowboy types."

I didn't know what kind of confession she was sharing with me. I wanted to ask her what she meant by "when he goes," but I remembered her instruction to mind my p's and q's. I wasn't about to throw away the perfect place for Faith and me over a question about some guy that I didn't care to know standing a quarter of a mile away in an arena. I looked at the ground and swiped my boot across the blades of grass, watching each one snap back to place, tall reaching for the sun.

"So, I'll have her shipped in tomorrow then?"

She gave me a single nod and turned back to the arena. She must have heard him approaching. I was either too excited about Faith's new surroundings or too confused about Sophia's lecture to notice that he had made his way up the hill and heard the tail end of our conversation. He stood a few feet from me, sweaty bay horse in tow, staring at Sophia.

"McKennon," she paused to acknowledge him and pressed her thin pink lips together. "I will discuss it with you this evening."

Sophia motioned toward me with both beautiful hands, the ones I couldn't stop looking at, and said, "This is Devon."

He turned his electric blue, weathered eyes on me and shot an untrusting glare. He shook his head, dark hair matted to his neck under a straw cowboy hat, pushed a heavy breath through his fine-lipped mouth then clucked to the horse, cueing him forward and disappeared over the backside of the hill toward the barn.

I couldn't help but watch him walk away, thin white shirt stuck to his sweaty back and molded to his wiry muscular frame. He was statuesque in the sunlight, a willing horse at his beck and call, anger evident in every step he took.

I wondered after him for a moment and then shook my head free.

Not my problem.

CHAPTER SIX

I t was a rainy Sunday when I moved Faith to Green Briar. I pulled in the driveway behind the horse-moving van, surveying the landscape. The farm looked like a ghost town. My eyes swept the grounds, looking for any signs of movement ... nothing.

Good. The staff must have Sundays off.

I climbed out of my car and motioned to the van driver to give me a moment. I wandered into the dark, damp barn, feeling the walls for light switches. Fumbling along, I finally flipped a switch, and the lights burned to life above me.

In front of me, on a dry erase board, was a cryptic, chicken-scratched note. It read, *'Pick any stall you want. On the other side,'* and it was signed, *'McKennon.'*

"Huh, the other side," I wondered aloud, allowing one eyebrow to rise.

I took a deep breath.

'On the other side' meant the aisle running parallel to the side where I assume all of Sophia's horses were kept. I had my pick of the 10 uninhabited stalls in the 20-stall barn. I browsed each one carefully, admiring their varnished sheen, touching the hardware on each door, feeling its cool purpose, gripping the bars jail-style and pulling myself up to peer down into them, looking over each board to make sure nothing was out of place that could injure my Faith.

Each stall was in impeccable condition. I could tell that someone had taken great pride in creating the layout of the barn and only selected the best materials to construct it from. I settled on a stall near the tack room and closest to the riding arena, better to mind my p's and q's if I don't have to wander too far to get to any one place.

As the moving truck idled outside with Faith inside, I began opening bags of wood shavings to bed down her stall. When I finished, I put my hands on my hips and nodded in approval over my stall choice and the fact that I still remembered how to bed one down.

When I unloaded Faith, she came off the trailer calmly and stood in the driveway for a moment, lifting her head and breathing in deeply. As I led her into the barn, her new home, I noticed her eyelashes were wet with the misty rain and that she looked alert, happy.

I unclipped the lead line and released her into her stall. She put her head down and moved the shavings around with her muzzle before lying down in the deep bedding with a contented, heavy sigh. She liked it here. I bid the movers goodbye, paid them the extra required for a Sunday delivery and set to settling us in.

I took comfort in the fact no one was around to scrutinize me on my first day here. I was able to take it all in gradually and in my own way. I breathed in the sweet alfalfa sweeping down from the hayloft on the cool, stormy breeze. I listened to the horses rustle, comfortable in their stalls, and I held my arms out to the soft rain. I felt clean standing in the open doorway of Faith's new home, looking out on green grass soaking up the light drizzle as far as the eye could see.

And then roaming back in the stable, there was Faith, her smell, her warm breath on my cheek, her easy, happy breathing, her soft coat. I ran my fingers through her mane and held them there, tangled in its soft, white tresses.

I was overwhelmed with a calm I hadn't felt in years. I heard the bird's song, the leaves billowing on the breeze, and noticed the dew drops on blades of grass. I didn't have to strain to notice these things here, they were just glaringly apparent. There weren't any horns blowing, machinery operating, people bustling to and fro, running you down if you missed a beat.

This was no city. This was the country. And in this moment, I was the country's girl.

As I was arranging the last of my online spending spree in the tack room, Sophia called. I answered my phone, and again she hypnotized me with her angelic voice.

"I see you have arrived and are acquainting yourself with our place."

She paused, and I wondered what she meant by *our* place. By tuning an ear into small-town gossip, I had gleaned some information on Sophia and this place from eavesdropping on locals.

I learned her husband had once run the town and passed away many, many years ago. He had left his young wife everything. She refused to remarry although, apparently, there had been many suitors when she was younger, presumably after her money or her body or both. Rumor has it she had gone to pieces after her husband's death, her love for him stronger than her will to live, and stopped eating. Something brought her back, but no one knew what made her decide to want to live again.

Sophia began speaking again, lifting me out of my thoughts and melting my heart with each syllable spoken.

"The staff have Sundays off here," she advised. "If you have any questions on Sundays, please reach out to me. Wander the ranch and get yourself familiar. I trust you, or you wouldn't be here, and for those I trust, nothing is off limits. I have great instinct when it comes to people. The horses are another story. Do we have a deal?"

"Yes, ma'am," I said into the phone.

"Dear, please call me Sophia," she said, so softly and gently, it sounded like a request, but I knew it was an order. She was the law on this land, and I knew she got her way on her farm.

"Yes, Sophia. Thank you," I said, grateful. "I love it here already."

"And oh, I wanted to mention that you won't be seeing McKennon for a while. He left very early this morning."

"No problem. Thank you for checking in with me, Sophia. I know this is going to work out for both of us."

"Have a nice day, dear. Enjoy." With that, she hung up.

Why did she keep calling my attention to this man? What exactly was his role here on the farm anyway?

I didn't know, and I vowed to mind my own business as I had promised to do. Again, I shook off the puzzling statement about some man I didn't care to know, probably a thousand miles away from my horse and me now.

CHAPTER SEVEN

There was truth to Sophia's words. I didn't see the McKennon fellow once in the first months I'd been at her barn. I had fit in nicely, and even gotten friendly with one of the farm hands, JD McCall. I had settled into a routine with Faith. I spent my days with her and found myself with plenty of time to write. I felt comfortable in my new surroundings.

For the first two months, I would arrive in the morning to feed Faith and clean her stall, and while she was finishing her breakfast, I would always set up my laptop at the picnic table at the top of the hill to write. It was a lovely view overlooking the empty, lonely riding arena. It was so peaceful; the words would just flow out of me.

I had completed several writing assignments since moving here, and my editor couldn't have been more pleased. She told me that my writing was better than it had ever been and asked me why I hadn't left the city sooner. New exciting assignments were pouring in, and I loved losing myself in the topics. My finances were sounder than they had ever been, and I couldn't help but throw my head back and laugh.

Fate. Fate had done it again.

I would work until mid-day or until the words stopped coming easily, whichever happened first, and then I would set my attention to Faith again.

Ah, Faith ...

It had been a hard two months because I was beginning to realize, despite my diligent research, I wasn't a horse trainer. Faith was sweet, affectionate, trusting, steadily gaining muscle and changing before my eyes. Best of all, we were bonding. She would prick her ears up and whinny when she heard me enter the barn in the mornings, but, on the flipside, she would test me every chance she got.

Occasionally, while I was brushing her, she would lean into me with such force that I'd wind up pinned to the wall, crushed, and gasping for air. Other times, she would resist me by standing with all four of her legs locked and wouldn't budge against my best efforts to pull, drag, bribe her into moving forward. She would swing her body this way and that to avoid being saddled. During some occasions, I would actually be riding her, and she would back up the entire distance of the riding arena when I thought I was cueing her to walk ahead.

I was growing frustrated but remained optimistic that we could work through these behaviors. I figured the end result would be so much sweeter if I had to work hard with her to achieve it. I reminded myself she was young.

Then McKennon came back ...

My heart surprised me when it fluttered as he swept by fresh from the road with an air of indifference.

Whatever. I committed to continue my daily routine with Faith uninterrupted.

One particular morning was no different than the rest as I exercised her on a lunge line. Faith moved around me in circles, performing the walk, trot and canter until she suddenly decided that she was going to dart into the center with ears pinned as if she were angry and wanted to bite my head off. Frustrated, I hung my head and ran my fingers through my long auburn ponytail.

"You little *snot!*" I shouted at her as she challenged me from the other end of the rope.

Defeated, I shook my head. Again, I found myself not knowing what to do with her.

"Don't let her do that to you."

"What?" I said, turning on my heels, letting the lunge whip fall to the dirt.

He surprised me.

"I said, don't let her do that to you."

McKennon was nonchalantly leaning against the railing of the arena.

How long had he been there?

"What?" I said again like an idiot, heat coming quickly to my cheeks.

"Look," he said, running his gloved hands over his chest to smooth his formfitting plaid shirt. "You have to show her you are the boss, or she is going to walk all over you. Whip her in the ass."

I picked up the whip and flicked it gently in Faith's general direction, missing her completely.

"I said, whip her *in the ass!*" he shouted, his voice startling me into action.

I heaved the end of the whip at her hindquarters, connecting with a crack, and she lurched forward, turning her head toward the center of the circle, eyeing me as if to say, 'Where did that come from? You are usually such a pushover!'

Faith moved and performed each gait perfectly without testing me again. McKennon stood silently at the fence with one dusty cowboy boot up on the lowest rail. He hooked his thumb in his belt loop, silver belt buckle gleaming in the high noon sun, and watched us.

I could feel his eyes on me. His stare felt like an arrow through my back, a bullet in my chest, each time I pivoted to follow Faith with my new whip weapon around and around. My stomach churned, and I was nervous. I felt my heart beating wildly inside my chest, and I noticed I was holding my breath. I hid my face beneath the brim of my baseball hat. I didn't want him to know that I wasn't wearing makeup.

What am I doing? Breathe, Devon, breathe! What do you care what he thinks? He will be gone again soon just like Sophia told you. Ignore him. Get yourself together. Hmmm, his advice did work though.

I was so busy finishing the conversation with myself in my mind and completing Faith's exercise for the day that I didn't even notice that McKennon had walked away.

I led Faith back to the barn, her sweaty, frothed coat smelling of fly repellant and salt. I guided her into the wash rack and proceeded to spray her down with cool water, letting the small training session settle into my brain.

I WAS a pushover. Yikes.

CHAPTER EIGHT

In the days following my little lesson with McKennon, it started to feel like all walls had eyes. Whether I was cleaning Faith's stall, bathing her in the wash rack, talking to her as I spoiled her with choice treats, or *attempting* to ride her, I could feel a constant presence. It was one that I wasn't accustomed to and didn't especially like. I knew McKennon was watching me, even though I never caught a glimpse of him.

Was this a game?

He brought his spying to my attention on a perfectly lovely mid-morning while I was perched in my favorite spot in a serene state of mind, hammering away at my laptop, putting down some of the best written lines of my career.

The seat of the picnic table bowed with his weight, popping me out of my trance, and there he was, sitting down next to me like poetry.

"I've been watching you and that horse," he said with an expressionless tone.

I couldn't bear to look at him, so I kept my eyes on the screen. I was leery of this man yet incredibly aware of his being.

His velvet voice riveted through me. I blushed beneath my hat.

Great, so he is fully aware, as is Faith, that I am completely incompetent and have no idea what I am doing!

My mind began to spin out of control again, accompanied by that throbbing heartbeat I remembered so well after I whipped Faith in the ass.

When was he watching me? Where was he hiding? Why doesn't he mind his own business? How do I respond to him when just his presence sends my pulse surging?

"Yeah ... I've sensed it."

Was that really the best I could come up with?

"She ain't a bad mover, you know," he said a little too optimistically.

My writer's mind cringed at his use of 'ain't.' I gasped as he ducked his head attempting to catch a glimpse of me hiding from him beneath the brim of my baseball hat.

Damn! I should start wearing at least a little makeup to the barn. Oh, shut up! You aren't out here to impress anyone!

"What're you writing?" McKennon inquired as he pointed the index finger of his lamb-skinned glove at my laptop, making circles in front of the screen in a teasing fashion, slight upturn to the corner of his mouth.

My eyes narrowed.

Was this cowboy even interested in the written word?

From somewhere inside of me, I shook off the nervous energy festering in my gut at his immediacy and slammed my computer shut. In a mighty gust of libido, I turned toward him and squared my shoulders with his. Confounded by my abrupt gear shifting, McKennon pulled back, eyes wide, and I looked upon him for the first time up close.

And he was ... *beautiful.*

I examined the smooth contour of his face, the rigid jaw line, the perfectly dished nose, the slight stubble of a day-old shave prickling from a square chin, his hair, dark beneath his cowboy hat, showing the signs of an overdue haircut, twisting into slight curls at the base of his skull, the blue eyes that looked like weather. He was so alarmingly well proportioned. It was heart stopping.

I couldn't stop looking into his eyes. They were rimmed with dark, long eyelashes that made me for a moment regret my own lack of mascara again. I tilted my head to the side and observed how, at the same time, his eyes were rimmed with lines – happy lines, stretching upward, the kind of lines that appear from years of laughing and beatings from the sun.

He was locked on my eyes too. I was hypnotized. The moment felt electric and made my spine tingle.

McKennon's lips, pressed together in surprise, were fine, supple and sexy. He let his pink tongue moisten them as if to speak and then thought better of it. He stopped leaning toward me and sat up straight as an arrow, running his gloved hand up his long, tan arm.

His skin was bronze and manly, smelling of horses and hard work, the perfect mixture of damp earth and the last trace of morning's cologne. I took a deep breath, holding his scent in my nostrils a little longer than a sane person should have. If I were his woman, I would hold his shirts to my face before throwing them in the washing machine just to smell him.

I clutched my hands to my lap because an overpowering place in me wanted to stroke his face. He was blinding in his construction, but I continued to look at him long and hard for about a minute.

I turned back to my laptop, flipped it open, and felt the words leap from my lips in an accusing tone.

"Why are you watching me?"

With that, McKennon rose from the picnic table, slowly, parting his lips painfully, gripping the brim of his cowboy hat with a gloved hand and tipping it to me.

"Uh ... I didn't mean to bother you, ma'am."

I looked after him as he walked away. His jeans were just the right kind of tight, and he had a slight bow to his long legs, spurs jingling with his stride as he again disappeared over the backside of the hill, hightailing it for the refuge of the stables.

I leaned forward, putting my chin in the palm of my hand, elbow cocked on the table, supporting the weight of my now-heavy face.

What on earth just happened?

CHAPTER NINE

I called Sophia.
"Hello, darling!" she gushed from the end of the line.

Her honey-like voice paired well with my moderately expensive red wine buzz and calmed me down instantly. Why she liked me, I didn't know, but she soothed me like a long lost grandparent, and I secretly hoped that I would amount to something like her in my old age.

"Sophia," I sputtered into the receiver.

"Darling, I sense you are awry. Tell me what happened immediately!"

Sophia had become my confidant. When I was stuck with an article, I would call her. When I was fed up with Faith, I would call to review all the ways that my mare was challenging my authority. Sophia never had any real advice, claiming that she didn't know a damn thing about horses or writing for magazines, but she would always listen, and I appreciated it.

"Sophia. Something just happened with McKennon."

"Oh! Well, out with it, dear."

"He told me he was watching me with Faith," I mewled.

"How do you feel about that?" Sophia inquired.

"I don't *think* I like it. I was kind of harsh with him."

"Hmm," she said, purring at me through my cell phone.

I wished I could speak the way she did. It was hypnotic.

"I know I don't often have any real advice to offer you, but when it comes to McKennon, I can tell you this," she said, and I leaned into the phone, straining, afraid to miss a single syllable.

"If McKennon is taking an interest in your horse, it must mean that you've got a good one. He doesn't waste his time with un-talented animals or with untalented people, for that matter. He will always assess a horse first, and then he'll examine the per-son attached to it. He thinks that people with a good head on their shoulders are the only ones who wind up with the really good animals."

"So he wasn't being creepy?" I pressed.

"Honey, I don't think McKennon Kelly could be creepy if he tried. He is just a good ol' boy looking to make his mark on the horse world. He has talent, but he has no idea what to do with it anymore. I have been watching that man for the last couple of years, and he keeps running himself like a dog chasing his tail in circles."

"What do you mean?" I encouraged.

"I've told you before that I have a special place for McKennon in my heart?"

"Yes?" I pretended to question her as I remembered full well our first conversation about McKennon Kelly.

"Well, I've made McKennon my silent partner here at Green Briar."

"Uh-huh," I urged, dying for more information.

This was the most Sophia had ever spoken to me about herself or about McKennon. Normally, I was dominating the conversa-tions, blabbing on and on about the complications of my own life.

"*So* ... after my husband died, rest his soul, I fell into a bad way. I never loved a man the way I loved my husband before or since. I just wanted to lie down and die when he left this world. I couldn't bring myself to leave the house or feed myself. I was desperately lost."

"Oh, Sophia, I am so sorry." My heart went out to Sophia.

"It was McKennon who saved me and pulled me out of the darkness," she continued, thoughtfully. "He came knockin' on my door, looking for work with horses and hoped for a place to keep his own. He found me laid out on the floor, too weak to move. I hadn't eaten in over a week. I remember that he let himself in through the screen door," she paused, and I held my breath as to not scare her away, clutching the phone in anticipation. "I will re-member that particular squeak for the rest of my life. That man, he just picked me up off the floor, a perfect stranger, and nursed me back to health. He fed me, encouraged me to bathe, and lis-tened to me lament about my dead husband. He didn't ask me for anything. In the end, he saved my life, a life I am grateful to have now, so I wanted to do what I could for him in return. I gave him the only thing I had to offer, and that was this ranch, these horses. And he is good at it. Every glimmering enhancement to this facility has been of his doing. He is an excellent horseman. I am afraid, though, he has lost his purpose."

"Purpose? What do you mean?" I was prodding.

"Oh my, Devon. It's been such a long time since I've shared that story. I haven't really talked about it since McKennon lost ..." she trailed off. "Darling, it is about time for my rest. Would you mind if I said adieu?"

Lost? Lost what? What did McKennon lose?

"No, no, of course not," I said, woeful that this conversation was coming to an end.

"You just steer clear of the cowboys, you hear?" she said, warn-ing clinging to her words.

"Yes, Sophia. Rest well."

I was confused, slightly annoyed.

Who was this McKennon anyway? Good cowboy or bad cowboy?

I couldn't tell.

My mind was reeling. Sophia had led me straight into a mystery.

The next morning, I arrived at the farm to find no trace of his one-ton diesel truck or eight-horse rig. I knew McKennon was gone again, and I didn't know how long it would be until he came back.

I found myself missing the walls with eyes already.

CHAPTER TEN

I tried to shake off his absence, but all too often, I found myself listening for the jingle of his spurs sauntering down the aisle or the mighty hum of his diesel truck pulling into the drive. McKennon had been gone for almost a month now, and I was feeling an uncertain loneliness. I kept silencing the voice in my head that secretly longed for his return, wished I hadn't been so harsh with him during that last encounter, and wondered after him.

Where was he? When was he coming back? Who was he ... really? Why did I care? Why was I so lonely now?

I was never much of one for a whole herd of friends. In the city, I had a couple girlfriends, a lot of acquaintances, my editor, and, of course, Michael. I could keep busy on my own for hours and often found being invited out for get-togethers spoiled how I had planned to spend my alone time. Being a writer was a solitary occupation and required space for thought and silence, aloneness.

I used to be so good at being alone.

I tried to shake off the emptiness festering within me. I filled my days with sitting by the pasture, contemplating my next writing piece while watching Faith peacefully grazing, with long grooming sessions, running the brush bristles over Faith's smooth summer coat until it reflected sunlight in its soft sheen, with languid walks over Sophia's grassy acres, just Faith, me and the earth. I filled my evenings with jamming to my latest favorite genre, country music, with cooking fabulous individual organic meals, with a glass of good red wine, with reading a good book snuggled up on the couch, with a hot bubble bath and candlelight. But I knew myself. And I could feel it coming.

Every once in a while I would get this bug, a devious urge. The one that sneaks up on a Friday night and begs you to rummage through the bottom of your closet in a heated search for that favorite pair of strappy heels, spend an hour picking out the perfect outfit, then call everyone you know, get a group together and fill the void with a night on the town. I had been on my own in this Southern town for months now, and I was itching to be social. That bug was coming on strong, buzzing my thoughts until I could no longer swat it away into the recesses of my mind.

The darn pest kept me up all night long, so the next morning, I stopped at the corner gas station and filled the largest cup available to the brim with steaming coffee. As I stirred in the sugar, I formed a plan to ask JD if there were any country western bars to go dancing in the area because this bug, quite honestly, was bugging me! I drove to the barn on a slightly spaced out mission after an evening spent with the nagging, nocturnal mental pictures of whirling around on dance floors.

JD and I were becoming fast friends. We had started eating lunch together after Mr. Mystery left town, sharing stories about our lives with each other. We didn't really discuss anything of substance. We just cracked a lot of jokes about stupid times in our lives and would end up doubling each other over in laughter. It felt nice to laugh with a man.

The time spent with JD was a refreshing shift. The last several years of my life were filled with a dark emotional repression as Michael and I passed each other in the halls of our own place with little regard. It was like coexisting in a prison for strangers rather than a home for lovers. It felt nice to express myself to another human without holding back.

I would tell JD tales about the city, in which he had profound interest having only known the wide open spaces of the South, about my writing, which he couldn't fathom me being paid for, let alone make a living from, and about my struggles with Faith's training. JD told me that if she were a bull, he could lend a hand with my troubles, but alas, Faith was not a bull, and my progress with her had stalled. Nonetheless, he was an attentive listener when I spoke and could turn just about anything I said into a joke. I appreciated that JD was lighthearted.

In return, JD told me about his escapades trying to earn enough points to secure a spot on the coveted *National Bull Riders* tour. He preached to me repeatedly that one day he wouldn't need to work on Sophia's land for extra money in between bull riding events. He envisioned himself winning the large purses once he got his big break on a really rank bull. 'Rank' was a term, he explained, reserved for only the meanest, toughest animals. The expression on his face when he paused was one of a faraway man lost in his dreams. I imagined his fantasies would consist of him tossing green bills in the air, captivated by them as they floated to the ground around him.

JD had big aspirations for his career. His dream was to ride bulls just like his uncle did. His passion was a tragic yet beautiful tribute to his father's brother who was killed when a bull stepped on his chest during a preliminary qualifying rodeo event. Those eight seconds happened during a time when protective vests and helmets weren't the norm in the dangerous sport. JD had been just a boy when he lost the family member he felt closest to. In one of our conversations, he conjured up a crumpled newspaper clipping of his uncle's big break into the rodeo scene from his wallet.

When he saw the empathy rise to my face, he said, "Ah, don't get like that."

I had to blink back a tear of compassion.

"No need to get all girly on me. I don't need no sympathy from you. It's not like that," he said, taking a big swallow himself.

Sadness wasn't in the cards for JD. He mustered his cowboy pride and told me that he chalked the loss of his loved one up to the fact that anything can happen in the bull riding pen. He thought of his uncle's death as a testament to the true cowboy his father's brother really was, out there living his dream from the back of a bull. JD aspired to the same grueling lifestyle and in return was disowned by his bitter father. In fact, I'd found that JD used this story and his cowboy status to his advantages any chance he got.

JD was young, 21 years young, with moves smoother than silk. He had a gleaming white, rock star smile, featuring all too perfect straight teeth, and alluring, big green eyes that pierced right through you. His eyes had just enough naughty glinting in them to serve as a warning that any smart woman should beware. To my entertainment, he never lacked stories about his latest buckle bunny conquest. When I asked him what the heck a buckle bunny was, he smiled that all too perfect grin at me, grabbed the tight crotch of his jeans, gave a downward tug and said with a smirk, "Basically they're the equivalent of the rock star's groupie." I rolled my eyes. *Hmmm, I gotta see one of these gems.*

JD was proud of the runner-up belt buckle that he'd won on the local bull riding circuit. He wore it proudly every day and never ceased to reference it when I asked him questions about the cowboy lifestyle, of which I had become increasingly curious. He used his cowboy status shamelessly with women, and I was no exception.

JD answered all my questions and took pride that I had started using him as my own personal western dictionary. Little did he know, though, that I longed for these answers, not because I was interested in how *he* lived his life, but to apply them to how *someone else* might be living his life while he was away. I even started watching *NBR* events on TV so I could have educated conversations with said cowboy.

My mission to plan a night out was abruptly interrupted as I took the turn into Green Briar's drive too quickly. Flabbergasted, I pumped my brakes hard, a jerky repeated pulse, spilling more than half of my caffeinated courage over the top of my foam cup and onto my boot. I surveyed the damage only allowing for a little annoyance about my soaking wet foot and sighed as I prepared for dampness to overtake my sock. My eyes swept over the scenery; there was more bustle than I had ever seen at the farm. To me, it was an ordinary Monday morning, but something about the excitement in the air voiced that *today's special.* I let my car creep into the drive and parked.

I held the top of my car door ajar, sipped what was left of my coffee, and took in the spectacle, jiggling my foot as if that would help my boot dry out. All the farm hands were gathered at their side of the barn aisle, and Sophia was already down, a rarity for her, given that she is a self-admitted non-early bird. She slowly circled the workers. I thought she seemed to be pacing, but Sophia's movements were so precisely calculated that she almost seemed to be ballerina dancing around the staff gathered before her, pacing would be an insult to her delicate movements. I was puzzled, scrambling for the puzzle pieces of the hoopla, when JD slipped up to me and gently whacked me on the back yet with enough force to send me lurching forward into the car door, causing me to lose the last of my much-needed coffee.

"Great," I said under my breath and chucked the empty cup onto the driver's side floor mat.

I observed the brown puddle and rolled my defeated eyes toward JD. *I'll clean that disaster up later.*

"Did you hear he is coming back with a surprise?" JD said intensely, staring straight ahead at the gathering in front of the barn. "Nobody's shut up about it all morning."

I swung my car door shut.

"What?" I said.

It was obvious that my caffeine and sleep-deprived mind wasn't absorbing anything at the moment.

Before JD could answer, the resident horses out to pasture started nickering to each other, and one by one galloped up to the front gates. I heard Faith holler from her stall. I'd know that whinny anywhere. Something *was* coming. The horses knew it, and everyone seemed to know it. Everyone that is, except for me.

Then I saw Sophia turn to the north and lift her luminescent face to the sun. I shifted from behind JD just in time to see the gleam of the chrome as the massive rig with an eight-horse trailer in tow, pulled into the drive. The driver was coming fast and with purpose, a whirl of dust kicked up from the dirt road.

JD leaned over and lifted my chin.

Apparently, my mouth had fallen open at the awareness of McKennon's homecoming.

CHAPTER ELEVEN

The rig pulled to a stop in the space between where JD stood next to me and the audience in front of the barn. The towering eight-horse trailer blocking our view, we hustled to the other side of the monstrosity to see what the commotion was all about. McKennon's door was ajar, and one of his spurred boots was propped on the chrome running board.

My heart skipped a beat, flush racing to my cheeks, and I yelled in my head, *Stop, stop, stop! Please don't let anyone notice what his presence does to me.*

The thunderous pawing and rustling coming from inside the trailer was merely a precursor to the huge *BANG!* that followed. It was obvious that whatever was in there wanted out, *pronto.* Responding to the ruckus, McKennon leapt from the truck and was at once at the side of the trailer. He gently pounded against the aluminum wheel well, shouted, "Hey now!" at the slightly cracked window, and looked over to Sophia.

"We got a live one in there!" he joshed as a crooked half grin slipped across his beautiful mouth.

Sophia clasped her fragile hands together and looked to McKennon in awe.

"Oh, McKennon! You've been missed. What surprise awaits us in there? I can hardly wait," she sung out to him as a slow, almost sweetly sinister smile turned her lips.

McKennon, face now blank, said nothing as he turned and leaned over the back of his truck bed, fumbled around for a moment and straightened up, grasping a lead rope. He looked to Sophia, looping the rope around his gloved hand, and gave her a shy grin.

Sophia melted into a bashful girl before him and did nothing but bat her long, elderly eyelashes. A butterfly swooped in my stomach. That grin of his reminded me of a little boy presenting his mother with an artistic creation, all rainbow scribbles and colored outside of the lines, in hopes that it would be refrigerator bound.

McKennon rounded the trailer, opened the rear door, lifted the ramp to the ground and disappeared inside.

We all hung in suspense. It felt like he had been inside for an eternity. We listened for signs of life as the trailer rocked back and forth. We tensed when we heard a scuffle and an abrupt "Whoa!" reel from inside. My stomach was a blaze of excited fluttering when I heard the first hoof on the ramp, then they appeared.

I caught my breath. I don't know which was more beautiful, McKennon in his pride, beaming over his prize, painted on plaid shirt outlining his lean, muscle-sculpted frame or the horse at his side, black, regal, majestic, nostrils a flare, pulsation with each breath, showing pink on the inside, skin frothed with sweat from his travel.

Once all fours were firmly on the ground, the stallion let out a long, low bellow and reared up onto his back legs. Showing off, he struck at the air with his front hooves, firing each one out independently and with electric force while shaking his head, mane flowing out in a wild expedition. The outburst shocked his onlookers.

In unison, we were jolted from our gawking and took a few hurried steps backward.

"Whoa there, boy," McKennon said, low and easy. "Whoa now."

Just as quickly as the horse went feral, he quieted within McKennon's world and inside of his words.

"This is Star," he said proudly. "He is named after the only white marking on his body. This white star smack in the middle of his forehead."

McKennon stood in front of the animal and smoothed his lush black forelock to the side, rubbing the middle of Star's star with his lambskin-gloved hand.

"Yep, when I am done with him, everybody'll be callin' him *Super* Star," he muttered.

McKennon's voice was low as if he were alone in the world, speaking only to his horse, and these words were a prediction of things to come, a hope for the future, a mark on time, his stamp of approval, a subtle wish for something better. To me, McKennon sounded like he was purring, and I rubbed my arms ferociously trying to send the goose bumps away.

Breaking his trance with Star, McKennon turned to Sophia, slapped his knee, shook his head and looked up at the heavens.

"This one's gonna win us the Congress!" he exclaimed, chiseled chest puffed with confidence.

It was obvious that Sophia was impressed. Enamored with their new acquisition, she languidly sauntered over to the horse's side and slid her lovely hand beneath his fuzzy, coffee bean colored muzzle.

"Super Star," she whispered up to the animal, and I knew her words swept straight into that horses soul.

Beaming, Sophia turned from Star to McKennon.

"Oh, McKennon! It hasn't been this exciting out here since ..." her voice trailed off, and I swear I saw a tear perched at the corner of her time worn, gossamer eye.

Swiftly wiping away the dewdrop, Sophia's demeanor changed in an instant from soft and open to hardened as she closed her arms tightly around her thin midsection, surveying her employees. Her gaze darted from McKennon to JD to the farm hands and then slowly to me as if she was wondering if I had been within hearing distance of her last comment. I looked straight ahead, doing my best to look as if I had heard nothing, and quickly released the space between my eyebrows that had intuitively crunched upward in response to the words I just heard.

JD and the others lowered their heads. McKennon moved toward Sophia, Star at his side, a faint hit of sadness sprawling over his face. He gently cupped his gloved hand over her lace-covered, achingly delicate shoulder and leaned to her ear. I strained to hear his reply. I prayed no one would notice as I angled myself closer hoping to scoot within earshot.

"Now then, let's not ruin this moment with stories of the past, Sophia," McKennon whispered. "Please." It was a quiet, heartstring-pulling plead. With that, he, too, lowered his head, clucked to Star to follow, and led the horse past me. To my dismay, he passed without so much as a sideways glance in my general direction and disappeared into the barn as the others trailed behind. My heart sank.

I followed the procession with my gaze as it filed into the barn. I didn't know what to do, who to be, how to act at that moment. I was an outsider. I didn't know why I had wanted McKennon to acknowledge me. I would've rather been a fly on the wall than standing witness to that in human form. I turned to JD, opened my mouth, and the words just fell out.

"So ... Um ... Do you know any good country western bars? I mean, you know, with dancing? I mean music for dancing?"

JD turned to me, puzzled yet polite. "So, you like dancing, eh?"

I had a thousand questions burning through my mind: where had he been, where did this new horse come from, what was Sophia

44

referencing, what did McKennon mean about the past. I had these and so many other questions bouncing around in my head that I would have rather asked JD other than about dancing, but I knew now was not the time. Then there was the burning feeling in me to run after McKennon, to cradle his face, to lift his head, to hold him and tell him it would all be OK.

What though? What would be OK?

Instead, all I could do was selfishly ask JD about dancing and pretend I hadn't born witness to any of this.

There. At least I can say mission accomplished.

I nodded my head, slowly. I felt like a ghost, like I wasn't even there.

"Uh-huh. Dancing. Uh, I like to dance."

I looked past JD when I answered, my mind elsewhere, as I gazed to the shadows of the barn, wondering after those who were now inside.

CHAPTER TWELVE

After Star arrived on the farm, I realized it was now me who watched McKennon. I watched him from my writing perch, admiring him from afar. I watched his determination to make Star a champion. It was written across his brow, crumpled in concentration, examining the way the horse's legs were moving.

"It is all in the way the legs move," I overheard him telling JD across the aisle and later Sophia over the telephone.

I watched how he was firm but also gentle, tough but never abusive, aggressive with his voice but also tender, almost soothing. With McKennon, every technique seemed to be an effort to protect the animal's spirit. I watched in awe as Star would come galloping to him like he was a god, leaving a pasture of perfectly delectable grass behind him to be in the man's presence. I, myself, knew this feeling, the desire to run into that man's arms.

I joined Sophia every day that week he came back to watch his training sessions. I watched how good he was with his hands, controlling his stallion with a mere two thin straps of leather looped between his gloved fingers. I watched as he eased Star's tension in a touch to the horse's sweat-strained neck, the horse's calm inside the width of his palm. I watched as he tended to his other chores, sometimes working on his truck tucked neatly beneath the hood, shirtless, glistening beads of sweat reflecting the sun as they traced the smooth contour of his masculinity. I watched how, when finished for the day, McKennon relaxed. I watched him in the late afternoon hours in the final moments of his routine as he would gracefully whisk away a fly from his lemonade, put his dusty boots up and turn his cowboy hat down, content with the day's work. I admired how when he relaxed, he really relaxed. It was something I don't think I'll ever master in this lifetime. My mind is always buzzing with thought, whereas I could tell by watching him that his was completely still.

How the tables had turned. In his homecoming, McKennon all but ignored me now. On the rare occasion he did acknowledge my existence, I would receive a passing, "Ma'am," with a nod, a slight tip of his cowboy hat or a gloved half wave.

That Friday night in the shower, preparing for a night on the town and some dancing with JD, I went over the day's ride on Faith. I smiled to myself. I had started to see an uptick in her positive responses to me. As I twisted the shampoo out of my long hair under the showerhead, my thoughts turned to this week's training sessions that I had watched with Sophia. I reviewed McKennon's techniques with Star over and over in my mind. I snorted at the realization that I was starting to use them with Faith, and they were working.

Smoothing conditioner over my locks, my mind wandered further, and I began wondering what McKennon would be like with a woman … *with me* … then I shook my head, hard, at the thought. I felt the idea fly right out of my brain to the wet end of my tresses, lashing my back and falling away from me with the drops of hot water down the drain.

Colder. Turn the water colder!

Forcing myself back to reality, I knew I needed this man's help with Faith if I was ever going to get anywhere with her. I had to apologize to McKennon for being so curt with him the last time we talked.

"I'll figure that out later," I said aloud as I wiped the steam away from the shower door and wrapped myself in a towel.

Here I was, Friday night, wondering what to wear and standing in front of my full-length mirror wearing only my under thingies. It had taken some searching, but I was able to salvage my few best pieces of club gear, remnants of my city life, from the recesses of my closet. These days, I had been wearing my cowgirl boots just a little longer outside of the barn walls. I used to change out of them when I had finished with Faith, but now I just left them on when I was running errands after the barn, spurs and all. I was definitely wearing my boots more than my heels, which were now buried at the back of my closet. I loved how the South allows for such things. It required some additional digging, but I'd finally found my favorite strappy heels, a constant companion of mine in the city, buried beneath a pile of my dirty, haphazardly discarded, weeks' worth of barn wardrobe.

Could it be that I was more comfortable in my country boots than my city shoes?

Definitely, I nodded to myself.

I put my hands under my breasts and lifted them in my bra. I giggled.

Yep, the girls are still there! They've just been hiding out in baggy T-shirts for months.

I pulled a deep plunging, clingy black halter top over my head. I stepped into a pair of tight, hip-hugging jeans and took a step back to reflect in the mirror once more. I had forgotten how good I actually looked when I was all done up. I didn't feel the need to get all gussied up anymore. I had to do it so frequently in the city that it lost its luster in my recreated life. Michael wouldn't take me anywhere sans makeup or perfectly coiffed hair, and it felt deceptively evil, wonderful, to go natural, knowing Michael would hate my defiance at his preferences.

I put my hands on my hips, gave a shimmy and said, "Darn it! I look good! Let's do this, Devon!"

I strapped on my heels, swiped my car keys off the counter and headed for the door.

CHAPTER THIRTEEN

At 6:45 p.m., I picked my way over the gravel drive, carefully balancing on the balls of my feet to keep my heels from sinking between the rocks and located JD in the tack room, polishing his prized belt buckle.

When he heard the *click-clack-click* of my heels on the paved aisle, he looked up from buffing the silver, raised both eyebrows and said, "Well, don't we clean up nice! You do realize that at this joint, you're gonna have to shun those $12 city cosmos for some good ol' fashion dollar drafts, don't ya?" He gave me a head-to-toe once over. "We'll deal with them heels another time," he said, pointing at my feet. "You look good though, Devon. Real good! You ain't gonna ruin my reputation all dolled up like that and hanging on to my arm."

I blushed as he put his belt and blindingly gleaming buckle back on, sauntered over to me, and offered the crook of his arm for me to take.

As I took JD's elbow, McKennon came barreling around the corner, carrying a western saddle, bridle slung over his shoulder, and saw us together. I felt like I had been caught. His breathtaking blue eyes fell on me and instantly widened. My skin felt hot as he let those eyes take a long walk all over me. He stood there holding that saddle for a long time. I swear I saw his eye twitch, just a little.

Was it jealousy?

After some time, McKennon turned his back on us, tossed the saddle on a rack, and took another peek at me over his shoulder.

"You two kids have fun now," he said as we started toward the door. His voice was without emotion, and he tossed a condescending jut of his chin in our direction.

Kids?

JD leaned over and whispered in my ear, "I'm thinkin' he thinks you're kinda pretty. Lucky me! Already got one man jealous, now I just have one whole bar full of 'em to go!"

JD lifted his cowboy hat and scratched the top of his head, scrutinizing my racy shoes. "I'm guessin' there'll be no walkin' in them heels on that gravel out there?" he razzed.

Laughing, JD whisked me up into his muscled arms and carried me over-the-threshold style out to his truck. JD knew women. Keyed up, I threw my arm around his neck, laughed too, and looked over JD's broad shoulder just in time to see McKennon peek out of the tack room as we exited the barn.

The bar was everything I expected: country music blaring from the jukebox, a plethora of line dancers stomping the dance floor, and the smell of cheap beer and cigarettes floating heavily on the air. I, however, was unexpected. My arrival in city slicker gear ordered up interested stares from the regulars. A good ol' boy heckled JD from his bar stool, "Where'd you find that one, JD, *NEW ... YORK ... CITY?*"

JD shot him a, '*You'd better shut the hell up* look' and lobbed back, "As a matter of fact, maybe I did, Willy. How'd you guess?"

Then he looked at me, lips twisted in an *I-told-you-so* manner, and said, "See what I mean about them heels?"

It had never occurred to me that in the South, you actually can wear your boots to the barn *and* the bar. Everyone around me was dressed like cowboys and cowgirls, donning Wrangler jeans, perfectly-shaped felt western hats, and boots. I suddenly felt out of place. I scanned the dance floor and knew that my plain round-toed black cowgirl boots circa the 1990s wouldn't have cut it here anyway, but I also knew they would have fit in better than my painted-toe bearing six-inch heels. All the boots in this saloon were fancy. JD pointed out the different types: leather, ostrich, alligator, sting ray, even elephant. I needed a drink, and I needed it fast. I sent JD to the bar as I tried to make myself small at a table in the corner.

JD returned with two beers and two shots. "One for sippin', and one for shootin'," he said. "The sooner you get a couple in your gullet, the more you'll feel at home."

I threw the alcohol down my hatch, and it burned as it descended. I welcomed the warming sensation and waited for the slow buzz to come.

"Mmm, that was good," I hummed.

"Want another one, Devon?" JD asked. It occurred to me that he seemed a tad too eager to see me under the influence. I shrugged the thought off. I was determined to have some social fun.

"Sure, I'll have a cosmo," I said, flicking my wrist, waving him off to the bar again, batting my lashes, and smiling. I felt naughty. JD shook his head, turned on his heels, and hit the bartender up for another round.

JD returned with a pretty waitress holding a tray of six shot glasses. Her white oxford shirt was open at the buttons, exposing her ample cleavage, and tied in a knot above her svelte navel. I looked at her feet, and even she had on a great pair cowgirl boots, broken in black leather ones embossed with a red rose pattern up each side. "Here you go, honey," she said as she lined up three shots in front of me and three in front of JD between snaps of her chewing gum.

"Thanks, Trudie," he said, slapping her on the butt and handing her a fiver. I was slightly aghast but figured it must be OK around here for a regular to slap the wait staff's behinds. *She seemed all right with it. As long as it isn't mine. It's cool. I guess.* Then he turned his attention to me.

"You ready?" he said, leaning in, low over the liquor and hooding his eyelids into a squinty slit daring me to dive in.

Feeling courageous, I did my duty and finished the whole row. "*Whoosh!* What were those?" I asked.

"Mind erasers. They're good for the soul. Want to dance, missy? That's what we came here for, isn't it?"

"Sure," I replied, extending my hand like a princess for him to take.

I had to admit, getting this kind of attention from a tall, dark, handsome, *younger* cowboy felt kind of nice after swearing off men, and especially after Michael, so we danced. JD spun me around and around the dance floor until I stopped caring about my poor choice of attire. At the end of our fifth song in a row, JD dipped me backwards, cradling me in the strong span of his bull rider arms, and I let my neck fall limp behind me. The ends of my hair touched the beer puddled dance floor, and I didn't mind. I laughed out loud and brought my buzzing head back up, only to find that I was shockingly the object of JD's green-eyed, dream machine stare. Taken aback when his pretty little face leaned in to kiss me, I put my hand to his firm chest and searched for my bearings. I turned my head to the side just in time as he pressed his pillow-like lips to my left cheek. I stood up quickly yet wobbly and bashfully offered him an apologetic sweet, half smile.

"Don't you think I am a little old for you, JD?" I inquired.

"Nah, haven't you heard?" he said, fielding the question like the playboy I imagined he was. "I dig cougars."

"Hey, YOU! I wouldn't say I am a cougar yet! I am still in my twenties!" I snapped, poking him in the chest.

"Sooo, you're 28, and I am 21. That's only seven years," he added.

JD sauntered out of chest-poking position, nudged me with his elbow and released his 21-year-old gleaming white megawatt smile. It was an attempt to dazzle me. I swear I saw a star twinkle in his eye as I glowered at him.

It's no wonder he beds so many of those buckle bunnies. This kid is good. I nervously glanced around the dance floor in an alcohol-induced haze.

There was a long awkward pause before JD addressed me. He pointed at me with his free hand, eyes squinting in accusation, and exclaimed, "Oh, I get it now! You dig McKennon, don't ya? I thought I saw you gettin' all girly when he came back 'round. Isn't he a little *old* for *you*?"

He poked me in the upper arm, twisting his finger into my bare skin, while grinning. I grimaced.

"I figured you out, didn't I? That's why you ask me all those questions! They are about him. Aren't they?"

"No, no, that's not it," I said over my shoulder, abruptly as I dipped under his extended arm, making my way back to our little corner table, bumping into a barstool along the way. JD dropped his arm and followed.

Sitting down, JD leaned back in his seat, arms behind his head, legs outstretched in front of him, eyeballing me.

"I just think his behavior is kind of weird. You know? Coming and going like he does," I felt a little warm under the collar. "Plus, I don't even know how old he is," I slurred this one, wrinkled my nose at myself, and immediately wished I hadn't had so much to drink.

JD rocked his chair back on its hind legs and rolled his eyes. "He's 36. Don't worry about it. All the chicks go gaga for that guy."

He let the front legs of the chair hit the floor with a crack and put his elbows on the table, clasped his hands together. "I don't get it ..."

Great. I repeated JD's words in my head, '*All the chicks go gaga for that guy.*' I wrinkled my nose again and tilted my head from side to side on each word as it filtered through my mind.

"What're you doin'?" JD said, looking at me quizzically.

"Nothing," I felt the blush of embarrassment rising to my already flushed cheeks. "Just feeling a little tipsy. That's all."

"Want another mind eraser?" he said.

"Sure," I said, shrugging my shoulders.

JD returned to the table with two more shots and two more beers. I looked up at him, and he gingerly sat down, balancing the tray of drinks.

"Where does he go anyway?" I asked.

"Goes to horse shows mostly or sometimes sales. Buyin' horses. Sophia usually provides the funds. Or sometimes he'll use his winnings. Sometimes no one really knows where he goes," JD replied, a faraway look in his emerald eyes. "He just leaves whenever he feels like it or when he feels like he is getting too close to people. He's the type that pulls away. It used to drive Sophia crazy. He'd take off on her any time she asked him anything personal or if they didn't agree on somethin'. Now she doesn't ask him too much. I think she just learned to believe in him. He's a pretty private guy."

"Huh," was all I could muster.

"You know, rumor has it McKennon got all excited about going off to find his next winner when he saw you with that horse of yours."

"What?" I clucked and drained my shot glass. "I can't get Faith to do anything," I huffed.

"You've done a good job with her, Devon. Don't you underestimate yourself. I don't know much about horse training, but I'd say you've done a pretty great job building a connection with Faith.

She might not be perfect right now, but I think McKennon saw the potential in you and your horse," he said empathically.

Switching gears, JD threw his liquor down the hatch and set the shot glass on the table, giving it a twirl. I watched as it bobbled in a bouncy circle, reminding me of one of those spinning tops that children play with.

"Christ, I haven't seen him this worked up about finding a horse since before the accident," JD said as he nonchalantly took a sip from his pint and focused in on a girl on the dance floor wearing a belly-baring, cut-off T-shirt with huge breasts overflowing from inside the deep cut V-neck.

"What? What sort of accident?"

Licking his lips, JD scooted the wooden chair forward with a screech, tuning in, as she danced seductively. He let out a long, low whistle and rubbed his jaw thoughtfully as the cheeks of her buns made an appearance from the bottom of her cut-off daisy duke jean shorts. JD was entranced with the miles of lean leg. Mouth in an O, he tipped his head from one side to the other, examining the length of them ending in her hot red cowgirl boots like a pot of gold at the end of a rainbow.

"Hello ... JD?"

JD turned back to me, lowered his head, and gave it a shake.

"Ah, Devon. I'm real sorry, but it's not my story to tell," he paused for a moment and sighed. He knew he had said too much.

Without looking at me, JD shoved off from our shared table and shimmied up to the red-booted cowgirl. He bowed low and put his turkey-feathered hat to his chest.

The girl was a goner.

CHAPTER FOURTEEN

All it took was one slow dance with the bodacious cowgirl for JD to acquire her phone number. Satisfied with his quick work and the probability of another conquest, he drove my intoxicated body back to the barn. Along the ride, we laughed off the attempted kiss and plotted his plan to bed red boots. It didn't take long before all was back to normal with JD and me. We half-hugged as I fumbled for my car keys buried deep in my bottomless purse.

"Friends?" I said, offering him my hand to shake.

"Friends with benefits would be better," he said, pouting as a hopeful glimmer hung momentarily in his eyes before we both broke down laughing.

In my drunken stupor, I punched him in his giant shoulder and reached into his shirt pocket, stealing one of his smokes.

"These will kill ya, cowboy!" I teased, holding the cigarette upright in front of his face, wiggling it between my thumb and forefinger.

"Aw, shucks. I know they're bad for me. Just can't help it. You all right to drive, Devon?" JD asked.

"Sure," I lied.

"OK, see ya tomorrow then."

Before I could reply, he pressed his warm, soft lips to my cheek and gave me a wink. I blushed.

"See ya tomorrow, *friend*," he said as he climbed into his truck, slammed the door, revved his engine, and floored it out of the drive.

I leaned back against my car. I felt a little dizzy as I watched JD pull away. I reclined my head on the cool roof and looked up at the clear night sky, millions of stars blanketing black. I lifted my head slowly and swung my alcohol-heavy body to sit on the wooden landscaping barrier of the parking area. I put my elbows on my knees and fingered the cigarette I stole. *It must be late,* I thought as I struck a pack of bar matches and brought the flame to my mouth.

"What 'cha doin' out here?" said a booming voice from somewhere in the night, startling me.

I jumped. Both the match and cigarette fell to the ground. McKennon, suddenly at my feet, stubbed out the match and smashed the unlit cigarette under the toe of his boot.

"Um, I was just sitting here for a minute before I head home. I think JD may have gotten me one too many from the bar."

"That kid," he said, shaking his head, putting his hands on his hips and looking down on me like my dad did when I misbehaved as a child. "Who gets a girl drunk by 8:30 p.m.?" he continued disgruntled. "And, even worse, just leaves her out here all alone to fend for her drunken self afterward?"

EIGHT stinking THIRTY? I am so lame.

"I told JD I was fine," I said, dropping my head into my hands. I wasn't sure which to be more embarrassed about, having to have this conversation or my being in this condition so early, or at all.

"I don't think you should be driving anywhere just yet, ma'am. Come on now. Come on with me, then," McKennon coaxed, lifting me up by my limp elbow.

Upon rising, I veered to the right then leaned backward. I felt faint in the presence of this cowboy Adonis. I was grateful, excited and flustered that McKennon had a hold of me.

"Stupid! Drunk! Stupid! Get it together, Devon!" I hollered, teetering on my ridiculous high heels.

McKennon chuckled and looped his warm, muscular arm around my waist. He was tall. My head barely reached his armpit. He smelled of earth and soap. I pushed into him and wrapped my arm around his waist too. My pulse was racing.

We didn't walk far, and he sat me down on a front porch somewhere in a rocking chair. I sighed with relief. Walking in my heels, even if a short distance, was no small feat in my condition.

"Be right back," McKennon said. I nodded and took a deep breath. The air was moist and warm.

I closed my eyes, rocked myself, and listened to the chirping and the buzzing of the evening in the distance until I heard a window behind me open, then the soft lullaby of Mozart billowed into my ears.

"Mozart?" I questioned when he reappeared, obviously wearing my confusion at his musical selection.

"What, you think cowboys only listen to country western music? Thought you could use something soothing. Here," McKennon perched on the edge of the chair next to me, leaned forward, and offered me a cup of tea. "To help you detox," he murmured. I took the warm cup between my palms and held his gaze. McKennon blinked wildly, leaned back and sucked in breath.

As he situated himself a good distance away in another rocker, I sipped the earthy smelling tea. Thankful. Bashful. Embarrassed.

"You live here?" I asked.

"Yep. Close to the horses. That's where I want to be. Sophia, she's good to me. This is her guest house. I work in exchange for rent."

The single story, brick house was nothing fancy, tucked away in the recesses of Sophia's spread of land. It was small, and in the silence, I found myself judging it, like perhaps I had judged him as small.

"You hungry?" he asked. "I always wanna eat when I've tied one on. I make a mean breakfast."

"Breakfast?" I questioned.

"It's the only thing that'll soak up all that alcohol in ya. Plus, it's the only thing on my menu," he winked and opened the screen door with a creak.

I eyed him hesitantly as my female instincts kicked in.

I didn't know this man.

"C'mon then," he gestured to the open door. "Don't you be worryin'. I'm a perfect gentleman. Promise. Now let's get some food in ya. Ladies first."

Maybe I didn't want him to be a gentleman.

Lethargically, I rose from my chair. My eyes were blurred, and my head woozy, but somehow I made my way through his front door. The open floor plan of the house was simple: a kitchen, eating nook, living room and a hall to what I figured was a bedroom. It was spotless, unusual for a bachelor. The hide of a bull made for a rug under the kitchen table, the fireplace mantle was lined with trophies, above it was a vividly-colored abstract painting, and bookcases lined the far end of the room. I walked toward them and ran my fingers over the colorful bindings. Shakespeare, Frost, Whitman, Twain, all the greats lined his shelves. I took an astonished glance at McKennon, busy building me breakfast in the kitchen.

I rounded the room, taking in all the details and reached what could only be a self-made showcase, the craftsmanship exquisite, filled with belt buckles. Congress, World, NSBA, National Rodeo

Association, all the great shows lined these shelves as well. Mozart, books, trophies, belt buckles, art, stainless steel pots and pans, and even a wine rack, but no pictures though. Not a single one. No snapshot signs of his life or anyone else's for that matter. I realized then and there that no, this man was not small, this man was BIG. A big mystery, that is.

I sat down on the couch, tired, still buzzed, and leaned against the soft sofa cushion. I closed my heavy eyes.

Just for a second.

Then I was hot. I sat up abruptly and gave my eyes a moment to focus. Blinding light was streaming in and cooking me through the slats in the shades.

The sun is up?!

I flung an afghan that must have been placed on me to the side, stood up, and slung my purse from the floor to my shoulder.

"Oh, my head," I said as I massaged my temples. It was pulsating with pain. I needed sunglasses *now*. I stood up, took a few barefooted steps forward, and bumped into a coffee table as I tried to get my bearings. My eyes widened, putting together the pieces of the evening.

Oh, my gosh! I am in McKennon's house!

I had to go to the bathroom. When I finally located it, it was like everything else, shamelessly clean. I looked in the mirror and was horrified at my reflection. My damp hair was matted to my face, and what was left of my eye makeup now formed black half-moons under my puffy eyes. I furiously pawed the toilet paper roll, acquiring a clump of tissue from the spool and rubbed to no avail. I found a hair tie in my purse and pulled my sweaty mane back.

I have to get out of here! I don't want him to see me like this! I didn't want to see me like this!

I tiptoed out of the bathroom, looking for signs of life. Nothing. I made my way to the kitchen and saw a note on the counter. The chicken-scratch handwriting was familiar. It read,

'*You passed out on me last night. Your breakfast is in the fridge. Hope you slept well. Help yourself to anything. I put those crazy shoes of yours by the front door. Work was calling. McKennon.*'

My tense shoulders immediately relaxed, at least I was alone. I opened the refrigerator, cringing at the fact he took off my stupid shoes. A beautiful ham and asparagus omelet, hash browns, and an English muffin stared back at me from a plastic wrapped paper plate. I leaned in closer, squinting through bloodshot eyes.

Did he really slice fresh strawberries as a garnish?

In disbelief, I grabbed my carry out and flew through the door into the blinding morning sun. I was a hot mess, running in heels, breakfast plate in hand, for the sanctuary of my automobile.

CHAPTER FIFTEEN

I scurried across the lot to my car like some nocturnal animal caught in the daylight hoping not to be seen. I shot quick looks from left to right, bobbling on the darn rocks in my stupid non-Southern heels and hit unlock on my keychain pad.

Hearing the locks click, I reached for the door and threw it open, landing safely inside. I jammed the key into the ignition and sighed as the engine sprang to life. I slammed the gearshift into reverse and hit the gas a little too intensely, shooting rock from under my tires up into the landscape embankment. The only thing on my mind was getting the heck out of dodge. As I reversed, I felt a pang of sickness hit my belly and paused to roll down the window.

Air. I need fresh air.

I whirled the window down, dropped my head, closed my eyes tight and breathed deeply.

Slow down. I counted my breath, *one ... two ... three,* all the way up to 10 until I no longer felt the urge to puke. I swallowed, momentarily relieved, as the sickness in my stomach leveled off. Just the slightest bit composed again, I reached for the gear and carefully dragged the stick to drive. As I started to roll, my thoughts drifted to Faith.

Today would be the first day in months I hadn't held to our daily routine. I wondered if she wondered where I was. I gazed at the barn toward her stall, then felt eyes on me. I slowly panned to the left to see McKennon bearing witness to my ordeal. He was standing there, leaning against the barn expressionless, his shirt sleeves rolled up, exposing the bronzed sheen of his forearms, crossed in front of his chest. His stance made me feel like he was silently mocking me. I shook my head side to side, hit the gas, gave him a quick, jerked half wave, and blazed past him.

I angled my rearview mirror to catch a last glimpse of McKennon. He removed his cowboy hat from his head, exposing his full head of dark bay locks, and wiped his forearm across his forehead. I cocked my head as he shook his own, laughing to himself before he wandered back inside the barn. My headache made a pounding reappearance.

Home.

I drove straight home. My mouth was parched and felt rough.

If I licked a blindfolded person right now, they would think I was a cat.

My head pounded, and the occasional jolt from my stomach made the 20-minute drive to my apartment feel like a 48-hour road trip to hell. Once inside, I threw my city clothes in the bathroom garbage can, taking special joy in pitching those heels of harassment, and took a long, hot shower. I sat in the bottom of the bathtub, bracing my knees to my chest as the steaming water blasted my back and squeezed my eyes shut.

McKennon's face, those piercing blue eyes, his smell, his warm arm around me last night, his chivalrous way of looking after me, his boyish manhood, his chest muscles perfectly framed in all of his shirts, flooded the forefront of my mind. The very thought of him stirred something in me, something I hadn't felt in a long while. The urge radiated through me until, right there in the shower, I took myself, my womanhood, in my own hands, and put an end to the wanting.

I just want to feel better, anything to just feel better ...

I laid my head back on the edge of the tub and let the rush come over me as I satisfied myself, candied cowboy dreams of McKennon dancing through my foggy hungover head.

I spent the rest of the day holed up in the darkness of my home, snuggled into the nook of my oversized couch, curtains drawn, cool wash cloth pressed to my pounding forehead, then to the back of my neck, now pressed into my eye sockets.

Mind erasers, all right.

Alcohol feels fun and risky when you are drinking it. It's like letting out the inner wild child you harbor deep inside. The problem was, I couldn't quite unscramble the evening as hard as I tried. I reminded myself that this awful feeling was the reason why I hated drinking. I never said no to that next drink because, at the time, it felt so good, plus JD was buying, but now here I am, losing the whole next day to recovery.

In the midst of ranting to myself about recovery, the ring of my cell jolted me out of my half-conscious narcosis. Groaning, I pressed the heel of my hand into the damp washcloth over my eye socket to hold it in place and dangled my other hand over the side of the couch. Unable to raise my pounding head, I patted the carpet searching the floor for my phone, remembering that I had put it down there somewhere so I could easily reach it.

Nothing is coming easily right now.

Finally fingering the phone, I swooped it up into eyesight and put it to my ear.

"Sophia?" I quietly questioned into the phone. My voice was flat and full of effort.

Her voice like an angel sailed to me from the other end of the line. "Are you OK, dear?" she inquired. "I missed you today. It isn't like you to not arrive at the barn."

"I know, Sophia, I know. Is Faith OK?" I asked, trying to add pep to my downtrodden voice.

"Oh, yes, dear. She is OK now, but I think she sensed something was awry today. Faith was just carrying on and on in her stall all morning long, whinnying away. I think she was wondering where you were."

"Oh, great! That's what I was worried about. I wasn't sure if she'd know I was out of routine," I huffed, running my fingers through my hair.

The grim image of Faith locked in her stall, forlorn, took hold of me.

"Oh, Devon. Don't worry, dear. McKennon looked after her for you. He just went right into her stall and settled her right down."

I shot straight up. The washcloth fell from my face and flopped its wet surface onto my bare skin, just above my knee.

"What? What did he do to her?" I blurted, ignoring the washcloth's relocation.

"He calmed her. That man just has his way with those animals. I was down the aisle, but I saw him slip into her stall. I reckon he spoke to her, gave her a good rubbing, and let her know you'd be there soon. She's been quiet as a baby since, napping all afternoon."

I lay back again, pushing my tired body into the couch cushions, attempting to get the comfort just right. I felt like a dog might when circling a spot before lying down. The pounding in my head had turned to a dull, annoying ache. Talking with Sophia seemed to help speed my recovery.

"Goodness, Sophia! I am not as young as I used to be. I used to be able to go out and have a bunch of drinks in the city, but now I am afraid I am not much of a drinker. I went to the country bar with JD last night and had a few too many. That's why I am not on my usual schedule," I confided.

"Oh my! I hope you feel better, dear. Have you eaten? You should eat something! That will help clear that poison right out of you," her voice billowed into my head like a cool breeze on a humid day, clearing the fog that had spread over my mind.

"You are right, Doctor Sophia," I joked. "It would probably do me well to put something in my stomach." I faintly recollected a certain someone else had provided the same advice not so long ago.

"Well, dear. There is another reason I called. I don't know if you'll be up for it after your escapade last night, but it is a beautiful Saturday. You are becoming like part of the family out here, so I wanted to invite you to a little barbecue and bonfire this evening."

My heart grew 10 times its size when she said I was starting to feel like family to her.

She continued. "It's nothing spectacular, just me and the boys filling an early summer eve with good food and good company. We like to do it from time to time," she sounded whimsical. I pictured Sophia's face as she said it, faraway, thinking of the past Green Briar barbecues, spinning them into a weave of storyline like something out of a fairytale published in her good-natured mind.

I appraised my body before responding; I felt terrible and was sure I looked terrible.

"Sounds lovely! Count me in. Thank you for the invitation, Sophia. I might just make a full recovery after all. Would you like me to bring anything?" I replied, wondering how in the world I was going to get off this couch without feeling like I might vomit, but the thought of admiring McKennon's glow in the light of a bonfire was too tempting to not at least consider abandoning the comfort of my couch. I wanted to see him again with every fiber of my being.

"Oh, wonderful, dear! We'll see you tonight around 7:30. And no, you don't need to bring a single thing. Adieu."

With that, she was gone. I envisioned Sophia's delicate hands clasping in excitement, phone cradled between her ear and shoulder, as she bid me goodbye. The promise of Sophia's happiness and seeing McKennon again was enough to coax my destroyed body from its home firmly rooted on the couch.

Heeding Sophia's words of wisdom, I opened the refrigerator in search of something to consume. I had all but forgotten about McKennon's chef-du-jour preparation, but there it was, staring back at me from the shelf, strawberry garnish and all. I reached for it and peeled back the plastic wrap questioning whether I could stomach it. Its smell was aromatic, its freshness undeniable as if he had harvested his own herbs and bred the chickens for the eggs himself. My mouth began to water.

I flipped the plate into the microwave and zapped his cold creation into edible warmth, before feeding it to my body. Delighted, I reveled in the fact that I was keeping the breakfast down. Astonished at how much better I felt with each bite, I ate slowly, relishing the fact that this cowboy Romeo had made a restaurant-worthy omelet just for me. I savored each mouthful as the asparagus and ham exploded on my palate, the egg saluted with the perfect equation of aged cheddar and fresh dill.

I saved the strawberries for last and felt my face flush as red as their sweet pulp in thought of what I had done in Chef McKennon's honor just hours before alone in my bathtub.

CHAPTER SIXTEEN

I pulled myself together, albeit not as nicely as I had the night before. Lacking the same zest for makeup and evening wear, I washed my face, swept my hair into a ponytail, pulled on a fresh pair of jeans, layered on a tank top, and tied a sweatshirt around my waist in case the balmy heat of the day turned cool.

As I cursed myself and JD for my horrendous hangover, I rummaged through my cabinets and the refrigerator praying that I had something I could whip up for the barbecue. Even though Sophia said not to bring anything, I didn't feel comfortable arriving empty handed. Random thoughts about Southern hospitality swiveled around my mind as I took stock of my options.

OK, pasta, check. OK, Italian dressing, check. OK, a nice block of parmesan cheese, some black olives, broccoli and peppers. I am golden. Pasta salad it is!

I arrived to Green Briar early. I needed Faith. I knew she would make me feel complete. She was the only thing that made me feel better when I was low. I pulled up in front of the barn and unbuckled the large pasta salad bowl from the passenger seat.

With the way I had been feeling, I felt like one crazy turn would create a pasta salad explosion in my car and decided it would be safer if I buckled it in.

I put the large bowl in the crook of my arm, salvaging it from the sun blaring through the windshield, and carried it into the cool barn with me. I set the bowl down just outside of Faith's stall and peeked in at her through the bars.

She was asleep, legs folded in a deep bed of fresh wood shavings. I watched her sides gently expand and release, in and out, in and out, and I sighed admiring her peaceful slumber. I carefully unlatched the stall door, closing it quietly behind me, and moved gingerly attempting not to stir her. I didn't go unnoticed. Faith groaned at the awareness of me, then splayed herself out flat on her side, eyes open but with no desire to rise. She breathed softly, and the shavings rustled as she blew breath.

I dropped to my knees as I approached her. Reaching her neck, I placed my hand on her shoulder and combed the fingers of my other hand through her soft white mane. Her neck made a perfect U around my body, and I heard her sigh at my touch. I turned toward her, folded my legs inside the bow of her body, picked up her soft velvet muzzle, and lifted her head into my lap. Faith didn't resist. She nestled into my crossed legs, and I stroked her white blaze, combed through her forelock, ran my palms over the triangular tip of her lovely brown ears, and wished I could stay in this moment forever. I didn't have to say a word to her. She knew what I was saying. I felt linked to this horse, felt like she could read my mind. And in these stolen moments between a horse and her owner, in the cool quiet of an empty barn, I knew I was forgiven.

My private commune with Faith was broken when a voice I recognized all too well broke the silence with a start. I knew immediately what was happening when I heard the bowl bouncing and scrapping its way across the cement.

"*Dang!* What the heck is that?!" I heard McKennon grunt. It was clear to me that he had rounded the corner from the tack room and produced an accidental walk-kick that rocket launched my pasta bowl halfway down the barn aisle.

Faith was startled by the noisy outburst and flailed on her side for a moment before scrambling to her feet. I had to jump up quickly to avoid accidentally being struck by one of her hooves. McKennon looked into Faith's stall and took a step back when he saw me emerge from behind Faith. He seemed shocked to see me there beside her, one jean leg covered with shavings.

"That would be my pasta salad for the barbecue," I said, addressing his question as I brushed down my side, loosening the wood chips.

Then quickly added, my heart skipping a beat, "Sophia invited me," realizing I may not be welcomed by him at the get-together.

McKennon just looked at me blankly and then turned his head slightly investigating me. He was calm and cool while I felt wild and hot under his scrutiny.

How is he just always suddenly here, catching me off guard?

I felt a flush come to my cheeks.

"Hmm," he purred, rubbing his strong, stubble-ridden chin between his thumb and forefinger, still examining me as if he enjoyed seeing me flustered, seeing me bashfully childlike in the moment. "Thinkin' I like ya better without all that face paint you had on last night," he continued.

Was McKennon admiring me? Was this some kind of backward cowboy compliment?

I furrowed my brow and looked at the ground, dipping the toe of my boot under the bedding in Faith's stall. "Uh, thanks," I managed, slightly under my breath.

"What're you doing in there anyways?" he inquired, pointing his finger at me still behind the closed door of the stall. He peered at me through the steel bars. Those bars felt like the only thing keeping me from leaping into the man's arms and burying the curve of my nose into the nook of his tan neck to just breathe him in. In this moment, the stall became my own personal jail cell. I was prisoner to my hidden desire for this man, yet safe from doing any harm.

"I was just making amends for not riding her today," I said over my shoulder as I turned to knead the muscle of her chest. I couldn't bear to look at him. I was afraid my eyes would deceive me, and he would see the longing that resided in them.

"You've got yourself a real nice animal there, Devon. It isn't just the horse though. You two make a good fit, a nice pair. That horse feels your presence ... *no* ... almost needs it," he paused to shift himself outside of the stall, and the sound of his spurs tingled in my ears. I couldn't resist. I had to look at him and cast a glance as he put his gloved hands on the bars, one on either side of his breathtakingly beautiful face. I turned away before our eyes could meet.

"You know she was throwin' a dang fit today when you didn't come for your ride."

His voice was deep, easy and satin. It sent a thrill up my spine. My writer's mind still couldn't help but cringe at his English, but something about it was endearing, earnest and real, and even though the words weren't perfect, I knew the sentiment was. He was telling me he could see what I had with this horse, and that meant more than anything. I felt understood.

"Sophia mentioned that you calmed her. Thank you. What did you do to her?" I asked.

"Oh, she just needed to know she wasn't alone out here. I knew she was missing her hungover mama, so I just gave her a little lovin'. No big deal," he said as our eyes finally met. His softened as our gazes joined. Diffident, I looked away, letting my eyes cast to Faith's; hers felt safe, all deep brown and trusting.

"Well, thank you. I appreciate it. And about last night –" I looked back to his eyes like oceans. He interrupted me by raising a hand and turning his weather blue eyes away from me.

"Don't mention it. We'll just pretend like it didn't happen," he said, waving a gloved palm at me as he walked down the aisle to retrieve the spun out pasta bowl. I thanked heaven that it had stayed closed during McKennon's field goal attempt.

Turning his words over in my mind, I realized that I didn't want to pretend like it didn't happen. I wanted to build on it, keep our evening in reality so perhaps there would be more.

I let myself out of my self-proclaimed jail cell and looked after him.

"You comin'?" he said, over his shoulder, my unharmed pasta bowl tucked in the crook of his arm like a football.

CHAPTER SEVENTEEN

I slid Faith's stall door shut and bid goodbye to the safety of being behind her bars. I followed McKennon out into the sunlight, letting my eyes fall on his perfect rear end, consciously suppressing the urge to race up behind him and put my palms on it.

He waited for me to catch up to him outside the barn, and we walked side by side in silence for a while, making our way along the white-fenced pastures toward the main house. The pastures were lush, dappled with the yellow heads of dandelions, and accented with the wedding-dress white of Queen Anne's Lace. May had given much rain, and the glossy blades of green reached the horse's knees as they rummaged through it, nature's perfect lawn mowers.

I watched the way he surveyed the land, every now and then reaching out to grab an overgrown stem of some kind and twirling it between two gloved fingertips. He took long sweeping gazes over the fence lines as we walked past, checking for any signs of fixing, I imagined. The day was still hot, and I held my breath as he unbuttoned his long sleeve shirt and stripped down to a form hugging white V-neck T-shirt, a soft tuff of chest hair exposed in its nook, just enough but not too much. I found myself thinking how I would love to graze that hair with my fingertips. After some time, I managed the courage to speak, and when I said his name, it felt good on my lips.

"McKennon?" I said, my internal temperature escalating a notch higher as he wordlessly turned those blue eyes on me. "Um, I want to apologize for all of it," I pressed on.

"All'a what?" he asked, adjusting his cowboy hat lower over his eyes to block the last blast of the evening sun.

I felt bashful. "For being so rude when you tried to talk to me before and for being so drunk last night. And the omelet was really incredible. I just can't get over those fresh strawberries."

He eyed me, still squinting in the sun. "I *said*, don't mention it."

"But I wanted you to know," I said somberly, feeling rejected in my apology.

"Well, I am glad to know you liked my cookin'. Thank you, ma'am," he tipped the brim of his hat and chuckled. Obviously, he hadn't put as much thought into it as I had.

"So you think Faith and I have something special?" I probed.

"Yes, I reckon I do."

"I'd like to ask you something then," I said, mustering my courage.

"Go on," I felt his eyes on my hot cheek, caught there in my pause.

"I think Faith and I could use a trainer. I've been thinking about it a lot, and I would like the trainer to be you."

There. I'd said it.

He stopped and squared his shoulders to me. He looked almost sad.

"I'm sorry, miss, but I don't train people anymore. Not since ..." he trailed off and looked to the sky.

"Not since?" I said gently, bracing for the letdown.

"Nah, never mind," he said, quickly pawing the air with a downcast, gloved hand. "Just don't do it no more is all."

"Oh," I said, trying not to sound like I had taken his rejection personally.

"Don't think too much about it. You hear?" he seemed to beg, in hopes that I would drop it. "C'mon, there's some good barbecue waiting for us up there. I'll have you know I made the sauce!" he taunted as he shifted from me on the heels of his boots and loped away, hightailing it toward the bonfire that had started without us.

There it was again, this mystery everyone around here referenced and knew but never expanded on.

I looked dejectedly in the direction of the party and did my best to put on a happy face, falling in behind him.

Winded from my pursuit, I closed the distance McKennon had created as we made our way up the gentle, sloping, grassy knoll that led to the main house. We arrived together just past 7:30 p.m. The circle around the bonfire slowed their happy chatting and looked at us as we settled into empty chairs across from each other, completing the circle. A smile smoothed across Sophia's luminescent face as she laid her beautiful eyes on his face then on mine. It reminded me of the kind of smile you'd see a proud parent wear during their child's wedding day vows.

"Welcome, McKennon. Devon. So glad you've made it!" she nodded to us, and the fire set a twinkle burning in her eye.

JD's expression couldn't have been more different. He elbowed me in the side from his foldout chair next to me and accused me with a loud, "What've you been up to?" and tossed his head in McKennon's direction.

I elbowed JD back as hard as I could and stole a quick glance at McKennon. He had his eyes dead set on JD, legs out in front of him crossed over at his boots, with a mischievous smile spread over his full pink lips, hands folded across his washboard stomach.

JD proceeded to quietly interrogate me about why my car was still in the driveway this morning and why I am now showing up to the barbecue with McKennon. I tried to tell him that I spent an innocent blacked out night on his couch to sleep off the mind erasers, but JD just leaned away from me like a boyfriend scorned.

"JD, I asked him to train us. That's all. And I am sure you'll feel better to know he said no."

"Whatever," JD said, still distraught over the whole ordeal. He sounded like a snotty little kid.

I spent most of the evening trying to rebuild my bizarre bond with JD but would find my eyes most often settling in McKennon's general direction. Our eyes seemed to gravitate toward each other's. We were like magnets. I'd feel him on me and catch him looking, then he'd feel me on him and catch me looking at him. It was agony. I longed to sit next to him, to ask him questions, to admire the smooth contour of his face in the burnt glow of the flames as it met the unshaven stubble that framed his perfect lips. I was too embarrassed though that he had rejected my request for training. I dared not speak to him again beyond the occasional laugh to punctuate his jokes or a faint smile to make him aware I was listening. I didn't want to be rude after all. At least my pasta salad was a hit. Even Southern belle Sophia wanted a second helping *and* the recipe.

The evening air was heavy, but the fire accompanied by a light breeze kept the mosquitoes and heat at bay. We ate, laughed and talked, deepening the bond of our little circle at the base of Sophia's big white house. We filled our plates with heaps of brisket, sausage, ribs and pulled pork. We slathered our meat in McKennon's homemade barbecue sauce, laced with the perfect amount of heat and sweet. Sophia's beans bubbled and spurted from a nearby crockpot. When I put them in my mouth, they melted on my tongue, leaving traces of brown sugar and maple syrup on my taste buds. An icy tub, boasting several varieties of bottled beer along with a few floating spring waters, made a sloshing sound every time someone reached for another. JD offered me a brew, which I politely declined in favor of bottled water.

"Hair of the dog will make it better," he said, laughing at me while exchanging the beer for my water. "Still feeling the effect of last night, do ya?"

"Um, yeah it was a doozy, JD. Don't let me drink like that again. OK?"

"OK," he said, smiling his JD smile at me now, seeming to have gotten over the chip on his shoulder about McKennon and me.

JD took his seat at my side and propped up his boots on a rock lining the campfire. He turned his attention to McKennon.

"So, cowboy, what're your plans for our new arrival here?" JD said loudly as his hand slapped down on my knee and gave a squeeze, a sly self-pleasing smile spreading over his lips.

I shot JD a fast, furious glance.

"JD!" I protested. "*Please*," I begged.

McKennon leaned forward onto his forearms in his chair, addressed Sophia with his eyes and said unaffected, "Would you explain the question, JD?" He seemed amused as he looked to me, delivering a sinister half grin.

JD took his hand away from my leg, straightened up in his chair, shoulders tipped in toward his opponent, and locked eyes with McKennon. This seemed like some sort of territorial male dance or a bizarre game of truth or dare to me. I tore my gaze from McKennon's reaction and studied Sophia. She was enveloped with calm, the words of warning she spoke to me seemed to be part of another world now, and she seemed pleasantly occupied by this exhibition of male hormone going on over her bonfire. I observed her lean forward in her chair intrigued, fine hair floating on the breeze, venerable face glowing peach in the firelight.

"I assume you're talkin' about Star here, JD?" McKennon said, teeth slightly clenched.

"Yeeeah," JD replied long and low, folding his arms across his chest.

"Oh, boys! What a wonderful topic. McKennon, won't you please tell us more of Star's progress and your plans?" Sophia asked, softening the situation with her harmonious utterance. The sheer joy in her voice when it came to Star settled the tension quickly. Both men relaxed their shoulders and gave each other 'aw shucks' kind of grins. The strain quickly dispersed in the hem of Sophia's presence. She was queen bee. We all knew she dictated how things were going to go on her land, and we were happy to oblige.

In a sign of surrender, McKennon sat up, opened the wide span of his arms out, and then back behind his torso, arching his back. I pretended in my head that it was a call for me to come to him so he could envelope me against his firm, lean frame to protect me from the night and JD, but alas, it was only a stretch. He laced his gloved fingers above his head, released his big hands and reached for Sophia's fragile, small, baubled ones, pressing hers in the tips of his fingers.

"Well, everyone, we've got our Congress prospect. I'm takin' him. I'm takin' Star to Congress this year," McKennon beamed.

Everyone was very quiet. The only sound was the hissing of the flames lapping the wood atop the fire. A log tumbled to its side, setting alive a firework display of embers and ashes, spurting into the night, then falling like snow around us as they cooled in the heavy air. I bit my lip and looked from face to face around the circle.

Someone say something. Darn it!

Finally, Sophia broke the stillness of the group, "That's wonderful, McKennon. We haven't had ourselves a Congress prospect for some years now. I think it is a perfect year to return to the show pen."

She caught my eye and offered me a slow smile. It made me feel nervous.

"Think he'll be ready by October?" JD spoke out. I sensed a transitory honest concern in his comment.

"He'll be ready. He's already lopin' like a ballerina. Just gotta give him the polish in the next months to make sure all the parts are workin' as good as the sum of the whole. Can't have the pretty picture without the proper paint, can ya?" McKennon assured.

"Well, it's a good show to choose," JD went on, glazing the next bit with sheen of bravado. "If you can't get laid at Congress, then you're doing something wrong," he sneered.

Peering at me, JD took a swig of his beer. It was an evil attempt to sliver my desire as if it were his duty to leave me with an obvious message about what McKennon might *really* be doing when he goes to Congress.

One, two, three people began to slowly rise to say their good-nights and leave the barbecue. I couldn't determine if it was because of the tension or the mere fact nothing much was left of the fire to stoke. McKennon, Sophia, JD and I remained.

As the last bit of flame grew low and lost its luster, the embers took on a life of their own, glowing brightly like little copper phosphorescent stars in their black sky of soot and ash. McKennon rose from his perch across the fire and made his way around the pit; orange, red and yellow reflecting off his teeth as he lay his eyes on me with an easy smile. I looked up at him not daring to move, afraid I might scare him away again.

"Devon?"

"Yes?" I stared into his hypnotic blue eyes, and he stared back into mine.

"I'd like you to ride with me tomorrow morning."

JD grunted and tossed his beer bottle into the fire. Sophia, listening like a school girl eavesdropping on her best friend with a new boyfriend, leaned forward. I saw the same slow smile cross her face that appeared on her angelic lips earlier in the evening.

"I'd like that," I said, clearly ignoring the arm JD had just strung across my back.

"OK, then. See you at 6:30 a.m.," he said as he moved away from me and leaned over Sophia, embracing her without saying goodnight. McKennon shot JD a satisfied look and left.

I looked down at my clamped together hands, dappled with the firelight, and felt a slow smile spread, too, across my lips.

CHAPTER EIGHTEEN

*A*rgh! I shot straight up, and, with bleary eyes, attempted to focus on the alarm clock.

What? 5:45 a.m.!?

I scrunched my eyebrows in horror. I swore I had set it for 5 a.m. last night in my McKennon-invite afterglow.

So much for looking lovely.

Heart pounding, I untangled myself from the warm sheets, blasted out of bed, and stood in last night's T-shirt barefooted on the linoleum bathroom floor, splashing cool water on my face. I managed to smooth my auburn sleepy locks into a hair tie, swiped the mascara brush through my top lashes and hastily glazed my lips with a sheer pink gloss.

I am so not a morning person. Who the heck rides at 6:30 a.m.?

The memory of McKennon saying he liked me better without face paint came blazing back to me.

OK, then this will have to do.

I stirred around in my dresser drawers and fished out a clean tank top, socks, bra and underwear. I threw open the closet door, and hopping on one foot, completed my ensemble as I thrust the second of my legs into my favorite pair of riding jeans. The pair that looks best with my cowgirl boots, just the right length, bunching nicely at my ankles, and hanging perfectly when my feet are in the stirrups. I had found that most of my jeans were unbearably short when I rode, exposing far too much ankle in a so-not-cowgirl-like fashion and calling unnecessary attention to my totally dated cowgirl boots circa the '90s.

I'll have to do something about that eventually.

At least I had invested in some proper jeans for this ride. I looked myself over and shook my head in disapproval. I looked like a zombie, sleep still hooding my eyes, lips in a frustrated twist.

Why did my alarm have to let me down today!

I sighed, scanning the contents of my closet and realized how much I had changed from my city days.

Was I actually becoming a bona fide cowgirl?

Standing there in my riding attire, it dawned on me that when I first came on to Green Briar, I would bring a change of shoes with me to the barn. My right eyebrow arched at this discovery as I looked at myself one more time with a less judgmental eye and snorted out loud, "This girl's more comfortable in her old school boots than in her shoes." I smoothed my shirt, slipped my thumbs into my belt loops, and shimmied my hips, thinking to myself McKennon-style, *Well, ain't that something.*

I blazed into the driveway without a moment to spare. It had been a long while since I had to arrive anywhere at a certain time. No office to clock into, no fiancé to report to, the only time I had to keep these days were the hard deadlines my editor set for my writing assignments.

Shoot!

I had been in such a rush to get to Green Briar that it hadn't even occurred to me that *I WAS ABOUT TO RIDE WITH MCKENNON.*

When I set my foot on the crunching gravel outside of my car and spotted McKennon, everything changed. My heart began that steady racing I was becoming accustomed to in his presence.

Thump, thump, thump.

Speeding, speeding, rapidly increasing, hotness touching my cheeks when I laid eyes on him, lazily leaned back against the entry to the barn, tanned arms crossed in front of his chest, hands tucked into his armpits, blue burning eyes set on me.

I slammed the car door still in frantic hurry mode.

"Hey," I said, gesturing toward him with my chin, sounding winded like I had just run a half marathon.

"Too early for ya, little lady?" he uttered with a hint of humor. A slight shadow was cast over his face beneath the brim of his cowboy hat. I could faintly see that he was wearing a sly smirk across his amazingly sexy, stubble-lined, perfect pillow lips.

Disarmed, I stuttered, "Uh, um. Alarm didn't go off."

I closed the distance between us, turning my eyes down, away from him, obliviously rubbing my chest just above my breasts in an apologetic fashion. McKennon merely nodded and let his eyes fall to my hand. Noticing him, noticing me, I immediately stopped, and he lingered just a moment too long where my hand once had been. My mouth fell open.

Did McKennon just check out my boobs?

He caught himself and met my widened eyes.

"Well, let's get on with it then," he said, turning to saunter into the barn. I shrugged my shoulders and followed him in. Under the buzzing of the aisle lights, I saw Star already saddled and impatiently jittering in the cross ties.

Shoot! He is ready to go. Darn.

As if he knew what I was thinking, McKennon addressed me, "Habit. Used to ask my clients to be tacked and ready to go for start time, figured they ain't paying me to watch 'em saddle up."

I felt hot, embarrassed and self-conscious. If I was going to win this cowboy over and get him to train us, I was going to have to learn his rules and follow them. A soft nicker broke my self-admonishment, and there she was. Faith was calling to me, soothing my frayed nerves, slowing the pace of my heart, offering peace in her wide brown eyes, ears pricked forward at my presence almost as if she sensed this was a different kind of day, the kind of day plump with opportunity and heavy with newness.

Faith was my gravity. She brought me back to earth and out of my head. I opened the heavy stall door, and she blinked expectantly at me, pushing her muzzle into the palm of my hand, her breath warm and moist on my skin. I put my chin to my shoulder and demurely peeked over it to catch a glimpse of McKennon. He was at Star's side, hand on his stallion's neck as Star continued his strain against the cross ties.

"Whoa now, boy," he purred, steely eyes on me, catching my glance. "Whoa," he murmured, his voice like silk running over my eardrums.

The stallion flexed his neck upward, ear turned toward him, and relaxed his head low in the cross ties at McKennon's wiry hip, calm again in the width of his palm.

Watching, I clung to Faith as she pressed her blaze to my chest. I took a slight step backward as she nudged me out of the stall into the aisle. I wrapped my arms around her sorrel and white painted head, across either side of her jowl, and under her throat, letting Faith's contentment at my presence press into me. Calm washed over me, and I stole a second over-the-shoulder look at McKennon as he adjusted the leathers at Star's side. I sighed at the spectacular realization that I had never really allowed myself to believe that real cowboys might actually exist, especially not one with brains and killer blue eyes, alive and breathing in my barn. This man was a real cowboy, not on the big screen, in my dreams or in my imagination, but here in my barn.

There was a heady, heaviness in the air as I saddled Faith in silence. McKennon slid down the wall, crouched in the aisle, tipping on the heels of his ostrich boots, and propped himself beneath Faith's stall. He twisted a long piece of hay retrieved from the ground between the fingertips of his lamb-skinned glove, relaxed, waiting patiently for me.

The only sounds between us were the bristles of Faith's brush as I gave her body a quick once over, the subtle squeak of leather as I tightened straps, horses shuffling in their stalls, searching for the last remnants of their breakfast flakes of hay, nostrils on muzzles blowing breath, serene chirping accented by the early morning coo of doves. There was a satisfying lack of and need for words.

Beside Faith, managing the cool metal bit into her mouth and lifting the headstall over her ears, I admired McKennon. Awe washed over me as I examined him. His eyes cast down, face hidden by the brim of his straw cowboy hat, twirling that piece of dried grass, he occurred as almost boy-like. This silence would be so much easier if I could only get beyond his model-like frame, lean muscles flexing easily with minimal motion, and the stirring in my blood that just looking at him caused. For but a moment though, I felt an easygoing bond between us, a shared silence like old friends or secret lovers. We had no need for words. We were just ourselves, enwrapped in the beauty of this horse world.

"You ready?" McKennon hummed as he cast the strand of hay away and stood to face me, penetrating blue bullets for eyes.

"Yes," I said breezily, feeling all melty on the inside like an ice cream cone that someone needed to hurry up and lick. Standing there facing his god-like gaze, I was thawing in the heat between us. Nervously biting my lower lip, I watched him examine my completed work of saddling Faith.

His eyes fell on my mouth, blinking; I released my lip, and his eyes shot back up to meet mine for a moment. Satisfied with my job well done, he squinted at me and said, "All right then."

McKennon moved to unhinge Star from the cross ties. He unwrapped the reins from the saddle horn and with his stallion in tow, languidly glided out into the morning rays of sun.

I slipped my hand down Faith's neck under her mane, gathered up her reins, and followed him, eyes unable to avoid admiring that all too perfect behind.

CHAPTER NINETEEN

We rode side by side through Sophia's sprawling acres, a short-lived spurt of jealousy pained through my stomach as my eyes surveyed her land, blades of long grass billowing on the breeze like waves of the tide.

I'd love to live here for the rest of my life.

We were silent for a long while, a peaceful permanent slight smile across McKennon's contented lips. I don't remember ever sharing silence with someone and being this comfortable, this calm. Of course, in my traditional way of being in my mind rather than enjoying the peace, I had to break the silence and spoke.

"So where are we heading?" I shifted in the saddle, facing him with my torso, arching my back a little to push my breasts forward, gleeful that I had selected a form-hugging top.

I had caught him admiring my breasts earlier, hadn't I?

"Checkin' on the foals. Do it every mornin' this way. Good bunch this year," he said, turning in his saddle, mocking my move to face me with the wide span of his shoulders.

Oh!

I couldn't help but notice the flex of his bicep as he grasped the back of the saddle to distribute his weight into the new position.

He narrowed his weathered eyes and circled a finger of his gloved, free hand in my direction, reins looped easily in his other, "And … *if* … you're lucky, I might just show ya where those strawberries you seem to like so much came from."

I felt my face flush pink just like the pulp of those berries. I thought back to the other night, me in McKennon's house, drunk as a darn skunk. I caught myself cursing JD to hell in that moment and then shook my head, whisking the thought away with a wave of my hand through the air. I giggled aloud in a throaty outburst, tossed my head back, ponytail trailing my spine, and flipped it forward. McKennon's eyes widened, and he gave me a sideways tilt of his head accompanied by a heavenly quizzical look, pressing his fine lips together.

McKennon puzzled. Sexy.

"Err, what's that all about?" he asked, all eyebrows furrowed and looking hot as hell in his confusion.

"Hmm, nothing," I answered, succumbing to the next wave of flush flowing fast and furiously to my cheeks.

"Come now," he probed, obviously intrigued by my outburst.

"Fine," I said slightly huffy. "I was just thinking that if JD hadn't gotten me all of those mind erasers, I wouldn't know a thing about those strawberries of yours."

Amusement spread across McKennon's face. I could see what looked like a repressed slight smile slip across his tightly clamped lips. He moistened them, grazed his lower lip with his front teeth, leaned forward in his saddle and clucked to Star. Star moved out immediately, on command, into a languorous, slow-paced trot. McKennon sat back deeply into the leather as if reclining in a favorite oversized chair to settle in and watch a ball game. Only then did he beam a real smile in my direction.

"You see, this is what it is all about. Don't call it western plea-sure for nothin'. Should feel effortless, natural to the horse, a real pleasure to ride. Should never be about holdin' 'em back. Either they've got slow in 'em, or they don't. Should be as easy as sittin' on a couch. This one here … well … he's a natural."

Ha! He said it just like I had witnessed it.

"You got one too, ya know? Go on and move her up."

I cued Faith, and she effortlessly shifted into a slow jog. My heart poured open with warmth. I giggled again, covering my mouth to smile into my hand.

"What?" McKennon questioned.

"I think it's funny. I guess Faith feels like a couch to me too." "All righty. Maybe we can come up with somethin' a little better than a couch. How's 'bout a real nice luxury car. Should be that smooth. And as fast or slow as you'd want 'em to go. Like easin' on and off the gas pedal."

Good. Now we're talking equine! Maybe I can get him to reconsider, rather consider, training us.

He reached out and gave Star a wide palmed pat to his thick muscular neck. The stallion tossed his head out and forward as if he was proud of McKennon's recognition.

Boy, would I like to be that horse.

Replaying my failed attempt at requesting McKennon's servic-es, I contemplated a careful choice of words, searching every single nook and cranny tucked deep inside a writer's mind. We hadn't shared so many words this morning, and I didn't want to scare him off when we'd just begun.

"So," I paused, feeling a hitch in my breath, bracing for the familiar flush to meet my cheeks whenever I attempted to engage this man. "Um, what would you recommend I do with her now?"

My thoughtfully-selected words hung heavily between us.

If he won't train me, at least I can probe for information and hope he provides me some direction because I am stuck.

I just didn't know what to do with her. Faith and I had reached some undefined plateau. Our bond was stronger than ever, but I didn't have the experience for the next steps, the world champion steps. My mind flashed to the trophy case in McKennon's place, lined with sparkling reminders of greatness that I could only hope to aspire to and incessantly dreamed of being good enough to achieve.

Yes, I needed to ask some questions.

I mustered up my courage and continued, "I think I've got something here, but – "

His husky, deep voice cut me off, low and guttural. "Well," he hesitated, tilting his chin upward looking to the sky. I looked up too. It was so blue, dappled with tufts of white clouds, buoyant in the heavens, permitting the sun to play an occasional game of hide and seek with us. When the daylight did slip behind a cloud, I was grateful in its choosing to generously shade us, offering momentary relief from penetrating rays.

What was he thinking about?

A nervous wave washed over me. It was like he was asking permission from above to speak. McKennon gazed upward a moment longer, looked down at Star, grazed his gloved hand down his bay mane, shifted his straw cowboy hat a little lower over his face, and put his free hand on his hip. "Well," he began again.

Did I just see him swallow hard? Is he going to break the bad news to me that I am delusional, and Faith isn't all that I had hoped? Was he going to break my heart and crush my dreams in a single breath?

I held all the oxygen I could muster in my lungs, clutched the saddle horn, and closed my eyes, teeth clenched, waiting for the gauntlet to fall. My heart was aching. I didn't want to hear. I had to stop him.

"Never mind," I said, dropping my head. I couldn't hide my disappointment if I tried and didn't want to. I shrugged and said meekly, "I just thought you saw something in her too."

McKennon pulled Star up, stopped dead in his tracks, and looked after me as I walked Faith on a few more paces, unprepared for his abrupt reaction.

"Whoa," I sounded, and Faith rolled to a halt. I positioned myself in the saddle to see where he had gone, and McKennon just gazed at me for a moment, his becoming face blank.

What was he thinking?

Arching an eyebrow, he clucked his stallion forward, arriving at Faith's side. I cast my eyes down, afraid to look at him. He was close, as close as two people on horseback could be, when his knee bumped mine, an electric jolt shot through my body.

Whoa!

He put his lamb-skinned glove on my knee, and the current coursed through me again.

McKennon was TOUCHING my knee.

My blood boiled hot, hotter than in the shower.

I turned to him defensive, mixed with a pinch of lust, and slivered my eyes, glaring at him. Preparing for his negative appraisal, my demeanor caused his hand to come away from my knee almost instantly. Overwrought with anxiety, I combatively shook my head, reminding myself that I had asked for this.

"All right, let me have it," I hissed. "She's no good, right? Is that what you want to say to me?" I continued, firmly planting an angry arm on my hip, jutting my chin at him in disdain.

McKennon remained unruffled by my outburst. As if preparing for how to deal with me, he furrowed his brow, took off his cowboy hat, ran his fingers through his dark damp locks, put it back on his head, setting it back a little too far then laughed.

Now, he is laughing at me?

My insides were a blaze, and I felt myself sneer. He looked up at the sky again and shook his head, clearly amused.

"Nah, nothin' like that, Devon," he said, matter of fact.

I couldn't help but notice that my name sounded nice on his lips.

"I was just wonderin', well, how many times have you actually had her off this farm since you got her? I was gatherin' you don't have a trailer of your own, guessin' no truck either since you drive that little car of yours."

"Uh, none," I answered. "I've never taken her off of Green Briar since I got here."

Now, I was curious.

Did he think I was less of a horsewoman because I didn't have a nice shiny trailer or super-diesel chugging rig like his?

I grimaced. I was fond of my little import.

Not very American or cowgirl-like, I suppose.

"Well, what about where you got her from? How many times did she leave there?" he probed on.

I winced and forced a faint smile, "Never. Just to here." I shrugged my shoulders.

McKennon looked at me all wide-eyed, blue blazing through me. After a moment, he said, distractedly, "Uh, OK, that's OK then."

He puffed a rather large breath, lips vibrating to punctuate the exchange, and rode on, leaving me with that disapproving shake of his head. I had to scramble to move Faith up to join with them.

"What?" I exclaimed, falling in line again.

"How old is she? Faith?" he began, jutting his chin at my horse. "I'm guessin' she's about four years old."

He paused, looking Faith over from head to tail and rubbed his strong chin, "Gotta get 'em used to new faces and places, Devon."

Oh, he said my name again.

With his words, I felt that risqué little spark sneak up inside of me. Trying to maintain my composure, I swallowed hard and sturdied myself by grabbing the saddle horn.

"Horses are flight animals. You know, like deer? Gotta get 'em to experience new places, or they get too attached to home, too scared of everything. Look up there ..." he trailed off and launched into a full gallop up the hill, looking over his shoulder at me falling behind.

Faith and I were still at a walk as he sprinted away, flashing me an all-American, dazzling, white-toothed, child-at-play kind of smile. McKennon leaned forward, riding low over the saddle horn, free arm and gloved finger pointing ahead, pumping his rein hand, and hightailing it on Star toward the far end pasture and the foals.

Bewildered, I slumped forward in the saddle.

Great. What the heck do I know about acquiring a truck and trailer?

CHAPTER TWENTY

I'll figure that whole getting Faith off the farm truck and trailer thing *another time.*

Furiously shuffling the thought away into my mind's *deal-with-it-later* folder, I mustered what was left of my confidence and, in spontaneous glee, urged Faith forward, chasing down this cowboy Adonis and his steed.

I'd never galloped Faith full out. It felt sensational. The breeze blasting my face, my cheeks raw, hot, not under McKennon's scrutiny this time, but by natural causes. Holding my breath and the saddle horn, I leaned in. Briefly, I feared holes in the earth, visions of tumbling momentarily stealing the thrill, but I quickly shook the thought from my mind and pressed on. Hovering low and forward, mimicking McKennon, I urged her faster, pumping my arm. I held that horn tight, and the exhilaration surged through me.

I couldn't help but conjure up images of racecar drivers whizzing their speedsters around the track. My heart was in my throat, and all I could think about was catching up to him, passing him, leaving him in my dust, proving my cowgirl-ness, and winning the race. My mind, it was a flutter of wilder days when this sort of freedom was the way of life. I felt at one with my animal, this man, this forgotten kind of being, the blades of grass tidaling around us, and the heads of dandelions a blur of yellow, electricity in my veins.

What a rush!

Even Faith surprised me. I felt her surge forward increasing in speed, intensity in her agile movements, legs flowing freely with ease, nostrils blowing hard.

This was fun!

I think Faith felt it too. We were free, wild, rooted in the past. She shook her head, white mane flying out in a wave, ears pricked forward as if seeking out my same goal. She wanted to run them down too. Faith easily closed the distance, and I smiled to myself.

We'll show him! Me and my girl.

Closer, closer, closer until suddenly, we were measly lengths behind them.

Fleetingly, I took up the tail of the reins in my right hand and in one harsh wallop, flung them in the air, landing the leathers with a smack on Faith's hip. In shock, she put on the brakes and slammed to a halt when I had expected her to surge forward faster.

This isn't how it happened in the movies.

I had no time to brace myself and was heaved up over the saddle horn onto her neck. Frightened, Faith shimmied to the left, and then to the right before spinning hard on her hindquarters. Unsteady, I lost my stirrups and shrieked.

From the corner of my eye as I clung to an uneasy Faith, I observed McKennon yell out in horror, slide Star to a stop, whirl him around, and gallop back in my direction. He pulled up next to me just in time to watch Faith spiral in the other direction. Aghast, I lost my grip and slipped off to the side. She stopped dead and dumped me into the long blades of grass. I hit the ground with a thud, landing smack on my tailbone. I rolled over onto my shoulder and clutched the back pocket of my new jeans.

Ow!

McKennon was off Star in an instant and at my side, panic in his wider than wild, blue eyes. Without hesitation, he scooped me up into his arms.

"Are you OK?" he demanded into my neck, his breath hot and sweet, holding me a little too tightly to his warm, strong, athletic body.

I felt like a little girl, my self-confidence bruised.

"Yes," I murmured, winded, back into his neck. He smelled of earth and soap. His scent intoxicated me. I closed my eyes. My heart was in my throat from the fall.

Or was it his proximity?

I wasn't sure.

"You're not hurt?" he asked softly, but with swift urgency, holding my slack body out and away from his body to examine me. As I lay spent in the crook of his able arms, he frantically searched my eyes.

McKennon pulled me back to his solid chest, and I could feel the stubble on his chin scrape my forehead when he spoke, "I ... I just couldn't deal with it again."

"No," I said, enjoying being cradled like a child by this mysterious man.

"Tell. Me. You're. Not. Hurt," he croaked, his voice hoarse.

"No, I'm not hurt. I. Am. Embarrassed!" I squawked as I squirmed in his arms, defeated. Mid-squirm, I felt a momentary tightening, his biceps swelling at my upper arm and thigh before he set me down, placing my feet on land again.

"You ever galloped her before?" he asked, giving me the same once over I'd admired him imparting upon the farm fence line, as if assessing for bruises or breaks.

"Um ... No," I paused, momentarily brightening. "Was pretty fun though until I whipped her in the ass." We both chuckled. It was a shared moment from what seemed so long ago.

McKennon brushed a clump of dirt and grass from my shoulder and said, "Tough. I like that. Good thing she wasn't full tilt when ya fell though. Let's save that ass smackin' for when she is doing something wrong, eh?"

Guiltily, I nodded and searched for my mare. Off in the distance, Star and Faith grazed, side by side, lazily as if nothing had happened. For a moment, I wondered if my mare had it as bad for Star as I did for his loner cowboy owner.

Did they put something in the water around here at Green Briar?

"Come on then," McKennon said, taking hold of me by the bend at my elbow. "I think you'll live. No more fallin' though. You darn near gave me a heart attack," he scolded as the anxiousness started to dissipate from his resplendent face. "Just couldn't deal with that again," he breathed, shaking his head. McKennon looked up to the sky and closed his eyes for a moment.

Deal with what?

Visibly more relaxed, he gave me a little tug. My brow furrowed, mind busy figuring out his words, as he tempted me forward.

We waded through the long viridian grass, spreading the blades in our wake, leaving the horses undisturbed. Complacent, I lolled in McKennon's protective eminence as he blazed a trail for us. I let my arm go limp in his clutch, and he looked back at me narrowing his eyes.

"Just over there," he said, pointing that gloved finger. I looked to my left and laid my eyes on a sprawling herd of about 20 mares and their foals; some sauntered about scavenging in the huge pasture, patient mothers nursed their young while others grazed, their babies lying on their sides, lazy, in the sun. I sighed.

This IS the life.

When we reached the pasture edge, McKennon easily leapt up, ostrich boot to bottom rail, and vaulted himself to a perch atop the fence. With effort, I climbed my way up the rails to join him. Sitting side by side, we were close enough, but not too close. I had assured an appropriate distance was spaced between us, but inside of me, I felt a burning desire to close the gap I had just created. I wanted to scoot closer, slide up next to him, with candied hopes in the back of my mind that his arm might fall around my back, but I reined myself in, controlled the want, and held my position.

"The next bunch, they'll all be Star's foals," McKennon said, splayed fingers moving from left to right, surveying the pasture before us. "This is a good lot, but I think we'll probably sell most of 'em. Soon we'll be ready to be breedin' from our own champion. I'm bringin' him back to Green Briar a champion." McKennon declared, slapping his hands together with a pop. Startled by the sound, the majority of the herd looked up, ears pricked in our direction as McKennon leapt from the top rail down into the paddock. I watched after him as he loped off toward one of the foals.

Gingerly, I dismounted the rail and slowly trailed after, examining him in action. McKennon slowed his gait as he approached one of the foals, a pretty Palomino with a golden coat, copper sheen gleaming with sunlight, mane and tail white as snow, and a single patch of white on her yellow belly. I held my breath as he dropped to his knees just feet from the foal and mother. The filly lowered her head and sheepishly pushed a boney, adolescent hip into the mare. With its nose near the ground in inspection mode, the foal put one foot hesitantly in front of the other, guardedly approaching McKennon. Sitting still as a statue, McKennon gestured me forward with a slight tip of his head.

I started toward them, but stopped in my tracks. I gasped as the pretty Palomino reached McKennon and put its tiny, velveteen muzzle right in the palm of his hand. This god of animals had me in awe. He stroked her golden forehead, for but a moment, before an airliner streaked the sky overhead. Alarmed, the foal turned, releasing a shocked holler from its lips and leapt urgently away from McKennon back to its mama.

McKennon rose from his crouch, smiling that million-dollar smile I'd begun to wait for. He shook his head and turned his eyes to me. My heart started thundering in my chest as he walked with purpose in my direction.

Reaching me, he put his covered hand to my shoulder, giving it a squeeze, and said warmly, "Not that one though. Keepin' that filly. She'll make a good mama someday. Maybe even have some show pen promise. She's a Paint, ya know?" he asked, eyeing me cautiously as if I had caught an admission. "We'll see anyway. Come on then."

Again, he hooked me by the crook of the elbow. I didn't resist, falling behind his drag, happy to let my eyes settle on his fine, fine cowboy backside.

CHAPTER TWENTY-ONE

"I haven't brought anyone here in a long while," McKennon said, crouching low in a garden row to admire his bushes, pregnant with heavy, ripe ornaments. The wispy branches were draped low from the weight of their bountiful produce.

Standing there silent, my mouth began to water at the thought of McKennon and his strawberries. McKennon smiled to himself as he cupped a huge berry still attached to its stem in the palm of his gloved hand. He glanced upward toward the sky again and then plucked the confection from its bush. I wondered, momentarily, which would taste sweeter to my tongue, the strawberry or McKennon?

"Here," McKennon said, offering me the lusty fruit as he rose from the well-tended turf. "They're best right off the bush. I hope you're not one of them city chicks that has to wash everything first. Are ya?" he asked with a smirk, pointing his finger at my chest, holding that glorious strawberry high and away from my reach in his other sheathed hand.

I scrunched my nose in response. The idea of McKennon viewing me as a highbrow, big-city dweller made me cringe, but I couldn't ignore the scenario at hand. McKennon, my muse, sent my mind fluttering away to movies I'd seen. The tantalizing fashion in which he kept his harvest lingering in the air made me yearn to tip my head back, open my mouth wide, and give in to fantasy. Greedily, I eyed his red berry tempting me up there in that hand.

All at once, I was playing a part, and it resulted in my momentary checkout from reality. Building castles in the air, I drifted away to a chaise lounge and draped myself across its soft upholstery, dressed in a flowing gown with gold accents, bejeweled, and propped up on a silken cushion. My eyes hooded and heavily lined, waiting to be fed by this cowboy god.

If only his offering were a bunch of luscious grapes! Then he wouldn't be offering his queen just one bite of fruit, but many to languish and pleasure. Oh, and some champagne, that'd be nice too. So, OK, I'll take any bite offered to me by McKennon. Anytime.

I heard him clear his throat.

Snap back, Devon!

As I gained consciousness, McKennon considered me, scratched his jaw, and shrugged his shoulders, oblivious to the sultry leading role he just performed in my daydream. Unsuspecting of the flush in my cheeks, he simply dropped the strawberry into my cupped hands.

Thank heaven.

I turned the perfect, plump berry over in my palm then picked it up by its unwashed tuft of green, and tore into it with my front teeth.

Oh, my goodness!

There was an eruption on my tongue, a missile sent from the earth, exploding across my palate.

Mmmmm. Yes, so much sweeter and full of flavor than those store-bought, plastic-contained organic strawberries that I once coveted in my urban living days.

"Sooo?" McKennon's sexy-as-hell cowboy drawl interrupted my erotic episode with the berry. "I was wonderin'. What do you really want to do with your writing? I see ya banging them articles out on your laptop all the time, eyebrows all crunched, hammering them keys. You don't look very, um, relaxed doin' that kind of work. I can't imagine writing about *tomaters* is really your life's passion?"

I stopped midchew, licked my lips, and allowed the last of the juicy strawberry pulp to slip down my throat.

I tilted my head to the side. *Huh, actually, no; I really don't want to write about 'tomaters' for the rest of my life.*

I narrowed my eyes and analyzed this inquisitive cowboy.

He's been talking to Sofia. I've never told him what I write about.

"Well, yes, recently I did a piece on organic gardening for *Whole Earth* magazine. It paid quite nicely, but honestly I'd really like to write a collection of poetry. Unfortunately, that kind of aspirational writing rarely pays the bills," I felt myself start to shift into an unwelcomed, somber mood. It was necessary to change the subject. "So, is this an organic garden?"

"*Organic?* Is that what you city folk call it? Yeah, I've heard that's the 'in' thing these days," McKennon blurted, pressing his lips into a fine line, and shaking his head. "Funny that you feel like you have to ask somethin' like that about your food. It's always been that way for me down here, *organic*, as you'd say," he snorted, raising both eyebrows in what I interpreted as boyish remembrance. "Do it like my grandpops did. Never needed any fancy bug spray or fertilizers back then, and don't see why you would need it now. Nothin' like good ol' horse shit and hard work. So *yeah*, guess you'd say that strawberry I just watched you enjoy is organic."

Trying to make myself small, I looked down as he pierced me with those weather blue eyes.

"Don't need no sticker to prove it's natural neither," he added. It was his final remark on the topic.

I felt thoroughly beaten down for my city slicker ways by this hot country boy. McKennon, not allowing me to wallow in my defeat, slipped a gloved hand beneath my chin, and lifted my eyes to him.

"I'd sure like to read one of those poems one day," he affirmed, locking eyes with me for what felt like eternity, my heart in my throat, skin a fire, my mouth parted slightly. I wanted to comment, but I struggled to find the right words.

Before I could respond, McKennon dropped his grasp, squeezed the tips of his fingers at the bridge of his perfectly straight nose, and clenched his jaw.

There, standing at the base of a meticulously maintained *organic* garden, visible richness in its soil, fragrant and lush, I witnessed McKennon wishing he could take his words back. He put his hands on his hips, rolled his eyes to the sky, and said, "OK, then. Time to be movin' along, Devon." Hurt, a little downtrodden even, I still couldn't help but like the way my name sounded on his lips.

We rode back in silence, side by side. Unable to enjoy the silence, I distracted myself with some of the lessons I had learned in my attempts at meditation in the big city. I moved my thoughts away from the buzzing conversation in my head that kept repeating over and over *and over.* I'd try anything to distract myself from the fact that I, and my writing, was unattractive in you-know-who's mind.

What the heck just happened?

I forced my focus on appreciation for the leaves billowing on the trees, the wind through the overgrown grasses, moving the blades like the sea, the feel of Faith beneath my seat, sturdy, slow, and strong, the sound of the birds, the passing of the white tufts

above, the blueness of the sky. These were all the real reasons I
came here.

I felt uneasy though. I couldn't wait to get back to the barn, put
Faith up, and make my way home. I had this burning sensation
that McKennon was about to leave again.

As we re-entered reality and approached the barn, my eyes
fixed on JD leaning up against his truck, chewing hard on a long
piece of straw, held tight between his lips, arms pinned across his
chest, one gleaming cowboy boot up against the side of his slightly
banged up quarter-ton pickup.

Wow. He looks really mad.

I made a quick, slightly awkward wave at him, glanced at
McKennon, and imagined how great it would be to magically
transform myself into an ostrich so I could seek out a hole to stuff
my head in. Hastily, I dismounted Faith. I was desperate to get
out of dodge.

Slowly, McKennon lifted himself from the saddle and gracefully set his boots back to the earth, looping Star's reins over the
saddle horn. In silence, he turned to me, put his big hands on
my small shoulders, and squared my diminutive frame to his tall,
wiry one. The top of my head barely reached his chest. Cautious
weather blue eyes on mine, McKennon removed his cowboy hat
with one hand and kept the other firmly planted on my shoulder.
Holding the brim of his well-worn and supple straw hat between
his forefinger and thumb, he swirled his gloved hand around the
top of his head then ran his fingers through his dark silken locks
from back to front.

*Was this an attempt to smooth his hair, or an effort to gather his
thoughts?*

"It was a real pleasure ridin' with you today, Devon," he said.
"I'll be seein' you around."

In a chivalrous manner, McKennon put his hat to his chest and
gave a slight bow, torso lowered, but smoldering eyes never leaving

mine. No visible signs of a last haircut, his hair was overgrown, damp tendrils slightly curling around and up toward his ears. I yearned to tangle my fists in his tresses.

I stood frozen aware that JD was witnessing the whole scene. I was all wide eyes and weirdness. Not knowing what to say, I blurted out, "Yeah, sweet ride!"

Argh! What am I, a teenager?

His grin broadened as he gave me a tip of his replaced hat and moseyed back into the barn to address his stead in tow.

In the burn of the sun's rays and under the glare of JD's stare, I turned to my Faith, embraced her muzzle in my arms and sighed into her cheek low so no one could hear, "He's leaving again. I just know it."

CHAPTER TWENTY-TWO

My intuition proved legitimate. It had been a week since I'd seen any signs of McKennon. However, JD was everywhere he wasn't: lounging on a hay bale, cracking jokes while I secured straps preparing for my daily ride, leaning through the bars of Faith's stall, hands dangling just above her feed bucket, flashing his big white 'I am glad McKennon's gone' grin.

I couldn't help but notice JD's filthy fingernails and wonder why he didn't wear gloves to manage his chores like McKennon did. I tried to welcome JD's lighthearted company, but there was a ghostly, heavy vacancy in me. I was an empty void lingering in the aisles of the barn in this absence. Something was missing at Green Briar without that big rig in the drive, the steed in his stall, or the rhythmic jingle of spurs on the man. I'd become so accustomed to listening for the sounds of McKennon in hopes I could catch a glimpse of him as he sauntered past my stall. Now, there was only his silence.

I couldn't stand it anymore. I hadn't seen him in days. I interacted with him more in those last three days before he went missing than we ever had. I had to know where he had gone and conjure up an estimate of how long he'd be away. I thought about going to Sophia, but figured the better of it. Asking Sophia would mean not complying with her 'mind your p's & q's' rule, and the last thing I wanted was the boot. So, I opted for the easier route.

JD had backed his truck into the adjacent aisle. Peeking around the corner of the hallway joining his aisle to mine, I zeroed in on him as he effortlessly heaved huge bags of wood shavings, just about bursting at their plastic seams, off the back of his dinged up pick up. His biceps bulged with effort, purple veins running close to the surface of his skin, pumping the blood through, and his back muscles rippled like a current beneath his thin T-shirt. Today, he was wearing a ball cap, bits of blonde peeking out through the hole above the adjustable band.

If I were half my age and maybe half as smart, I'd certainly be gaga over JD. He *was* very handsome. Wearing that baseball hat, deep in concentration, a certain innocence about him, working so hard yet with ease, he looked very much like the young man he was, rather than the tough, bull riding, buckle bunny teasing man he claimed to be. I liked him this way and felt a sad little pang in my stomach remembering our get-to-know-you conversations.

Oh, his father disowned him when he was so young over the loss of his uncle to a bull ride gone wrong.

I felt a wave of empathy for JD wash through me, softened my tough cookie approach, and made my way to the side of his truck.

"JD?" I asked, looking up at him through my lashes, giving him my best cowgirl in distress voice. "Can I ask you something?"

"Sure, little lady. You can ask me anything."

He stood up in the back of the truck and dusted off his hands on the thighs of his jeans. I tried to pay no mind to his dirty fingernails as he coiled his thumbs through the belt loops at his hips, and jutted his crotch, a triangle of tight denim topped with a just-polished belt buckle all twinkle and shine, in the general direction of my face. I stiffened and jerked my head back an inch. "I'd prefer it be askin' for a date though," he smirked.

I just blinked up at him through my lashes again, a momentary deer in headlights. I should have expected this type of behavior from JD, but my mind was still caught up with my earlier revere for him.

"Aw, shucks, Devon," he said, shaking his head as he dropped back. Putting the seat of his wrangler jeans on one of the remaining shavings bags yet to be heaved from the truck, he looked down at me.

Was there tenderness in his eyes? Did he feel bad about putting his junk in my face?

His expression was soft.

Why did I get the feeling JD suddenly felt bad for me?

He huffed, "You wanna know where he's gone, don't ya?"

"Yes," I breathed. I sounded too desperate, but it was all I could manage. My heart was racing through my chest like a herd of a thousand wild horses under pursuit.

JD shook his head in distain, but his eyes were rimmed with pure empathy.

JD did feel bad for me.

"Just don't know what it is with that guy." He took off his baseball hat, gave it a dusting and put it back on, taming his damp blonde locks. "All right, Devon, he's gone to a show. When he was showing regularly, he always took 'em in early to get 'em used to the place. You happy now?"

"Is he going to show Star?" I questioned calmly, but inside I felt giddy.

"Don't know. Probably not. Probably just usin' it for prep. You know, for the big show."

JD turned away from me, picked up a new bag of shavings, and tossed it off the truck. It landed awkwardly in the aisle and burst open at the corner seam.

"Dang it!" JD hollered as he leapt from the back of the truck like an action star might leap from a building in the movies.

"I'll get you a broom," I offered over my shoulder as I scurried off into the tack room. This was my attempt to keep his annoyance to a minimum and the questioning session online. The scent of the split shavings bag filled the air with the aroma of pine. I passed JD the broom, proffered a smile and pressed on, "So, how do you know so much about how he does things anyway? Doesn't seem like you two are all that close from what I can see."

JD visibly tensed, and his mood turned dark before my eyes. As he hardened his stance, I tried to decipher whether it was a defensive or an aggressive personality shift.

"I lost her too," he growled, then as if surprised at his reaction, he tempered down and continued, "– err, we had a mutual acquaintance. Uh, that's all I mean."

Her? What's this? Have JD and McKennon shared a conquest?

Ugh! I don't want to know this right now! Gauging JD's expression, I decided not to press it. Not at this exact moment anyway, but later for sure. I had to change my approach.

"JD, did you know that Faith had never been off the farm she grew up on until she came here?" I asked, and JD's shoulders relaxed.

He paused his sweeping, perched on the push broom, both hands at the tip, and leaned forward, resting his chin atop his intertwined fingers and peered at me. "No. Didn't know that." His eyes narrowed, quizzing me, obviously relieved at the change in subject, but cautious about where I was going.

"Did you know I haven't had her off Green Briar since I've had her here?" I continued.

"That I knew, missy. I'm always keepin' an eye on you," he purred in a velvety voice, slivering his eyes, smacking his plush lips, and giving my body a long lingering once over. In his assessment of me, JD released a low, slow whistle through his now-pursed mouth before stowing the broom and leaping up on his tailgate.

"Come on, JD. Be serious!" I scolded as he looked down on me from the truck, hands on his hips. I could feel the heat of his young eyes on me, and I rushed to fasten an upper button on my shirt in an attempt to hide my cleavage.

There, damage control!

"Your bra'wls pink," he hummed, proud in his dismantling of me, pleasure spread across his face. He was enjoying watching me squirm.

I sighed and dropped my hands to my side in a failed attempt to hide my assets.

What do I have to lose?

"JD?" I cooed. "Would you take me to the show?"

"Why don't you just drive your little car there yourself if you want to see Mr. Dreamy so bad?" he sneered, ego bruised.

"No, JD, Faith and me. Take us to the show. You know I don't have a truck or a trailer," I mumbled, shrugging my shoulders and casting my eyes down.

I am so NOT cowgirl tough right now.

"Why would you want to do that?" he asked, baffled by my request.

"Well," I shrugged my shoulders and offered my arms out to the side, palms up in surrender. "McKennon won't train us, so I've been asking him for tips."

"Tips? You're askin' him for tips?" he exclaimed. Perplexed, he scrunched the skin between his brows.

"Yes, *tips*, and he said that I should get her used to new places. So I'd like to start by going to this show." I peeked up at him. It registered that he might be mulling it over.

"You really think that's a good idea?" he questioned, rubbing the stubble on his chin, and looking me over normally, with a pinch of bewilderment, as opposed to a piece of meat. "I like your mare, Devon, but she can get a little jumpy."

"Please, JD," I begged, batting my lashes, leaning forward just enough so I could feel my breasts shift into view, and fill the front of that pink bra JD had been working so hard to admire. "I have an overnight bag in my trunk, and I'll pay for gas," I continued as I feigned a stretch, turning it into a cat-like yoga pose. The top button of my blouse, the one I had just hastily done up, popped wide open with the pressure of my bosom right there in the aisle of a horse barn.

He stared straight at my peach flesh plunged forward in pink. "Uh, uh, um. OK, what the heck! I'll take you. It's not that far from here anyhow," JD said shocked, blinking wildly. He was clearly taken aback that I had exposed myself so willingly.

I arched forward, hands at the base of my back, a sly smile slipping to my lips.

"Great! When can we leave?"

CHAPTER TWENTY-THREE

As JD pulled around the corner, my breath hitched and a wave of terror washed over me. His rickety, bucket-of-bolts horse trailer, if you could call it that, was deafening. The exterior was canvased by a dull, red, peeling paint job faded by the sun's constant beating. Its steel edges were encrusted in rust and protruded like daggers. One would think the tiny rocks in Green Briar's impeccably-kept gravel driveway were enormous boulders. The fifth wheel creaked and groaned with effort above six tread-less tires, flexing its straining axles, as they met the meager wheel-worn potholes beneath them.

Like my old school boots, JD's stock trailer was a product of the early '90s. It was dated, made-of-steel heavy, and honestly scared the living daylights out of me. It was nothing like Green Briar's sleek white and chrome accented, eight-horse gooseneck, aluminum trailer with human living quarters fit for a king. I imagined McKennon leaning back inside that trailer after a long day of riding Star at the horse show. I could almost hear him recounting the highlights in his landmark Southern drawl over the phone to an anticipatory Sophia, her hands clasped in elation. I pictured his muscled, free arm crossed behind his head, cell held to his ear, boots up on an adjacent chair, satisfied, and relaxed in a job well done. I wondered if one day I might be allowed inside that pristine trailer with them, with him.

Calling me back to the situation at hand, Faith, once standing calmly at my side, jerked her head up high as JD creaked and clunked passed us. Her sudden movement took all the slack from the lead rope and just about dislocated my shoulder in the process. Steadying her, I realized I must have a screw loose, something in common with his six-wheeled deathtrap, for even considering putting my horse in there.

If only I had a gigantic can of squeak lubricant, I'd give that thing a once over for sure.

Lost in skepticism, I hadn't even noticed Sophia slip up next to me. Her scent, all citrus and clean, lifted me out of my scrutinizing daze. Sophia's soft, wrinkle-hooded, but luminous eyes were alert. They grew even wider as she watched the trailer bump and crash down Green Briar's driveway. Metal on metal screeching, she clenched her jaw bearing witness as it bounced along behind JD's beat up black quarter-ton truck.

Driving the getup way too fast, JD circled at the far end of the farm, spewing gravel, and creating a dust cloud that hovered in the air. Tempted but unable to cover my eyes, I watched as he cut the turn so tight that I feared the trailer would jackknife, or worse yet, slam into the sprawling live oak in its direct path. Luckily, the truck and trailer cleared the turn, but clipped a branch on the tree. With a crack followed by a thud, JD succeeded in bringing a large, low-hanging limb down into his truck bed. Its thunderous fall was surrounded by a furious rainstorm of leaves.

JD slammed on the brakes, and the trailer wheels locked, sliding to a stop in front of the barn, Sophia, Faith and me. Apparently unaffected by having half of a tree hanging out of the back of his truck, he leapt from the cab with a swing from the driver's side door and gave it a heavy heave shut. Faith's head shot up in alarm with the clamor, nostrils blowing in a rapid rhythm. Her wide, brown eyes, rimmed in white, were dead set on the tree branch, its remaining green leaves flittering from the abrupt ending of motion. Sophia put her delicate hand to my horse's anxious muzzle. As Faith pressed into her palm, she gave me a weak smile and turned back to the circus unfolding before us.

JD worked the back gate of the trailer open with effort. He clenched his bottom lip between his front teeth, beads of sweat forming at the base of his hairline, as the rusty hinges of the doors cried out, stiff, and in decline.

With the entryway finally pried open, JD swung his torso toward us with pride that quickly dissipated when he realized our trepidation toward his trailer.

"Hey now, ladies! I know it don't look like much, but it always gets me where I'm want'n to go. Shucks, I've had some really rank bulls in there, and they never complained! Devon, we doin' this or what?" He shifted his hips to the left and planted his hands on them in expectation. "I hooked this beast up at your request. You wanna follow that T-I-P McKennon gave you and get that horse used to new places? Well, this is your chance, cowgirrrrrl," he spelled out 'tip', tapping his boot to each letter, and let the cowgirl roll off his tongue, long and slow, taunting me.

My heart started thumping in my chest.

Darn it! I'm going to show them all!

I put my apprehension at bay, gave Sophia a reassuring nod, and walked Faith toward the tail end of the trailer. Peering into the back of the monstrosity, I could see that JD had been thoughtful and laid down fresh shavings for Faith. I investigated the interior further.

No sharp edges inside of it at least.

It looked in good working order. I stepped inside, bounced up and down on the floorboards. I picked up the mat below the new bedding and examined the trailer floor while Faith stood outside at the long end of my lead rope, head out smelling the air, ears pricked toward my ongoing efforts inside.

It's now or never. Can't come this far and back down.

Hopeful, I gave a gentle tug on Faith's lead, pulling it taut, and encouraging her forward.

"Come on, girl. It's OK," I begged.

She hesitated, setting back on her hind end, and braced her front legs out in front of her. Panicked, she locked her knees and tension rippled across her muscular conformation. Without warning, JD strutted up behind her, uttered "Get up now," and swiftly swatted Faith across her tail with a broom. Nearly running me down, she shot into the trailer. I had to leap to the side to avoid her rush. Thrusting me out of the way, JD jumped into the trailer behind her, swung the cross bar shut, grabbed the lead from my hands, and hastily tied Faith's head in front of her.

"Don't worry, Devon. I've done this before," JD consoled, thrusting a bag overflowing with flakes of hay in her face. I sighed as Faith investigated the food in front of her.

JD helped me pack my work saddle, tack box, a bale of hay, and enough grain to get us through three feedings. He tossed a couple spare Green Briar buckets into the bed of his truck and ripped the tree branch out. The shrill sound of bark on metal and flickering of leaves sent Faith stomping and calling from the back of the trailer.

"Well. Think that's all you'll need this time around," JD said, brushing his palms together. Aware of Sophia's proximity, he leaned in closer to my ear and put his hand on my shoulder to pull me closer, "Devon, you're sure about this, right?" To allow his jade eyes to search my face, he lifted from my ear, pushed my shoulder out, and gave me a pleading nod, prodding me to respond.

"Yes," I said, strong, squaring myself to him, and shrugging off his hand. "I'm sure." I couldn't look at Sophia.

He put his hand back to my shoulder, paused to give me room to back out, and eyed me over once last time. "All right then. Let's talk sleepin' arrangements," he said, closing our distance. His whisper was hot in my ear, and I shoved him off as his trademark smirk crept back across his lips. He pulled away, satisfied at having ruffled my feathers yet again, stealing a glance at an unimpressed Sophia.

I apologetically admired Sophia, and she quietly returned my gaze. I was grateful that she hadn't said a word. Her feelings about what was happening were transparent. I could see her concern for our safety. The worry was clearly sprawled across her incandescent peach face, and her lips were set in a firm line. I knew she was holding her tongue. She did not approve. Honestly, if she decided to speak up, her lovely voice singing out, to convince me to rethink this, I could guarantee that I would cave instantly. However, it seemed as though a higher power kept her silent, perched on the shaded bench just outside of the barn, merely observing this impromptu travel attempt of mine.

"In the TRUCK!" I demanded, pointing at JD's rig.

Shoot! I hadn't really given any thought to where I'd actually be sleeping tonight. Darn it!

I stomped to the passenger side, stepped on the running board, looked back towards Faith, gave a halfhearted wave to Sophia, and planted myself in the seat beside JD.

"Please go slow, JD," I pleaded. "She and I haven't done this much. OK?"

"OK," he said, softening toward me. "Ready?"

"It's now or never," I replied, strapping myself in.

JD jerked the shifter down to drive, and we crept forward, tires crunching below us. As we pulled out of the driveway, I looked in the side mirror and caught a last glimpse of Sophia. She was off the bench and pacing.

What was she doing?

Just before we cleared the crest of the hill out of Green Briar, I realized her baubled fingers were flying across the face of her cell. As my caravan sank up and over, I watched her swiftly raise the phone to her ear in urgency, then she disappeared.

I turned in my seat, hoping to catch a last glimpse of her, but I was startled into the present and back inside the truck. JD's open palm came down with a slap on my knee. He moved his hand slightly higher, and, with a squeeze, cupped the inseam of my jeans. Laying his best sultry gaze, thick and slick, all over me, he crooned, "Now, how's about we talk about them sleeping arrangements?"

CHAPTER TWENTY-FOUR

I clutched JD's grip on my leg with both hands and tossed him off.

"Hey! You've got my precious cargo back there! Keep your eyes on the road and your hands to yourself, mister! Stop with that smirking, or I will slap that smile right off your face," I warned, narrowing my eyes at him and raising my palm above my head. I was trying to appear as mean as possible, but inside, I found the whole thing slightly amusing. I had to turn my head to the window to avoid having my grin tattletale on me. JD was obnoxious and constantly coming on to me, but deep down, I knew he didn't mean me any harm. We were friends.

"Aw, come on, Devon. I was just joshin' with you," JD chirped, voice sounding temporarily burned. Quickly regaining his form, he quipped, "You know, I got me some friends, err, girlfriends with horses and living quarters of their own up at that show. You can use my bed in this trailer. Built that living space myself. Figured I'd hang at the show for a night. You know, get me some action."

"What are you going to do, JD?" I asked. "Are you going to just hop from trailer to trailer in your underwear, pulling your pants up and your boots on as you leave?" I snapped, bothered that my sidekick found it necessary to share the details of spreading himself around, playboy-style, while on the road with me. "Never mind," I said, shaking my head. "I'd really rather not know. I just hope you're careful. That's all, JD."

"Always figured you for the jealous type," he chuckled before beginning again, more sincere this time. "Just thought I'd stay up at the show for the night. You know, to make sure you're cool. Didn't just want to drop ya with my trailer and leave. I'm worried you might ding up my paint job."

Dumbfounded, I shifted in my seat, giving him a blank look.

JD gingerly knuckled me in the shoulder. "Aw, come on, Devon! Lighten up, will ya?" And with that, we broke the heaviness and shared a good, hard laugh out loud.

Somehow we managed to make the 60-mile drive from Green Briar to the fairgrounds without a collision, breakdown or equine meltdown. Butterflies were fast forming and had set to fluttering around my insides as we pulled in through the large front gate and meandered down the blacktop drive. We passed rows and rows of gleaming rigs with monogrammed trailers in tow, hooked up to electricity poles as we wound our way to the main barn in search of the office for a stall selection. I was thankful that JD knew his way around the grounds from competing there when the big rodeo tour came into town. Anxious, I searched for any sign of McKennon as my eyes took in the sights around me. I felt blazingly out of my league arriving in this manner, crazy bull rider at the wheel, clunker of a stock trailer creaking in drag, frenzied horse hollering from inside, but here I was anyway, following his *tip*, following *him*.

"Well, lookie here," JD grumbled as he eased on the brakes and slid the gear into park. He thumped both hands on the steering wheel, shook his head, and cupped the brim of his ball cap, squeezing it into a deep U, before hopping out of the cab, letting the heavy driver's side door bang shut behind him. He rounded the front of the truck and shook McKennon's hand. I turned ashen. As I eyeballed the two of them, I knew I was failing to keep my composure, succumbing to the familiar pounding at my chest, holding my breath, and clutching Faith's lead rope. They exchanged a few words. JD turned and glanced at me from under the brim of his baseball hat. He looked ashamed, like a boy getting a talking-to by his father, then shrugged his shoulders, making his way back to the truck.

He leaned in the rolled-down window and said, "He wants to talk to you." His head gesturing in McKennon's general direction, then he added, "He's such a wet blanket. You still serious about doin' this?"

Seeing my unwavering expression, he dismissed me with a wave of his hand and rolled to the side of his truck, leaning back against it, arms folded across his chest, one boot up on the tire, preparing to wait us out.

"Apparently, we are here, aren't we?" I murmured under my breath when JD turned away. I didn't care if he heard me or not. I released my seatbelt and swung open the truck door. And there he was, all Romeo in Wranglers, standing under an awning in the shade, blocking the entrance to the stall reservation office, tapping his elephant hide boot on the cement, plaid fitted shirt with the sleeves folded back molded to his frame, hands tucked into the crooks of his arms, hat low so I couldn't see his eyes, only his firm lips locked in a disapproving but arousing frown. I approached him mustering all the cowgirl confidence I could find.

McKennon removed his straw hat, ran his hand over his dark hair, and regarded me steadily. I kept my chin up. I wanted to be here. I wasn't backing down. I met his deep blue eyes, defined by thick eyelashes, like the sky just before a storm.

Why did I feel like I owed him an explanation?

"I … I," I struggled out. I felt like my lungs had stopped functioning. There was no breath to make words with. He put his gloved finger to his lip and hushed me.

"Come on then," he directed and put his hand on the small of my back. A burst of heat expanded in my groin. I looked over my shoulder at JD, eyes pleading for him to look after Faith. He caught my eye, and with an annoyed but reassuring shake of his head, waved me on pumping his right hand in the air twice. With that, McKennon pressed me through the office door.

"Sallie Mae?" he called out.

The timeworn show secretary looked up, propped her glasses atop of her gray head, and smiled as if she'd known him for years. Sitting low on a stool behind a tall counter, her face reminded me of a raisin, oval and sunken from too much sun, brown with deep lines at the corners of her eyes, but jovial. McKennon offered me forward with slight pressure to my spine. The slow burn below turned to a raging forest fire inside me.

"This here is Devon. She's just arrived. One horse. That stall next to mine still available?" he asked.

"Hmmm. Let me see," Sally Mae clucked, pulling a thick white binder from beneath the ledge of the counter. Dropping her bifocals to the bridge of her nose, she leaned forward, flipped open the pages, and examined a hand-drawn layout of the stalls in the show barn. Her finger dragged across the page until it settled on his last name, Kelly.

"Ah, here you are, Kelly. Stall number 22 and 23. Let's see. Why, yes, it looks like stall 24 hasn't been taken yet." Looking up from her book, she observed me kindly. "You're in luck, darling! You get to stall next to this hunk of a cowboy for the weekend."

Blushing, I clutched my purse. "How much do I owe, ma'am?"

"Well, that depends. Are you going to show your horse, dear? Here's the show bill," she said, sliding the paper across the counter with her weathered hand.

I picked up the white page, printed front and back, and examined the line listing of all of the offered classes. My eyes widened as I reviewed it. I knew I wasn't ready for this. I stole a glimpse at McKennon, and he mirrored my extreme apprehension. With his baby blues locked on the show bill in my quivering hands, his expression clearly was one of hope that I wouldn't say yes.

Sallie Mae openly registered the shock on our faces and rescinded, "Well, if you aren't sure now, you could always come back later and add a class or two. All you have to do is leave an open check and then settle up with me tomorrow."

"Um. OK," I said, swiftly placing the leaflet back on the counter. "I think I'll just pay for the stall."

McKennon released an audible sigh of relief, and I tensed before rummaging through my bag for the checkbook.

Sallie Mae pressed a pen to a carbon copy receipt book. "The stall will be $50, miss. Shavings are $10 a bag."

McKennon stepped forward. Leaning in, fingers through his belt loops, he said, "She'll be needin' four bags, Sallie Mae. Gotta watch out for those horse's legs." He winked at her, and she passed her quizzical hazel eyes from McKennon to me. It seemed that their history made her question our relationship.

She offered me a reassuring grin, then a brief, almost knowing, glint of sadness toward him. I handed over the payment for one stall and four bags of shavings.

"OK. That'll do it. Welcome to the show. Byron will be by shortly to drop those shavings off." Finished with me, she picked up a walkie-talkie and barked into the receiver, "Four bags to 24, Byron. A new one just arrived."

She slapped a paid sticker on the counter and instructed me to put it on my stall.

"Thank you," I said.

"You're an angel, Sallie Mae," McKennon added. "Be seeing you tonight?"

"Only if you buy me a cocktail, Mr. Kelly," she countered, batting her age-old lashes, obviously melting in his inviting presence.

"You got it!" He tipped his hat and motioned me toward the door with his chin.

As I breezed through the door, I felt on air knowing I'd be so close to McKennon during the show. Seconds later, reality set in.

"Whoa now!" I heard JD call out.

He was trying to calm my horse, turned wild animal, raging in the back of his trailer. Spotting us, JD called out with urgency, "She's getting pretty riled up in there, you two!"

We were only away for what seemed like minutes!

"Better get her out," McKennon ordered, dragging the lead line from my hand. Instantly, JD was at the back of that beat up trailer, wedging the rear doors loose to clear a path for McKennon. McKennon acknowledged JD's efforts with a nod and swooped into the trailer. Instinctively, they seemed to know how to work together.

I felt helpless. I peered in through the slats, grateful that they took charge. I hadn't done this in so long. McKennon snapped the lead to Faith's halter, releasing her from the tie inside.

"Easy, easy, easssssssy now," he coaxed, the gentle words falling from his stubble-fringed lips. He was calm with her crazy. JD pulled the screeching hinges wide, and McKennon attempted to ease Faith backwards, but she shot out of the steel cage like a bullet. Her coat was slick with sweat. She hollered into the air, ears flitting furiously, front to back then side to side, pink nostrils a flare smelling her surroundings.

Holy shit! What have I done?

Finally out of the trailer, McKennon held her firm as she danced and pranced, snorting and shuffling, on the paved drive. A few cowboys paused in their crossing of the grounds to watch our debacle. I was growing more and more uncomfortable.

"You want her?" McKennon asked, offering Faith's rope to me. Embarrassed, I shook my head, unable to meet his eyes, and stared at the ground.

"All right then," he said, walking away from me, aiming my bouncing, bellowing beast toward the barn.

JD whisked up beside me and put a reassuring arm around my shoulder. "You all right?" he inquired, giving me a squeeze. I shrugged into him, willing myself not to bury my face in his chest and sob. I felt the hot tears wanting to come. "Guess his tip was pretty spot on?" JD murmured as he towed me along in the crook of his arm.

Byron had already unloaded the shavings in front of stall 24. Like a business partner, sports teammate, or lifelong comrade, JD rushed to McKennon's aid, pocketknife in hand. I couldn't help but wonder if they had a deeper working relationship with each other in the past. JD dumped the first bag of pine into the stall haphazardly. Without thought, he tossed the white plastic bag into the aisle. Faith's eyes turned to alarm, white around the edges, and her head shot up at the sight. She tugged McKennon sideways a foot or two, catching him off guard for but a moment. He eyed me, registering my upset, dug his heels in and pulled the lead down hard then paused. I could see his mouth move, but I couldn't hear what he was saying. He was talking to her, coaxing her off the edge. He put his gloved hand to her neck and stroked beneath her white mane, running his fingers slow across her withers, down her shoulder.

Rather than being grateful, I wondered how his hands would feel on me.

Could I be jealous of the way he was touching my horse? Yep! I was.

I gasped as I watched Faith visibly relax in the spread of his palm. JD tended to the stall with urgency. Having learned his lesson, he rolled up the remaining bags and tucked them inside an empty sack before he hustled out down the aisle as McKennon led her in.

"Gotta tie 'em up when you first put 'em in, Devon," he explained, not looking at me, tying the lead in a quick release knot to the front bars of the makeshift show stall. "They get a whiff of those fresh pine chips, and all they wanna do is lie down and roll in 'em. Had one hang up on me that way, wound up ripping a tendon. Didn't have anyone to tell me better then, was out for the count because of it. Learned me a lesson on that one."

JD reappeared, kicking up dust in the aisle. He looked that boyish way again. He was lugging one of the Green Briar buckets with intensity, splashing water from its top along the way. He brushed past me and tied it up in Faith's stall with haste and a string of twine from one of McKennon's hay bales. Faith slurped and chugged the entire bucket with gratitude before lowering her head, letting her eyes fall closed.

"Think she's had one heck of a day," JD said, shifting his ball cap back on his head, examining her.

I felt like a stone, immobile. I hadn't done anything to handle my own animal. "Thanks for bringing water, JD."

Fearless cowgirl? Nope! Not me.

I just let the cowboys swoop in and take over, come to my rescue. As I considered this, something stirred in me, and I willed myself into action. I opened Faith's stall and went inside. I looked into her weary, big brown eyes. I had to apologize to her, and this was the only way I knew how.

I let my hands graze over her coat, and she was still slightly damp. I liked her warmth beneath my palm. I glided over her body, one side to the next, ending at her head. I stroked the white blaze between her eyes then embraced her face in the span of my arms. Faith let the weight of her head go. I just held her there, allowing connection to return between us. After a while, I reached out, unlatched her tie, released her chiseled face, and stepped back. She set free a long, low breath, circled the stall once, and dropped down in the deep bedding to rest. It reminded me of the first time I introduced her to the new stall at Green Briar.

"Think she's good now," McKennon witnessed. "JD, you go get Devon settled in since you know the grounds and how to park that million-dollar trailer of yours. You got electrical in there yet?"

"Workin' on it, *Ken*," JD spat, grimacing to himself. Undoubtedly, his intention was to annoy McKennon by uttering the nickname.

"I'll stay on here to look over Faith. And JD? Don't be callin' me Ken."

CHAPTER TWENTY-FIVE

I felt defeated as we headed out of the barn and back to the jalopy we left parked in front of the show office. JD bumped me easily in the shoulder with his and offered a reassuring smile.

"Maybe not what you expected, huh?" he quizzed.

"No, not exactly. Faith didn't act like that when I brought her to Green Briar. She is usually much more peaceful," I mumbled. "I guess there's a lot more commotion at horse shows."

"Exactly the reason I like bulls. They're always the same, acting like angry rank tanks. They may be mean, but at least they're consistent. You only have to think about three things with bulls. Stayin' on, stayin' out of their way, and stayin' alive. Horses, on the other hand, they can get, er, screwy."

"I think I know what you mean," I said, offering JD a weak smile. I shrugged, holding my palms up in defeat.

"Aw, come on now," he encouraged, hooking his elbow around my neck and tugging down as the truck and trailer came into our view. "Don't fret too much. It'll get better. Have a feelin' Ken'll be helpin' you out. Now let's get ya set up in my sweet rig!"

"Ken?" I wondered up at him, trying to tilt my eyes to his, but he flexed his bicep, bracing me from movement inside the headlock.

"Nah, long story."

JD waved an open palm in front of my restrained head and lengthened his strides, heading for his pickup in anticipation. I struggled to keep the long pace with my noggin tucked like a football in the bend of his flexed arm. JD released me just as Sallie Mae was making her way out of the show office. Paused on the porch, she took a quizzical gander at the two of us for a moment then contemplated me with an amused onceover.

"Ma'am," JD said, tipping his baseball brim to the little old raisin lady.

"This one here," Sallie Mae mused, pointing at me, her index finger crooked with age at the knuckle. "She's scoopin' up all the handsome cowboys in a butterfly net now, isn't she?" She beamed a mischievous smile, and I couldn't tell if she was teasing or serious as the wrinkles deepened at the corners of her eyes. "Will I be seeing the two of you on the dance floor tonight?" she pressed, needling JD and me.

"I've been known to give Miss Devon here a whirl around the dance floor, ma'am," JD retorted, fielding the question like a pro, turning his trademark mega-wattage, limelight smile on me. I clasped my hands in front of me at the waist, and looked down into them as if they were a crystal ball, visions of my last trip around the dance floor with JD visualized in my palms.

Yeah, your last whirl landed me a major headache and on McKennon's couch! I scrunched my eyebrows with concern, embarrassed at the recollection.

JD ignited the winning twinkle in his eye and continued enthusiastically, "Devon, Salle Mae's speaking of a Saturday night tradition! Every time there's an event on these fairgrounds, all the cowboys and cowgirls go to The Silver Spur to unwind. You know, to throw back a couple, warm the gullet, and give those old floorboards a stompin'. Isn't that right, Miss Sallie Mae?" Sallie Mae's entertained nod was her only response as JD rubbed his tight belly in anticipation of heating his insides with that first sip of whiskey.

"Started the tradition myself back when I was just a barrel-racing wisp of a thing," Sallie Mae responded, a whimsical wave of her timeworn hand and a glint of pride in her eye. She lowered her eyes and stole a sweet, secret smile in memory of her former youthful self. I knew it was a personal moment for her and watching made me feel like an intruder. I looked away.

"So? Will you be joining us this evening then?" JD nudged me.

Sallie Mae concluded her reminiscing, wrapped her age-old, circular body around the wooden porch pole, and leaned forward in anticipation of my answer. It occurred to me that this 'cowboy in a butterfly net' thing fluttering about her head was probably the best thing to happen to her since the invention of those carbon paper copies she pressed her pen down on.

I hesitated, hand clutching the handle to the passenger door, contemplating my response, and wondered if McKennon would be attending the festivities at The Silver Spur.

I certainly wouldn't balk at the opportunity to share a dance with him tonight. I shook the idea from my head.

I decided to respond quietly, carefully. Sallie Mae had clout with McKennon and the cowboys. I didn't want to get off on the wrong foot with her, although she already seemed to have me pegged as trouble.

"JD, please, let's move this beast of yours out of Sallie Mae's office space so she doesn't have to keep looking at it." The sun had moved in the sky, causing the hulking trailer to cast a shadow over the tiny one-room show office. "I'd really like to get back to Faith as quick as we can to make sure she is settling in OK. This is her first horse show after all. I promise I'll think about tonight once I know Faith will be all right. The Silver Spur sounds like a lot of, um, fun." My stomach turned as I made the word 'fun' audible. Half of me felt compelled to avoid any watering hole that JD might frequent, but the other half was curious to check out the scenery.

"All right, Devon. Best be gettin' you back to your mare then. Sallie Mae, I won't be lettin' her off the hook easily. Don't you worry."

JD flashed Sallie Mae his million-dollar smile and hopped into the driver's seat. Relieved, I hoisted myself into mine.

JD managed the trailer into a parking space, left hand on the wheel, head over his shoulder, olive eyes full with concentration, tongue to top lip, right arm spread across the bench seat behind me as the faint fragrant scent of cologned deodorant drifted to my nostrils.

I was shocked at the ease JD exemplified as he skillfully landed us in a spot in close proximity to the barn. I would have come apart at the seams attempting to navigate the grounds with his squeaky, screeching bucket of bolts bouncing in tow. I was also relieved because I had been silently worrying myself silly that we would have to set up camp a great distance away from Faith given our late arrival. Luckily, I'd learned that JD's trailer wasn't yet wired for electricity so we didn't have to seek one of the coveted spots available for plug-in.

"This lot is where people droppin' horses with their trainers then getting hotels for the weekend usually park trailers," JD explained, confirming that we were able to set up base between what looked like two very expensive, pristine and uninhabited trailers in a long row of abandoned horse totes.

"I'm not gonna unhook my truck since we'll just be leavin' tomorrow. I'll hitch a ride to The Silver Spur with a lucky lady this evening." He smirked at me then continued, "If you're nice, I might ask her to let you come with us too. Or you can walk if you want. It's just over there." My eyes traveled JD's outstretched arm to his pointing dirty fingernail and saw a lone, white, dilapidated building across the dusty gravel parking lot. I squinted at it to make out the sign, and, sure enough, it read, The Silver Spur.

"Got it. Think I'll walk if I end up coming, JD."

"Suit yourself. Come on, let me give you a tour."

I cringed as JD unlocked the side door of the beat up trailer and stepped aside.

"Ladies first," he said, bending low, wrapping his arm at his waist in his best royal bow. I curtseyed, mocking him. I knew that he had done that move a million times before.

I forced my head to peek inside his trailer in full expectation that I would be horrified by the interior, but felt my mouth fall open. It was completely the contrary. The trailer's interior was beautiful, cowboy chic, and impeccably clean. I stepped inside and took the contents in. I made my way around what would ordinarily feel like a tight space, opening doors as I went. JD's craftsmanship made the limited space feel roomy.

The floor was real hardwood. Oak. The walls rich mahogany and the large closet lined with cedar made the insides smell heavenly. It had a kitchenette, stainless steel appliances, a leather sofa accented by cowhide pillows wrapped around a circular table, and a bathroom, even, complete with standup shower. The bed was set up high in the gooseneck part of the trailer above the truck bed. It was made up romantically with a satin rainbow of pillows, all the shades of western brown accounted for. Its spread was plush and soft as I smoothed my hand over the embroidered design of a star encompassed by barbed wire woven in the fabric. I drew my hand back as I noticed the candles lining the ledges next to the mattress.

"You like it, Devon?" JD whispered, standing behind me and just a little too close.

Suddenly, I sensed the tightness of the quarters, his hot breath on the back of my neck. In an effort to create distance, I turned and put my fingertips to his chest, thinly veiled in a white undershirt, pressing him back.

"Yes, JD, it is lovely. Did you do this yourself?" JD outstretched his arm to the adjoining wall and leaned in. Seeing an opening for retreat, I ducked under his arm and gunned myself to the couch.

Disappointed, he turned after me and sat on the other end of the couch.

"Yeah. Done it myself. Just finishing the wirin' so I'll have electricity next time she's out. Then I'll have her really ready to show the ladies a good time. Well, Devon, I'll let you get settled and run your tack up to the barn."

"Thanks, JD. I really appreciate you letting me use your trailer. The living quarters are amazing. You did a great job. And JD?"

"Yeah?" JD turned back to me from the door, hopeful.

"You are *really* a good friend. I'm glad I know you."

He pressed his lips together, idle in the doorway. "Yeah. You're a good friend too, Devon. Glad to help." As he leapt from the trailer about to go, I couldn't help myself.

"JD?" I called after him. Eyes bright, he gleamed into the trailer from the ground. "I have some womanly advice on the trailer. You might want to consider getting the exterior of this thing a paint job." JD hooked his hands into the sides of the door and leaned back, looking over the faded red, rusty, chipping outer skin and nodded.

"You might be right there, Devon. I'll take that under advisement," he said, tipping his ball cap to me.

"Oh, and will you save a dance for me tonight?" I asked. I figured offering him a little encouragement was the least I could do to repay his generosity.

His lips quipped up with intrigue. "I'll figure you out yet, Devon Brooke. You best be careful what you ask for, miss." And with that, he slammed the trailer door shut with me still inside.

CHAPTER TWENTY-SIX

Hurriedly, I arranged my hastily-packed knapsack. I wanted to be able to easily find my belongings with only the light from my cell phone to illuminate the interior of JD's trailer.

You never realize just how much you depend on electricity until you don't have it.

Feeling satisfied, I bounded out of the trailer and ran toward the barn back to Faith. And McKennon.

By the time I arrived, JD had unloaded my saddle, bridle and tack box in front of Faith's stall. I figured he was already off seducing his evening's entertainment. As I assessed my gear, I grew aware that eyes were on me. This was a reoccurring sensation for me in recent months since meeting *him*. McKennon was always just suddenly there, catching me off guard. I was always in the middle of some unfortunate goofy conversation or an assumed private whisper meant only for Faith. He always chose the awkward moments when I would have preferred to avoid any personal inspection. My cheeks flushed in their usual way at his sudden appearance.

He stood there just studying me, as I grew hotter under his scrutiny. I had the odd thought that he liked catching me this way. I felt like a bashful child in his company. As my blush blossomed, I noticed he had swapped his straw cowboy hat, the one he always wore when he was working, for a fine, fine perfectly-shaped black felt hat. I'd never seen him adorned so lavishly. Just this small variation in hat-wear elevated his dreamboat status from breathtaking to heart-stopping, all tall, dark and handsome.

"Put any equipment you want up in my tack stall there," McKennon instructed, gesturing to the stall between Faith and Star. I surveyed its meager contents; stacked on top of his work saddle was Star's bridle, a body brush, and hoof pick, and to the right of the equipment was a half full sack of grain leaning against a mossy green hay bale.

Silently, I added my few items to the stall, the space between.

"You say you brought a lunge line?" McKennon questioned. As his hot, blue, come-hither eyes burned a hole through me under the brim of that black Stetson, a familiar yearning snuck up on me from below.

"Yes!" I said, too excitedly. Quickly, I rummaged around in my tack box and victoriously held up Faith's lunge line in my right hand above my head.

"Well, that's good. I think she's had enough for today, but that'll come in handy tomorrow," McKennon said, signaling to Faith with a roll of his head. "Take a look at her."

I exited the tack stall and wrapped my hands around the bars of her stall, rising on my tiptoes. Faith was nestled in the deep shavings, legs bent, supporting her resting head upright with her muzzle. If a horse could snore, she surely would have been. I felt the first happy wave of the day rush over me and finally relaxed a little myself.

"Wow. She's out like a light!" I giggled over my shoulder, feeling lighter in my cowgirl boots.

"What you just did to her, young lady, was a big deal," McKennon chastised.

"I know." I said, regretfully.

"Most horses would be running circles in that stall causing a fuss," he continued. "Pretty lucky she's just wiped out in there. I recommend just leavin' her be tonight, Devon."

Oh! He said my name again. My insides tingled.

"I gotta hunch that she's gonna have a lot of energy come tomorrow so you best be prepared. You hear? Don't do any ridin' until she's good and lunged. I am talking *good and tired.*"

"OK," I said, leaning back against Faith's stall, meeting his luminous, sultry gaze with my wide-eyed, nervous one. The cool purpose of the metal lining of the stall felt nice against my blazing skin. There was an internal war within me as I took a deep breath and held it in my lungs. This man had started to become my solace, my reason for existing, the only thing that stirred my blood besides my horse. I hadn't felt this way since the first days of my relationship with Michael back in the city, and I knew I had to try to push it down, bury these emotions, because I had no right to make a claim on McKennon. Yet I felt that we were linked somehow like magnets forced together by circumstance, but when flipped over in another moment, we were pushing each other away.

McKennon broke our silent stare with a cool request, "The show's on break now, but why don't you come watch some of the classes with me? See some of the grounds, and get some insight into ya on what to expect tomorrow."

I nodded, forcing myself to move forward and away from the protection of Faith's stall. McKennon tossed a small camouflage-colored, soft cooler over his shoulder, and we headed off quietly next to each other through the show stall aisles.

As we walked, McKennon would tip the squared off brim of that perfectly-shaped cowboy hat, sitting low atop his head, as we passed comrades and cowgirls. Most the men would take a second glance at us over their shoulder as we passed. All of the women gawked at me like I was a vagabond as McKennon toured me around the facility, pointing out the round pens for lunging, and the make-up arenas for show pen preparations.

Inside, the fear of what tomorrow would bring when I took Faith to those places was growing, and my anxiousness expanded with every weird look I received from our spectators.

Maybe keeping McKennon's company wasn't such a good idea?

I found some relief when we finally reached the bleachers. Gladly, I led the way up a set of stairs to the very top row. I wanted to be far away from the other groups that had gathered inside the air-conditioned indoor arena.

I surveyed the stands framing the show pen below us, and I noticed JD in the distance among the crowd. He had ditched his ball capped boyish look for his full on bull rider persona. He was surrounded by eight women, visibly all bubbly, busty and babbling. I couldn't help but assess JD in action. It was clear that he had the woman enthralled, hanging on his words. While his lips moved, his eyes surveyed their plunging necklines. I could tell he was satisfied with his eyeful, and I knew he was finishing one of his trademark jokes because all of his harlots tossed their heads back in laughter. I smiled to myself when JD gave an aw-shucks kind of slap to his knee.

McKennon nudged me. "That's a typical spectacle around here," he said, voice like velvet in warning. "Be careful with that one. Good kid. Young. Kinda stupid, but with potential, I suppose." His eyes wandered my face, looking for something.

Oh! Did he think I was interested in JD? Surely not, but maybe?

Feeling mischievous, I aimed to keep McKennon in suspense. I smirked, covered my mouth, leaned toward him, and asked in a cupped whisper, "Are you talking about the one in purple?"

Caught off guard by my question, McKennon let a deep, loud whoop escape as he teetered backward on his jean pockets. He raised his boots off the ground and slapped his gloved hand to his mouth to silence himself, blue steel eyes wide, shaking his head at me.

The group below stopped and looked up at us situated alone at the top of the stands. The super sleazy buckle bunny in lavender that I had just identified stood up in angry response at our outburst. Hastily, she gripped the top of her sliver-studded, blinged out tube top and gave her double-D boobies a fast, hard hike up under her chin. This move only enhanced the pale, soft muffin top that trickled over the waistline of her too tight, faded black jeans. McKennon stifled another chuckle and smiled into his glove. The wannabe cowgirl smoothed her overgrown, overly hair sprayed, brittle blonde roots and slivered her makeup-caked eyes of the same purple hue. It was obvious that she was shooting eye daggers at us in response to our unwelcomed disruption.

JD crunched his eyebrows in confusion and gave us an awkward wave. The other seven women joined the purple-painted lady and shot nasty looks in my direction then fluttered their lashes seductively at McKennon.

Wenches!

My mind growled, but I kept a cool disposition. I knew nothing productive would come from coming undone at the seams over this. Not to mention, I couldn't really blame them. McKennon *was* a beautiful man, and he was sitting next to *me*.

McKennon reached for the strap on his soft cooler, corner of his mouth turned up in amusement, wiggled a bottled beer out of the zipper, slipped a koozie over it, and took a lengthy, slow pull from the long neck. The loud speaker boomed that the show would continue in 10 minutes.

CHAPTER TWENTY-SEVEN

"Wanna sip?" McKennon asked, extending the light beer bottle to me.

I blinked at it, studying the camouflage koozie wrapped around it that read, *M&M Kelly Quarter Horse Training and Services.*

So, he did train people once.

I zeroed in on the second 'M' stamped to the foam and momentarily lost myself in distracted thoughts of the person that initial might belong to.

McKennon gave the bottle a jiggle, foam sloshing side to side, breaking my trance. He leaned to the side, examining me from under that hot black hat.

"Want some?"

Careful not to meet his placid blue eyes, I reached for the bottle he held extended to me.

The bottle that was just resting on his full, tempting, pink lips!

His lips of few words provoked me. They constantly taunted me, calling out 'come, hither,' not in reality, but in my tempestuous dreams. I placed the cool glass to my mouth, and his eyes shifted gears, shining bright with intrigue. Just the contact to the bottle, knowing it had been on his mouth, felt oddly illicit and intimate. I took a quick sip, swiped away any presence of moisture, bit my lower lip, and passed the impure prop back to McKennon. He flashed me a ghost of a smile, eyes luminous and holding mine. My pulse accelerated.

"So, are you planning on showing Star tomorrow?" I asked, feeling hot under the collar, heated in the cheeks, surely flush visible on my outside.

"Nah. Just here to get him practiced. Like you," he said, turning back to the arena and jutting his chin toward it. A new class had begun to enter the arena at a slow, languid jog.

"A few years back, they started mixin' up the show schedule. Used to always be hunt seat classes on Saturday and western on Sunday, no matter which shows you'd go to. Now you gotta always be checkin' them computers to see what the next show's gonna look like. That's why I love me some Sallie Mae. She always calls me and tells me how things are shapin' up before I head out. She knows a little something about all the shows no matter where they are. She's been a circuit staple for ages now."

"Hmm," I purred as the first wave of horses and their riders reached our side of the arena. I marveled at the rhinestone-covered show clothes, colors bouncing by us in every jewel tone across the spectrum. I was dazzled by the glimmer of crystals, in the thousands, adorning the cowgirls' riding jackets accompanied by the gleam of freshly polished ear-to-tail silver embellishments studding headstalls and saddles of their mounts. I took a deep nervous breath and clutched my elbows, squeezing my arms tight across my chest.

This was the big league.

"Hey," I felt a soft, knowing nudge to my upper arm.

"Them clothes, that silver you're droolin' over right now," McKennon shook his head slowly side to side and folded his arms in front of his chest, regarding me like a disappointed schoolteacher. "Just distractions, designed to take attention to the wrong places," he grunted as a really pretty blonde, lush ponytail swinging mid-back, glided past us. I watched McKennon's eyes sweep down her body to the horse, and I read disappointment in the alignment of his face.

"And sometimes distractions work in the show pen, depends on the morals of them judges standing out there in the middle of the arena." In a moment of pause, McKennon's beautiful mouth turned to a disturbed, tight line, jaw clearly clenched as he stared straight ahead, clear blue eyes like daggers into the center of the arena.

"Sometimes the most expensive package wins, sometimes the politics behind a name wins, and occasionally the real talent wins. Unfortunate as it is. Lots of ins and outs to learn in this business, miss. For me, always has been, is, and will forever be only about the talent. *Every time.*" His velvety voice hung on his last words as he turned those blue bullets on me and rested his forearm on the top of his thigh, leaning in, broad chest turned, engaging me.

"Talent?" I questioned, hooked by the way his eyes burned with desire when he let his mouth linger on the word. I idolized him even more in his instant of intensity, all fiery and talking passionately. The burst of a thousand butterflies in my belly made me squirm on the bench seat next to him.

"Let me ask you a question," McKennon said, shifting fully to me on his pockets, eyes like slits, honed in on my mouth, awaiting a proper answer. "What're you gawking at out there, them sparkly outfits or the legs?"

I laced my fingers and looked down into my palms, looking for answers. As usual, they turned up empty. I shrugged my shoulders.

"I guess I was looking at the pretty outfits and all that silver. I was wondering how on earth I am ever going to acquire show clothes and tack like that. One day, I mean."

Exasperated, he continued, "You just don't need all that dazzle. All that matters is the horse and the way that it moves. I don't take to the show pen in anything but a crisp white shirt, black tie, black chaps, and this here hat on top of my head." He gripped the brim of the felt as if to affirm its realness and gave it a downward tip.

"Don't use no fancy tack neither, minimal silver – clean, polished and shiny, mind you, but not excessive. I let the horse speak for itself rather than let my get up do the talkin'," McKennon paused for a moment as if to let his words sink all the way in then pressed his lips together. Immediately, I zeroed in on his tongue as it briefly made an appearance, peeking through his stubble-lined mouth, moistening his kisser.

"Let's work on somethin'. I want you to ignore those pretty faces, glitzy outfits, and slick tack. Think you can do that?" he asked, arching an eyebrow, challenge in his eyes, an easy smile spread across his mouth.

"OK," I squeaked, looking up from his carnal mouth to meet his smoldering sapphire stare. McKennon had just enough weather at the corner of his eyes to make him look like a man, seasoned, rugged almost, yet enough boyish coy in his grin to make him appear youthful, at peace almost.

"Look there," he directed.

Reluctantly, I shifted my eyes away from the smooth of McKennon's face to his shoulder, through to his pointed finger, and settled my sights on a pretty equine specimen. The horse was athletic, of perfect conformation, and radiated a chestnut sheen as it breezed across the far, long side of the arena.

"Do you see? That there's the winner. The good mover. If the judges are in it for the horse, that is. The gaits should look effortless for the animal. Should resemble gliding, dancing, soaring, you know, nothin' jerky or false. If the trainer done their job right, all the rider needs to do is sit there and look relaxed, good, pretty, *er*, whatever."

As class after class went by, I gradually began to see, really see. The mystery of the horse world was opening up to me like a rose unfurling for the sun. Through McKennon's words, my perception of horse showing and what real show pen success looked like changed. I was being cultivated, turned over like fresh soil in his garden, so new seeds could be planted and grow. I began to see the rhythm in the rides, the real reason for the battle to be the best.

According to McKennon, the judges at this particular show weren't 'a bunch of crooks.' The winning riders and their mounts were worthy of their prizes. Under McKennon's coaching, encouraging and gracious with his guidance, I actually picked out a couple of the winners. Smiling, I gave myself an imaginary pat on the back. Getting to the show may have felt like a circus act, but coming to the show hadn't been a foolish decision after all. Here I was, getting insights from a seasoned cowboy. The one I couldn't stop pondering about nonetheless. I may not be able to call him my trainer, but I was getting the training that I desperately wanted and needed, whether he was aware of what he was doing or not.

"Good work today," McKennon murmured as the results of the last class of the day were called, and the contestants began to exit the arena.

After placing the last empty bottle of our shared six-pack back in his cooler, McKennon yawned and stretched his lumbering arms above him. He let them hover in the air for a long time, arching his back. I couldn't help but take in breath and cover my mouth, copying his contagious yawn. I tipped my head forward, amused to watch this beautiful creature situate himself. An expressionless McKennon adjusted that sexy hat with his right hand and contemplated me out of the corner of his eye. Slowly, his left arm descended from above his head until a gloved hand settled in the middle of my back. I tensed. After a brief pause, I felt him slide lower, finding a new home at the small curve in my spine, the slightest pressure above the waistline of my jeans.

Was that just a temperature check?

I was very still. I didn't want to scare him away. My mind started to race.

Was this a gesture of reassurance? Or something new?

I couldn't tell, but this felt different than any previous interactions we'd had. The burst of butterflies came fast and furious again. I pressed my thighs together.

"You make sure you lunge her good tomorrow," he said, slicing my tension open, spreading it away like butter on toast with his serene, effortless vocalization. "Really good, you hear? And then, why don't you give ridin' in this arena a try. You can come in here during the lunch break. Came to get practiced, didn't you?"

It was as if he knew that I would have rather been out there riding than watching all day. I was only capable of a nod. Sitting awkwardly still, my senses were fully aware that his arm was now around my waist. My prickled skin pulsed where his fingers wrapped my side.

"So, you comin'," he paused, locking eyes with JD, who had taken notice of our proximity, then continued, "...to The Silver Spur tonight? JD tell you about the tradition?"

His velvet voice thrummed through my ear canal.

Leaving JD to glare, McKennon tightened his muscular arm around my midsection and slid me closer to him. As he towed me down the cool, metal bench seat of the arena stands, a wild, erotic grin spread across his lips, and an uncertain, unreadable desire set in his mature, sensuous eyes. Heart banging in my chest, my mouth fell open and empty of response to his inquiry.

Would I go to The Silver Spur tonight?

CHAPTER TWENTY-EIGHT

"So, I'll be seeing you tonight then," McKennon said in a matter-of fact-manner. He nodded as if it were certain, turned, and, over his shoulder, tipped his brim to me. Flustered, I watched him round the corner of Star's stall and disappear.

Once he was gone, I mulled his words over. They had landed as a statement, not as an invitation. Relieved, I leaned back against Faith's stall and let out a long sigh. My senses had been on high alert for hours now. My excited feminine nerves felt frayed.

Faith, eager to greet me and seemingly settled into her new enclosure, poked her muzzle through the feed slot at the front of her stall. I reached back, not turning toward her, afraid to remove my glued eyes from the path he just blazed away from me. I stroked the soft fuzz between her nostrils, and her warm breath fluttered tendrils of hair at my shoulder. I felt like my lungs had compressed. I needed to stabilize myself. He had left me a confused, sexed up, wanting mess.

Disoriented, I checked Faith's water level, tossed her a flake of hay, and wandered back to JD's trailer to freshen up for the evening's festivities.

An hour later, buzzing neon sign flashing blue and green on the bare skin of my forearms, my hands found my hips. I examined the exterior of The Silver Spur, contemplating my decision to follow McKennon here. The once-white paint on the outside of the aged saloon was weathered, crusty and peeling. I reached out and stripped a crunchy piece of veneer from its lifted exterior. Examining the crispy eggshell-like surface, I mustered my confidence, tossed the paint chip to the ground, crushed it under my boot like a discarded cigarette, and entered the bar.

It was roaring. It certainly seemed like everyone from the show was there in honor of the Saturday night celebration. My nostrils were immediately permeated with the tang of spilt beer, smoke, and the sweaty musk of tangled bodies. Adjusting to the new aroma, heavy on the air, I hovered just inside the threshold on tiptoes, but fell too short to see much from my position. Committed, I smoothed my tight, black shirt, sucked in breath, and pushed myself into the boisterous, energized crowd, angling for a better view. Memories of adolescent crowd maneuvering at summer music concerts flickered in my mind.

As I navigated the small spaces between crammed humid bodies, my eyes swept over the interior of The Silver Spur. It was heavily draped in western décor. There wasn't an empty cowhide-upholstered stool at the long mahogany bar that lined the back wall. Cowboys bending the brims of their hats and throwing back shots filled four-top tables at the overflowing, outer edges. Long-horned bulls with glass eyes, but without bodies, were bolted to the walls while a headless, mechanical one whirled a daisy-duke wearing woman slowly, seductively in a corner. Men crowded toward her with their mouth's drawn open and leaned on the railing to get a better view of her go around. Unimpressed, I observed them sipping beers, elbowing each other in the sides, sneers plastered to their faces.

A jukebox jammed a country tune over the centered dance floor, and there, a lone spotlight glinted off the rhinestones glued to the bustier of an entranced girl in purple. She held a beer bottle to her breasts, circling her soft center in a methodical, provocative slow dance, performing in front of an obviously boozed up and blurred JD. I snickered as he attempted to maintain some sort of rhythm wobbling back and forth, teetering from toe to heel on his clumsy cowboy boots. I shook my head and let my eyes trail past JD.

Train wreck waiting to happen. Not my business, I'm here for someone else.

Before I could move out of view, I caught JD take notice of me in my peripheral. Frantically, I searched for a space in the crowd to scoot through as he positioned his self in my direction, and, unfortunately, away from the girl in purple. I pretended not to notice him wave me over and decided it best to slip deeper into the refuge of the dance floor mob. Darting for an opening in the mass of swirling bodies, I pursued the other side of the tavern.

Safely out of JD's reach, I came up for air sandwiched between a pair of lovely, but barely covered, breasts and a beer belly blanketed by a red plaid shirt. A little too eager to share, the couple continued to bump and grind with me caught in the middle. Floundering, I squeezed out from between the pair.

Wobbly, I stood at the edge of the undulating dance floor, desperately scanning the room for my cowboy. Suddenly, the butterflies returned from their brief hibernation, swooping like a roller coaster hitting the bottom of a first hill through my belly.

At last.

McKennon was sitting with Sallie Mae, easily engaged in conversation, arm slung across the back of her barstool. A deer in headlights, I flushed immediately as he sensed my presence. Under his distant, hooded, sultry gaze, my pulse accelerated, zero to 60 in 0.1 second. Lifting from his stool, eyes still seductively set on me, I watched as he patted Sallie Mae's shoulder and started to make his way across the floor.

Confused at his sudden departure, Sallie Mae shifted in her seat, took a pull from her beer bottle, and narrowed her eyes in my direction. Her puny lips turned into a raisin-like smirk before she dragged the rest of the bottle down, returned to a forward facing position at the bar, and circled her pointer finger in the air. Immediately, she was delivered another long neck of ale. After witnessing her mannerisms, all I could think was that a belch would have been the perfect punctuation.

Disregarding thoughts of Sallie Mae's potential vulgarity, my heart hammered in my chest as I realized McKennon was slowly closing our gap. Finding my feet, I channeled my inner cowgirl, locked eyes with McKennon, and started to cross the muggy crowd toward him. Everything felt like it was moving in slow motion.

Was this really happening?

The anticipation was almost too much. I knew that I soon wouldn't be able to hide the idiotic, giddy grin that was growing across my mouth.

Step, step and step, I repeated.

There was merely a car length between us when I saw the girl in purple. Stumbling down a set of three stairs, she missed the handrail, swerved, and cut off a taken aback McKennon in mid-stride, interrupting our tryst.

Oh, no, not now!

Her face was twisted in an ugly, tense scowl resembling that of a seething ogre. Without warning, she began barreling toward me and, raging bull-like, rammed into me, hard. Upon impact, I staggered backwards and attempted to regain my balance.

"Are you hitting on my man?" she shrieked an inch from my face, beer and peanuts on her hot breath.

I was in shock. As the girl in purple circled me, I just stood there, wide-eyed and lost for words.

Coming to the rescue, JD stepped in. Facing me and turning his back to her, he put his hands on my shoulders.

"You OK?" he asked with a concerned slur, giving me a little shake.

"You get off of her!" bellowed the beast, clawing for his arm.

JD let go of my shoulders to address her, but reacted a moment too late. Aghast, I watched in horror as she dug her beefy shoulder into the middle of his back. Grunting like a linebacker crushing an opponent on the football field, the lavender hellion bulldozed him from behind. In an instant, JD was thrust past me and floundered in his stupor several steps forward, knocking into a bar stool. He grabbed a nearby table with a screech to sturdy himself, and his cigarettes tumbled out of his chest pocket to the damp, soupy bar floor. I scrambled to retrieve the pack. Feeling compelled to save his smokes before the oncoming group of line dancers did the boot scootin' boogie over them, I snatched them up and tucked the box into my purse.

Looking up from the commotion, I noticed McKennon's eyes had saddened; his disappointment evident after bearing witness to the messy brouhaha between me, the girl in purple, and JD. I just stood there in the center of the dance floor, movement all around me, transfixed on McKennon. The girl in purple transfixed on me. I was furious, but I didn't dare act.

Fortunately, JD had composed himself. With an angry grumble, he breezed by my frozen body and swooped in, catching the lavender terror under her doughy upper arm. JD escorted her with a jerk off of the dance floor.

He exchanged a few bitter words with her before turning to her friends, delivering an urgent request for them to take control. As he handed her over, the girl in purple burst into tears, her stomach jiggling with every sobbing heave. Her perfumed and primped posse fretted over her as they oh-so-gingerly coaxed her toward the exit. Just as they almost had her out, she gripped the door jamb, refusing to go.

She hollered at the top of her lungs, "That girl was trying to take my man!"

Gritting her teeth, all wild-eyed and crazed, she dug in, ignoring the baby coos and panicked pleads of her girlfriends. After what seemed like an eternity, an indifferent, towering bouncer stepped in and heaved her over his shoulder. Swinging to and fro across his broad back, she lifted her head with just enough time to shoot me one last 'this isn't over yet' makeup-smeared, evil-eyed glare before one of the twin swinging parlor doors clashed with her noggin as she was escorted out of The Silver Spur. Then, she was gone.

I was stock-still watching them, watching *him*. I felt like someone had zapped me with a stun gun. Before I knew it, JD had returned. He wrapped his arms around me and whispered words of comfort. Bewildered, I didn't protest as he swept me into a dance with him. A slow romantic song about a cowboy and his angel started to play.

It all had happened so fast. Why did that girl hate me? She didn't even know me.

I felt a hot, embarrassed tear start to form in the corner of my eye and gave up, gave in, to JD's embrace. I wiped my nose on his strong shoulder and searched myself for the strength to generate a glance in *his* direction.

Still standing there, McKennon was calmly assessing the situation. With a nod, he pressed his lips together, offered a defeated shake of his head, and took a step backward, eye on the dance floor for a moment, before turning back to Sallie Mae. I was sure he was thinking that JD had it all under control, and he did.

JD was the only one I really knew much about at the show after all, and we were friends. JD had my back. JD brought me here.

JD made sure I had a place to stay. McKennon and I, on the other hand, may have shared a moment in the stands today, and he secretly had a spot in my aching heart, but beyond that, where did he and I actually stand? I was safe right now dancing with JD.

Still, I watched painfully as McKennon finished his pint, pulled cash from his wallet, left bills on the bar, tipped his hat to Sallie Mae and turned to go. I sniffed, let my nose rest on JD's shoulder, and from a distance, watched him leave, not looking at me again. I peeked at Sallie Mae. Her lips quipped up in entertainment, wrinkled eyes fixed on me, and then she shifted in her seat to watch him go too.

"Don't be lookin' after him. I got you," JD murmured in my ear.

With those words, my eyes went so wide, I thought they might burst from my head.

I had to get out of here.

Disoriented, I broke away from JD's two-step and stared at him. I blinked wildly for a moment before bolting out of The Silver Spur's side entrance. Embarrassed, I needed to be alone and get away from all the crazy. I streaked across the parking lot, wind whipping through my hair, tears blazing trails across my cheeks. All I wanted to do was get back to the safety of JD's trailer. My mind was rampant with wandering thoughts.

Did I just tell McKennon in so many unsaid words that I really did prefer JD?

I swung the trailer door shut behind me, consumed in darkness.

What have I done? Did I just end it before it even began?

CHAPTER TWENTY-NINE

Tossing and turning, I couldn't sleep. My stomach was in my throat, and it felt parched as if desert sand had been funneled into my esophagus. It was late.

Or was it very early?

I couldn't tell. I lay in the darkness. Bar fights and purple sparkles had been impregnating my lackluster dreams ever since I hit the pillow, but now my insomnia was caused by more than just that awkward moment at The Silver Spur. Now, I was consumed by terrorized thoughts of riding Faith at the show for the first time tomorrow.

Great.

I had a bad case of the horse show jitters, and I wasn't even doing any showing.

How was I ever going to live my dream and be in World Show performance shape if I couldn't even be here now?

I just laid there in the darkness, staring up at the ceiling inside of JD's trailer, unable to enjoy the plush mattress fit for a queen *and* a king in JD's world. After all, boot knocking was what he had built these exquisite living quarters for. Frustrated, I fumbled for my wristwatch. Carefully, I flipped the covers off of me rising slowly in the blackness as to not hit my head on the low ceiling inside the gooseneck portion of the trailer.

I squinted and held the face of my watch to the parking lot light underneath the tied up piece of cloth that covered the window.

4:30 a.m.? Wow.

Lowering myself to the trailer floor, I decided to make my way to the barn to check on Faith. I smoothed the T-shirt I had worn to bed, stepped into my jeans, ferreted out my boots, and pulled them on. Leaving the trailer, I slipped a baseball hat over my unmanageable bedhead.

Yes, seeing Faith would help calm me down.

It was quiet when I entered Faith's temporary quarters, still cool in the early morning. I took a deep cleansing breath of earth, animals and fodder. At this hour, I relished the lack of people scurrying to and fro. I felt like I had traveled back in time to my first quiet days at Green Briar when solitude was easier to come by. I stabilized my mind, finding a meditative rhythm in the buzzing of the halogen lights humming high above my head.

Taking pleasure in this new, unexpected peace, I wandered into *our* shared tack room rummaging for Faith's brush. I wanted to stroke her, connect with her, and feel something without the confusing additive of human words. Grinning with the successful location of a blue-bristled body brush, I suddenly felt a presence.

Glancing over my shoulder, I met fierce, icy blue eyes, hooded and taking me in. *He* was there, standing in the doorway, thin, white T-shirt molded to his chest, jean loops holding the weight of a belt buckle hung low on his hips, boot tip in the dirt crossed over the other one as he leaned against the only exit, defined arms crossed in front of his torso.

Hurriedly, I reached back to pull down the hem of my top, which had ridden up my back, exposing my flesh to the cool air and his glare. I shifted from my crouch to stand and face him.

Unexpectedly, he rushed toward me, alert, and with urgency. My lips parted, and an audible gasp left my lungs. Surprised, I dropped Faith's brush as he swiftly swept his arms beneath mine and wandered his gloveless hands up the back of my shirt, soft fabric rising, and gently grazing me as he hungrily roamed my skin. *Gloveless!*

His fingers were all calloused, warm, and roused me without warning. I could feel the tinge of sweat caught up in the nook of his palms. It was a damp heat, *his heat*, spread across my body like lotion.

Was he as nervous as I was?

All of his glorious hotness pressed me up against the back wall of the tack stall; his weight bearing down on me, pinning me as he buried his face in my neck, my hair, his eager lips softly grazing my skin.

All I could do was keep taking my next breaths, one after another, and hope to hold oxygen in my lungs. I liked his hands on my hips, exploring my back, clutching my upper arms, and bringing me to him like a ragdoll.

"It'll be all right, ya hear?" he whispered. His lips were close to mine, his steel eyes scanning my face for compliance in the small space between.

Could he really sense my nervousness at riding my horse here tomorrow?

His eyes burned me as he leaned closer. My everything was charged, currents of electricity accelerating through my follicles. Every hair on my body might as well have been standing on end. This felt forbidden. Against better judgment, I inched forward, absorbed by his prowess.

Please, just TAKE ME! I can't stand it any longer.

I felt like a caged animal, all pheromones and feral. Held in place by his firm grip, my heartbeat throbbed in my veins, in my chest, behind my eyes, *everywhere.*

I let my nails drag down his shirted, tight back. He thrust into me and released a low guttural groan.

"Devon," he hummed into my ear. Pulling back, his eyes scanned my face before he moved in on me, angling his mouth moments from mine.

Here it comes.

My pulse was racing, my breath ragged, and my wanting washed over every inch of me. I knew I wouldn't resist his advances. I wanted this cowboy to take me here, now, any and every which way. Leaning in, I felt …

BANG!

Groggily, I rubbed my forehead. I had just collided with the low hanging ceiling inside the gooseneck of JD's horse trailer. And I had just woken up from the hottest dream of my entire life.

Ouch, that's going to leave a mark!

As the intense, tingling pain subsided to a numb throb, I blushed all alone in the dark. Covering my mouth, I smiled into my hand and allowed a little laugh to escape.

Was it late, or was it very early?

I wasn't sure. I let my achy head fall back into the warm pillow and pulled the blankets up under my chin.

CHAPTER THIRTY

"Shoot, shoot, *shoot*! What time is it?" I said, awaking in a full sweat.

In its non-electrical state, JD's trailer lacked air conditioning and had become a humid, hot box, baking in the blazing morning sunshine like an oven set on broil with me cooking inside.

Waking up late was not what I planned, but I'd been drifting between an alternate universe and reality trying to cling to the last remnants of my luscious dream starring McKennon. Lust had become the main course, so I added it to the menu and, against my best intentions, had stayed in bed.

Of course.

Forcing sleep from my eyes and racy dreams from my head, I burst out from under the covers, mindful of that nasty, low hanging ceiling and hastily dressed. I raked my fingers through my twisted locks, meeting tangled knot after knot. I gingerly fondled the tender bump pulsing at my hairline, a gift left over from hitting my head in the night. Disheartened, I pulled a ball cap over my battered crown to camouflage my matted hair.

Bet I look grrreat.

Rolling my eyes, I flung myself through the trailer door, hitting the ground at a jog on my way to Faith.

Adjusting my eyes to the dim of the barn after sprinting in the bright of day, I arrived to a message duct-taped to the front of my stall. Instantly, I recognized his chicken-scratched handwriting. The first note he left for me at Green Briar appeared in my mind, 'on the other side.' Today, that concept seemed foreign, a world away from me now. Now that I was this close to him. Now that I was sharing a block of horse stalls and a horse show with McKennon.

I reached out and lifted the message from the stall. It was scribbled on a torn piece of brown paper lining from the inside of a feedbag. The tape made a ripping sound that caused Faith to raise her head in alarm.

It read,

'*I fed your mare. Lunge her good! You hear?*' It was signed, '*McKennon.*'

I stood in the aisle, note in my grip, and kicked a dust cloud up with my boot in disgust. I battered myself, concerned with what McKennon must think of me right now.

Geez, I can't even get up to feed my own horse on time. I must seem like a train wreck to this guy.

I shook my head, took a deep breath in and out.

Oh gosh! Did he think I let JD into my trailer last night? Shoot, shoot, shoot!

I looked at the paper again like it was a shopping list.

OK, lunge her good. At least I can do that right and hopefully do right by him.

My eyes flittered to my watch.

Shoot! 11:00 a.m. He wants me to ride at lunch break in the real arena.

In a furry, I scoured through my belongings in the tack stall, gathering my lunge line, saddle and bridle. I left the grooming supplies in my tack box.

No time for brushing!

I'd never passed on grooming Faith before, but in the interest of saving time, I opted to get Faith ready in a hurry.

Go, Devon, go. I have to get her lunging, have to get to the arena, and have to ride inside it with McKennon during lunch break.

My mind was abuzz with thoughts of the pleased grin McKennon would wear when he saw Faith and me traveling gracefully around the arena. I envisioned him stopping Star in the center and just watching us go by, hand on his hip, reins loose through his fingers, eyes traveling all over me. I was moving so quickly and so in love with my daydreams, I hadn't even realized that I had Faith saddled already. Coming back to reality, I clipped the lunge line to her halter, slipped her bridle over the saddle horn, and snapped up my lunge whip.

To say that Faith was feeling fresh was an understatement. Making our way to the lunging area, she spooked at everything. I didn't expect such a challenge. A group of lawn chairs sitting empty near the corner of a stall section caused her to lower her head and snort. A mere plastic bag caught on the breeze sent all four of her legs splaying out to the sides.

This is going to be harder than I thought.

What should have been a five minute walk turned into 20 with a prancing painted pony at my side. Faith was jigging from side to side, nostrils flaring and blowing at everything that crossed our path. Cautious, show-goers tracked wide to avoid us, creasing their eyebrows in concern, as we went by. My face turned hot under their scrutiny.

Finally, I reached the circular pen and closed the gate behind us with a clang. I released an exasperated sigh, relieved just to have gotten my horse to the pen. There was no relief for Faith though. I examined her, standing tense in the center, slack taken up in the now-taut lunge line, eyes wide. At the sight of her, I ran my fingers over my face and down my mouth, instantly regretting the choice to not groom her. I had deprived her of the bonding experience that was always part of our routine. I scolded myself for selecting to do that here of all places.

Can't do anything about it now.

Determined to do right, I directed Faith to the rail with my body language, dropped her bridle at my feet, and gave my whip a snap. Instantly, she took off like a lightning bolt. She thundered around the enclosure at break-neck speed, hollering at the top of her lungs, ears flitting back and forth, nostrils wide, red and pink visible as they flared, tail raised high, mane flowing out, and eyes full of frantic fear. Her beautiful body was a blur of strained muscles, quivering with nervous energy and wild recklessness.

Around and around, my horse went faster and faster, stirrups slapping her sides. She kept gaining speed. In this moment, Faith had hotter blood than a Thoroughbred, was more high strung than an Arabian, and was less the likes of the calm languid Paint-Quarter Horse she was bred to be. The tips of my ears were on fire, and my heartbeat drummed in my chest, in my throat, behind my eyeballs as cowboys passed by, observing the train wreck we had become. A few hesitated at the edge of the pen, considering whether to step in, but then decided otherwise, acknowledging me with a tentative tip of their hats.

It felt like she had been speeding along for hours when I heard the loud speaker announce that lunch would follow the results of the current class.

Shoot, shoot, shoot!

I had to hurry up and get Faith to the arena to see *him*, to please him, to impress him. Faith had started to slow, but was still traveling the circumference of the arena at a strong canter.

At least I had gotten her to switch directions a few times.

"Whoa," I called out, praying that she would stop. After some time, Faith came to a halt and lowered her head. She was winded, but still alert, her neck slick and glistening. A bubbly froth of sweat had formed around the saddle pad.

"You OK, girl?" I whispered into her jowl with a pang of guilt as I wrapped my arms around her muzzle. I could feel her body rocking back and forth as her breath blew in a ragged rhythm through my embrace.

"Let's show them what we can do, huh? Do this for me, girl. OK?"

I guided the bit into Faith's mouth, lifted the headstall over her wet ears, gripped the reins, and made our way out of the round pen. Pleased, I nodded my head, a quick smile on my lips, proud that I had just followed McKennon's direction and 'lunged her good.' I headed for the main arena, sweaty horse in tow.

CHAPTER THIRTY-ONE

I stood in the center of the arena in awe. The riders, practiced and polished, made horsemanship look so effortless, a communion between horse and human. A nervous flurry of butterflies released in my gut the moment McKennon glided past us on Star. They were a vision of perfection, a steed and his master in union. As Star rounded the corner, I could see that McKennon had me in his side view. He offered a quick jut of his chin, encouraging me to get on.

This is it!

My stomach was in back flip mode. I twisted the leather stirrup, jammed my boot into it, and started to hoist myself onto Faith's breathless back. It took mere seconds for me to realize I wasn't going to reach my position. In my haste, I had forgotten to check and tighten the saddle's girth.

In slow motion, the saddle jerked to the side, and I slipped beneath Faith's body. Alarmed, Faith was off in a bolt, racing across the middle of the arena, jerking my leg hard, and catching my foot in the stirrup. The thud of my body rang in my ears as my back hit the ground and became a plow in the soft earth. Faith dragged me behind her, furiously trying to get away – dust, hooves, her white underbelly, the silver of four horseshoes whirled around me. The anxiety of being crushed coursed through my body.

Outside of myself, I banged and bumped along, trailing Faith in a limp heap. I was only present to the sound of her shrill whinnying, a desperate call for help. Each time I bounced from the ground and slammed back again, I knew I was both powerless and helpless in this situation. People were hollering out 'Whoa!' and stepping in front of Faith, waving their arms. I heard McKennon's voice mixed in with the commotion too, but it was no use. Faith was a freight train gone off the tracks. Her hooves only pumped faster, and I was a useless ragdoll. The arena was a blur of horses, faces, cowboy hats, and dirt spinning in Faith's dusty wake.

I heard the loud speaker click on.

"Hold on there, folks," the announcer said. "Let's all riders stay still while we work to help this young lady out. Let's get this horse under control …"

The rest of the announcement was lost in my scream.

"Faith! Faith!" I cried out to no avail. "Please someone stop her," I begged.

Then the blow came, Faith's hind leg to my head. A wave of pain instantly washed over me. I was afraid my brain might explode. My tears hot, I clenched my eyes.

Think, Devon. Think! I yelled in my mind determined to get out of this situation.

By some higher power, my body, pumping with adrenaline, returned to me, and suddenly I was able to move again. I wiggled and twisted my foot until it came loose from my boot. Released, I curled into a ball and rolled away from Faith's galloping feet. The arena still spinning, I just let my face rest in the dirt where I landed, unable to assess myself for any damage. I knew I would soon be the laughing stock of the horse show, an emotional pain I feared worse than any physical one.

It all happened so fast. I am definitely NOT a cowgirl!

CHAPTER THIRTY-TWO

*A*m *I still alive?*
Startled by my numbness, I tried to roll to my side. Breathless, I shook my dizzy head, vision clearing just in time to see JD make his way toward me in duress.

The thunderous hoof beats were still pounding in my ears, but not loud enough to drown out the girl in purple howling after JD.

"*Ooooh!* Stupid girlie! That's what you get for trying to steal my man!"

I clenched my teeth watching as an ugly scowl took shape, embossed across her makeup-caked face. Emphasizing her point, she leaned over the railing hard, clutching the top bar. The weight of her breasts visibly puckered where the skin connected to her chest.

Turning with a laugh to the other spectators, she continued, "Spotted devil horse threw her silly skinny little ass off. She deserved it as far as I see it." Hand on her hip, she pointed her index finger at my crumpled body lying in the arena. "What is she thinking bringing that crazy thing here anyway? That animal is dangerous!"

JD turned back toward the stands, and I could tell he was giving her a look. Then he fell to his knees next to me, hands on the top of his thighs.

"You all right, Devon? I'll never forgive myself if you're hurt bad. I feel like this is my darn fault. Shouldn't have brought you here. *Dang it!* Knew you weren't ready."

"It's not your fault, JD," I said, trying to sit up. Unable, I gave up, gripped my head, and let out a groan. Feeling woozy, I collapsed back into the dirt.

I looked up into JD's concerned green eyes and could see my pathetic stunt reflected in them. I felt my mouth begin to quiver. I wanted to cry as I replayed what just happened in my mind. I let my head tip to the right and closed my eyes.

"I'll take it from here, JD. I've seen how you've handled enough of these Devon situations. I'll be takin' her and the horse home too."

McKennon's velvet voice hummed through my achy body. I peered up at him. He had Star in tow. McKennon rested a gloved hand on top of my head. "Don't move," he ordered, low and with concern, his eyes franticly assessing me as I lay in the dust.

"JD, call the medic. Now!" McKennon demanded. I tensed at his intensity. JD snapped out of his blank stare and into action, hustling away from us, quickly closing the short distance to announcer's booth. "You hurt?" McKennon bellowed. "Just tell me you're OK. Then I can deal with this." His panic was evident as he sucked in breath.

"I ... I don't know," I wheezed, meeting his angry, vividly blue glare.

"They are on their way," JD called out, returning to the scene.

"Please, Faith. She's got to be scared. Please," I implored. McKennon softened just the slightest inside of my request and looked up searching the arena for my horse as he handed his own to JD. "Lay back, and be still. You hear? The medics are coming for you. Just please lay still. And *fine*, I *will* train you! You don't have to kill yourself to prove you need my help!" he said, rising to his feet, dusting off his knees as the medics rushed in.

Immediately, the medical staff started prodding me, feeling my arms, legs, head, stomach, pressing here, pushing there, assessing me.

A serious young man in scrubs asked a series of questions. He fired them at me one after the other, like rounds from a shotgun, "Are you OK? Where does it hurt? Do you know where you are? Can you feel this?"

Following McKennon's instruction, I remained still as the medics conducted their work. Numb to their actions, I only cared about the safety of my horse. I struggled to watch him gather up my mare as they treated me.

I have to keep him in my vision. I have to know she is OK. Hold on … Did McKennon just say that he would train me?

I kept my focus on his back as the medics completed their assessment of the situation. They placed me in a neck brace, raised me onto a backboard, and strapped me down.

I yearned for Faith. It pained me to see her in such a state. Her saddle was shifted to the side and a tangle of reins wrapped around her front legs. She was trembling in the far corner of the arena – as traumatized as her owner. Fighting to see between the racing arms adjusting me here and there, I watched McKennon approach her. He extended his arm out to her. His presence was calm and the complete opposite of hers – all wide-eyed and wild. Faith was laboring against the metal bit pulling at the corner of her mouth from the weight of her own front legs standing on the leathers.

What had I done?

"Nice one there, McKennon. Where'd you turn up this pair?" yelled a man from the stands. The crowd was growing larger by the second. McKennon clearly had history with these folks. "You a sucker for losers these days?'

Ignoring the taunt, McKennon reached Faith and settled his gloved hand to her strained neck. Slowly, he reached down to lift her front right hoof then her left, releasing the reins and the pressure from the bit on her mouth.

"Yeah, McKennon!" squealed the girl in lavender. "When did you start trade'n quality Quarter Horses for those wild ones with spots? Not quite like you, *cowbooooy*!"

Wordlessly, McKennon adjusted Faith's discombobulated saddle. With a heavy heave up, he tightened her girth and mounted a visibly, suddenly calm Faith.

This man was a zen horse master.

The final strap tightened me to the backboard, and my head throbbed with the jolt of being hoisted into the air. I managed to shift McKennon into view just in time to watch him glide past me on my horse. His reins dropped low, Faith going smooth and slow like a luxury sedan. My eyes closed, wishing to be back in that Green Briar field with him again.

Forcing myself to stay coherent through the pain, I heard McKennon's voice, "Y'all see what this so-called spotted devil horse can do? That girl there is still learning. Give her a year, and she be wiping up the show pen with you asses!"

A faint, satisfied smile pricked to my lips before I opened my eyes again, bright arena lights blaring against my aching head, and I am ushered out of the arena.

At the makeshift fairground nurse's station, I am diagnosed with nothing but a bruised ego and a headache. Martha, a smug, skinny, young nurse with thin lips and skin as white as her uniform, gives me three extra strength pain relievers, an ice pack for my noggin, and a healthy prescription for some riding lessons.

CHAPTER THIRTY-THREE

I climbed up the mountainous passenger side of McKennon's big rig diesel truck. I always wondered what it would be like to be his co-pilot. Sliding into the deep front seat, I stroked the soft, smooth, rich leather. Settling in, I gingerly kneaded my body into the lush seat, still tender from my fall. My fingertips followed the thick stitching, and I let out a long, laborious exhale. I wasn't sure what pained me more, my body or the fact that it hadn't been a very good horse show.

Clenching my eyes shut and gripping my hands together in my lap, I bit my lip in embarrassment, my heart and head aching. As a means to escape my bruised ego and booty, I started to daydream that I was McKennon's girl. I hoped to find some refuge in pretending that I actually belonged in his truck. Pensively, I leaned forward toward the dash and etched our initials into the thin coating of dust that had settled there.

As I completed my dusty dashboard inscription, my thoughts drifted back to reality. My eyebrows formed a hard 'V' as I thought about McKennon. He had been so quiet ever since my circus-style debacle in the arena. I couldn't help but think his behavior was right-fully so. Clearly, he couldn't have been pleased with my riding stunt. My heart sank realizing Faith and I had not, worse yet probably could not, meet the high expectations McKennon had set for us. Gasping, I held my breath, clutching my hand to my mouth. Stopped by my revelation, I sat stone still for what felt like a long time.

We are not as he had hoped.

Startling me, McKennon swung open the back quad cab door and tossed in an equipment bag. A cloud billowed into the air as it landed with a thud to the backseat floor, dispersing the sev-eral day accumulation of tack stall dust into the truck. A burst of frayed nerves awakened in my belly as I hurriedly wiped away our inscribed initials, erasing them just as he climbed in behind the steering wheel. McKennon had our horses loaded. We were ready to hit the road.

A nervous wave washed over me, heat rising behind my cheeks, I sat silent beside him. I'd become accustomed to reacting this way, the same familiar vibration swept through my being any time we were in close proximity.

Had I just been caught acting like a little girl again? Surely, he can't wait to get us back to Green Briar and out of his trailer, out of his hair, out of his sight.

Disgusted with myself, I rolled my eyes. *Ugh. I am such a disaster.*

Pinching the bridge of my nose with my left fingertips, I fum-bled inside my purse and touched the pack of cigarettes that had tumbled from JD's shirt pocket last night. As I reflected on retriev-ing them from the wet dance floor of The Silver Spur, a violent flashback of that beastly woman's body bulldozing JD sent a shud-der through me. I pressed my body against my seat, hard, teeth clenched at the thought of the girl in purple's oxen form rushing toward me.

I mulled the box over, right hand buried deep inside my purse, poking the corner of the cardboard into my palm.

Why did I have to pick up the darn pack? Why didn't I give them back to JD? Probably because my non-cowgirl self spent half the afternoon laid out on her back in the dirt! That's why!

Contemplating them, I worked up reasons to partake.

Maybe I could just have one to calm my nerves?

I had smoked a few times in college when I thought I was fitting in with my friends at keg parties.

Why does he make me want to have one now?

I fingered the pack over and over in my purse.

Why not? I am a grown woman!

I lifted the box from my purse, retrieved a tobacco stick, and, with conviction, put the prop to my lips.

Turning to McKennon, I asked quizzically, "Do you have a lighter?"

McKennon shifted slightly in his seat to look at me, using the steering wheel as leverage. Cocking his head in confusion, he blinked several times before furrowing his brow, pressing his chest to the steering wheel, and setting his lips in the tight line of contemplation. Wordlessly, seemingly baffled, he continued his inspection of me, resting his handsome head on his arms wrapping the wheel, probably expecting me to fill the pregnant silence with a cue that I was joking.

This was not a joke.

I just stared back at him through my lashes. After waiting a period for a response from me and realizing none was coming, he silently leaned toward and over me, sculpted chest bearing down on my lap. I welcomed the weight of him by clenching my thighs together, a slight smile slipping to my lips. My eyes wandered in wonder over his sculpted back, cloaked in the thin gauze of his white T-shirt, muscles rippling like a river beneath it. Pressing into me a little harder, McKennon opened the glove box.

My pulse surged through my veins, erupting in an electric shock that flowed through me. I could feel the rousing charge at the end of each tendril of my hair, spreading warm through my belly, and it was very present *there*. Gulping hard, I took a deep inhale of him and was immediately intoxicated with his aroma, leather, animal, man, and a hint of spice. I pressed my thighs even tighter. McKennon rummaged around for a second without looking at me before turning up a lighter and passing it to me.

I struck the lighter once, twice, again and again.

"This lighter doesn't work," I said, shaking it close to my ear, listening for fluid.

McKennon fumbled to his jeans, attempting to shimmy his hand into the tight front pocket with little success. Readjusting himself, he leaned way back in his seat for a more appropriate angle. My eyes widened as his jeans tightened just enough that I caught a glimpse of his seemingly well-endowed package.

Oh my! I nibbled my lower lip with my front teeth and held my breath. I turned my head away to look out the side window.

Finally, McKennon retrieved a book of matches and held them extended to me in the palm of his gloved hand directly in front of my chest. Dipping my chin to look at them, I saw the letters of The Silver Spur embossed on the cover. Closing my eyes, I reached for them. Forcing away thoughts of the horse show's calamity, I let my hand linger a little too long and ran my fingers across the smooth exterior of the lambskin glove, wishing I could feel beneath it, feel his heat and the tinge of sweat I knew were there, paused in the palm of his hand.

Why does he always wear those gloves?

Suddenly, I realized this whole smoking thing was a ploy for his attention, perhaps a ploy to touch him again. Waking up from my daze, I seized the matches, pulled a match loose, and struggled to strike it into flame. Cigarette clutched in my pursed lips, I imagined McKennon as mine. Awakening to a place deep inside me that I wasn't fully ready to admit actually existed or that

I was deeply ashamed of, I concluded that I desperately wanted McKennon to kiss me.

Lost in this aphrodisiac, I was startled when McKennon moved faster than I had ever seen him. His movements were usually so calculated, lethargic even. This time, he was like lightening.

Swatting the matches from my grasp, he pushed the cigarette away from my mouth, my lips sliding across his fingers as he dove at me.

Clutching me by both upper arms, he clenched my lean biceps hard, blue eyes blazing as he pulled me to him. It felt forbidden.

What is he going to do?

McKennon just held me there and searched my eyes. Overwhelmed with his good looks, I let myself completely collapse in his grasp, my body limp, head tipped back, throat exposed, supported by the strength of his hands, his scent overwhelming me. All of the things I loved were right there, hovering in front of me: horses, hard work, strength, knowledge, winning.

I lifted my head. He was so close to me. We just stared into each other's eyes, lost in utter connection. McKennon leaned closer, took a deep breath of me in, and parted his tempting mouth. It felt like we had been suspended, wordlessly, in time for hours. I watched McKennon wet his lips to …

To what? To speak? To touch them to mine?

I was standing at the edge of a ledge, ready to lean in and fall.

Then, from behind us and without warning, an anxious ear-piercing holler followed by a loud, forceful bang, penetrated our moment, and we were no longer suspended in time. The abrupt jolt rocked the whole truck and trailer, the result of the impatient kick.

Was Star or Faith the interrupter?

Whichever animal had delivered the blow was clearly irritable and ready to go. All at once, he and I became aware of time and place. McKennon released me from his grasp. Turning away, he slammed his hands on the steering wheel, gripping it tightly, twisting with an intense wringing motion. I could envision his knuckles going white inside those gloves he always wore.

Trembling with desire, I struggled to catch my breath. Putting my lips to my knuckles, I leaned over the still-open glove box. Clenching my teeth, I tried to calm the butterflies set loose in my stomach. I had felt this feeling before.

Yes, I desperately wanted McKennon to kiss me.

Staring straight ahead, McKennon turned the key over in the ignition. "Devon, I am damaged goods," he whispered. He was so soft-spoken that I had to make every effort to hear him. "I'll train you as I said, but that is where it ends," his whisper turned into a low growl. "This moment never happened. You hear?"

McKennon put the truck in gear. As his words settled in, disappointment took hold. Forcing focus, I fought to straighten my gaze, ahead, out over the dash, and through the windshield, a disenchanted cowgirl wannabe fighting back her tears. Yet there was still a hopeful anticipation bubbling up in me. I couldn't help but wonder what would happen next in our saga.

What did the future hold for McKennon, me, and my horse of different colors?

CHAPTER THIRTY-FOUR

I stepped into the damp cool of the barn, fondling the humid wallboards, and flipped the switch to awaken the overhead lights. As the halogens warmed and found their buzz, I lazily walked the aisle, breathing in the place.

After spending the weekend at the fairgrounds, I was happy to be back at Green Briar. Monday meant a fresh start, a new beginning. I was ready to turn the page. I felt secure again, serene in my femininity, certain of my surroundings. I opened Faith's stall door like a present and haltered my mare in the dewy early air. I welcomed the familiar flutter of happiness as I led Faith out of her stall, blinking sleep from her heavy brown eyes. She released a long, low, lethargic sigh at having to leave behind her bedspread of ankle-deep, aromatic pine shavings.

I was my real self here. I felt afresh, connected to the earth. I had two feet firmly on familiar ground. I was present to my life's energy source simply through the gentle awareness of my breath going in and flowing out of my lungs. My mind was now relatively under control as compared to the mind that I inhabited during the recent horse show craze. I wrapped my arms around Faith's muzzle, and she dropped her head low, offering her delicate face to the cradle of my arms. Her pink nostrils gently blowing warm air on my forearms.

Serenity.

"Today will be our first lesson," I whispered close to her cheek, giving Faith a light squeeze. Then I heard the jingling of his spurs coming toward us with urgency from the adjacent aisle, the clip-clopping of Star in tow. Not wanting to be caught in another one of my personal moments, I rushed to straighten myself from the embrace.

"All right," McKennon's voice struck me with the intensity of a wicked, wandering bullet. I was the bull's-eye, his words pierced my heart, and my pulse was shocked into a frenzied pace – a defibrillator designed just for me. Faith lifted her face from my hug and pricked her ears toward me as if she could feel my blood racing too.

Direct hit.

"I said I would train ya, didn't I?" he said, snapping his stallion into cross ties.

Was McKennon satisfied with his choice to offer his training, or was he wishing he hadn't committed to taking us on?

I reminded myself that I was standing on familiar turf and shook off the self-doubt. Regardless of my condition, his velvet voice thrummed through my ear canals.

In the early morning light, McKennon looked otherworldly. I was smitten watching him as he polished his mount. I smiled when he pawed the air near his face, wafting away the floating dust particles lifted by Star's body brush. My eyes explored his torso, thin white shirt gripping his sculpted pectoral muscles. His frame was defined, but not bulky, biceps flexing effortlessly as he shifted directions, following the flow of Star's silken, metallic, flecked coat.

"Don't be callin' me your trainer though. I'm only doin' this to keep you safe. You hear?"

Trying not to let his words bother me, I swallowed hard and picked up a brush to groom Faith.

"So ... so ... why did you ... um ... help me when Faith threw me off?" I asked. Eyes wide, I immediately chastised myself.

Foolish cowgirl.

Taking a moment to ponder my inquiry, McKennon adjusted his straw cowboy hat lower over his eyes, the one he worked in, the one that I was accustomed to, and the one I missed. He returned to working Star over, bristles revealing a coat of copper sheen, eyebrows knit tight in contemplation. I let my eyes linger on the chiseled edge of his right tricep, flexing and falling in swift movements, as he upped the intensity with which he groomed his stead.

"Well ... I guess ... uh. It's just ... um ... I just ..." he stumbled. "Fine. I feel like I need to watch over you. That's it." His penetrating blue eyes trailed across Star's big bay body and met mine.

Dropping his gaze to the concrete, he scraped his boot tip across the floor in an 'aw shucks' kind of manner. "There you have it. You satisfied, Devon?"

"Oh," I said, looking down at my own lame black 1990 boots and resorted to becoming the bashful version of Devon. It was all I could muster.

Interrupting the heaviness of our bittersweet silence, the grand twin barn doors began to split open. Their slow screech filled the space between us. Bursts of starting and stopping stabbed the air, conjuring up memories of a classmate's nails on a schoolteacher's chalkboard. I clamped my teeth. Both horses' ears instantly shot forward, pricked with anticipation, and our attention lifted to follow the clamor at the front entrance.

Sophia managed to move the doors just enough to squeeze her frail frame through. Once inside, I couldn't help but watch her weathered, purple veined, baubled hands wrap the handle and pull the 12 inches of gap shut again. Her strength surprised me.

"Good early morning to you two!" Sophia exclaimed. She breathed life back into the stable, suspending our awkward exchange. Shimmying up to Star, she enveloped his muzzle in her slender arms, wings of her gauzy, flowered blouse floating to either side of his jowls. Star leaned into her small frame, contented. After a moment of equine reconnection, she reached for McKennon and hugged him, fawning over him like a long lost son. McKennon's eyes beamed down upon her.

I wish he would look at me like that.

"Glad to have us back, Miss Sophia?" he teased, poking her ever so gently in the upper arm. She giggled. I grinned, a witness to their bond.

"Yes, McKennon. Always glad to have you back ... but," she turned her crooked thin index finger toward me and cupped her mouth as if to whisper but shouted down the aisle, "it was this one that I was really worried about."

It took all I had not to recoil in self-consciousness. I stood my ground, two cowgirl boots firmly planted, and retorted, "So, Sophia, I assume it was you who tattled on me. Isn't it so?" I jammed my hand to my waist and jutted my hip, punctuating my inquiry with a wink.

With a slight nod, Sophia responded coyly, hand raised, circling and uplifting the surrounding air in a queen-like fashion, "So, darling, I see you've returned in much better company than you departed. And with a lot less noise."

Sophia and I began to giggle like schoolgirls crushing on the new boy in school. My mind raced back to Sophia's bejeweled fingers flying across her cell phone, and my arrival to the impatient tapping of McKennon's boot at Sallie Mae's office door.

Once our female side splitting subsided, Sophia continued to probe.

"So, what's going on here?" she asked, her curved, index finger traveling back and forth between McKennon and me.

Certain blush rising to my cheeks, I left McKennon to answer. Returning to my duties, I lifted Faith's saddle up and over her back. Straightening the saddle pad, I moved to the opposite side, gripped the girth, and looped it through. At the same time, I couldn't help but position myself to get a better view of McKennon's tight frame as he leaned against a stall door, silver buckle slung low on his hips, one boot crossed over the other, addressing Sophia's question. He kept his voice low. I knew he was likely filling her in on the gap between JD's trailer bouncing out of the Green Briar driveway and the events that occurred at the horse show. I knew it was in the cards that their conversation would include my idiotic behavior.

Embarrassed, I didn't want to hear anything they were saying. I attempted to tune out Sophia, but it was a challenge. She repeatedly referenced me with a raised eyebrow and a quipped upper lip. Between McKennon's pauses, she regarded me like a beautiful disaster.

Out of the corner of my eye, I kept him in view, looking for signs of displeasure, but he wore his normal easy expression, punctuating sentences with a chuckle. That is until he took notice of me, leather strap in my grasp, leveraging my body into position, ready to heave the girth up, and tighten my western work saddle.

"No!" he barked. "No saddle today, Devon!"

The command was urgent and sudden. It stopped me in my tracks. His face grew stern as he pushed himself away from the wall. McKennon changed before my eyes. This was a new face, a new voice. An order. A certainty. He was the boss now, and I was required to stand at attention.

I felt the excitement drain from my frame.

"No saddle?" I peeped.

"No," he repeated. He was firm.

"Oh," I said, unwinding the leather strap from the girth. I let it swing beneath Faith's belly in defiance.

"Go on now, Devon. Take it off," he ordered.

In disappointment, I stripped the saddle from her back. Pouting like an angry 4-year-old, I returned it to the tack room, dragging its appendages behind me. This morning, I had been so excited to have him assess our riding. Now, I wondered if he was going to train us at all.

McKennon sure is good at talking, but was he ever going to get to work on us?

I flung my saddle back to the rack with a huff and returned to the aisle, trailed by a cloud of gloom. Upon my return, Sophia offered a weak smile from her glittery peach-glossed lips. I was clearly wearing my melancholy like an identification badge.

McKennon pondered me for a moment, rubbing his strong, stubble-covered chin between his forefinger and thumb, then shook his head. Eyes cast to the ground, he wandered down the aisle, covering his luscious lips. I slivered my eyes at his back. I knew he was wearing a grin.

Opening the heavy outer doors wide for Sophia, McKennon gestured her toward them with a tilt of his head. Sophia immediately responded to his cue. It was as if she knew the work was about to begin and, without question, understood it was time for her to go.

"I'll leave the two of you to it then," she said.

Pausing in the space between the doors, Sophia cast me a glance. It was a look of warning. I knew she was hoping to alert me to the talking-to that I already knew was coming. Then she disappeared through the parted doors. And we were alone again.

CHAPTER THIRTY-FIVE

"I won't be workin' with this kinda attitude, little missy," McKennon said over his shoulder as he closed the doors behind Sophia. I knew closing the doors was a last-ditch effort to contain the remnants of early morning cool inside the barn.

He strode over to me and hovered above. Tall, rooted and expansive like a live oak, he rested his lambskin-covered hands on his belted hips. I felt meek.

"You gonna straighten up?" he quizzed, wearing the expression of a disappointed father figure across his celestial face.

"Yes," I squeaked.

I was instantly entranced by his sudden shift. Once angelic and innocent, McKennon's demeanor had gone sultry through his come-hither sapphire eyes. His expression eliminated any feelings of defiance and turned me unequivocally weak in the knees, almost breathless, at his virile proximity.

As long as he keeps looking at me like that, I will willingly accept his command!

"Good. You ain't always gonna get it your way, little lady. You hear? You just gotta trust the process. Ridin' is the last thing we're gonna do. Getting to the ridin' part takes steps, a foundation. This mare here don't have none of that right now."

I nodded while my writer's heart clenched in my chest and my toes curled up in my cowgirl boots at his brutal assault on the English language ... and my horse.

"First things first, we gotta get her to stop being so dang scared of everything and keep you in the darn saddle," he scolded, blue eyes blazing.

He was right.

I seriously stopped counting how many times I'd almost lost my seat riding Faith since arriving at Green Briar and tried to put out of my mind how many times I'd actually fallen off of her especially this last time at the show.

He reached out with his gloved hand and caught my chin in his fingertips. "No more fallin' off! You hear?"

Giving my face a downward tug, he leaned into me, meeting my upward gaze with his sea-colored one.

Goodness, he is so beautiful!

I could see the flecks of hazel like golden streamers through the sapphire of his irises.

"OK," I said, finding my voice in lieu of his overwhelming allure. "No more falling off. I promise I'll try."

"Good. I'm gonna hold you to that. Stops my heart every time I think about it."

McKennon put his hand to his chest, tapping where his heart would be beneath that thin, tight shirt and pointed his sheathed index finger to the ceiling.

"Um, maybe we should buy some superglue for my rear just in case. Does that stuff work on leather and jeans?" I bit my lower lip and admired him, a warm flush quickly coming to my cheeks.

He lowered his arm and studied me, his eyes catching me like a butterfly in the net of his gaze.

"All right, let's get started then," he said, shaking his head in humor and exhaling a quick-pulsed snort from his perfectly straight nose. He headed down the aisle toward Faith and over his shoulder retorted, "I guess we'll have to try out that superglue thing. If it works, I'm investing in bulk! You know if they got that stuff at the feed store?"

"Are you just going to leave Star standing in the aisle?" I asked after him, observing the calm stallion standing, one hind leg cocked in the cross ties.

"Yep. Does 'em good to teach 'em to stand and wait. Patience is a virtue. In people and in horses, Devon. You gotta show 'em you're the leader, and no amount of jiggin' this way and that is gonna get 'em what they want. It's a respect thing. It's a safety thing. Star's been an ace student so far. He'll be fine. Come," he ordered, gesturing down the aisle with a motion of his hand.

Yes, patience is a virtue especially when you are waiting on your editor to send your next writing assignment ... or waiting for a hot cowboy to kiss you! Smitten, I followed in his enticing wake.

"OK. So remember how I told you they are flight animals? Well, fear and flight equals survival in their natural habitat, you know, a herd environment roamin' the plains. They are wired to react and run. Just about anything can show up to them as a predator, somethin' to fear. It's just in their nature. Understand?"

"You mean that anything can set them off? And it's a biological response that can be overridden?" I asked, exchanging my cowgirl-in-distress insignia for my studious, journalist's cap. It felt good to try it back on after the disempowering experience of the horse show.

Momentarily, I envisioned myself with notepad in hand, hair in a bun, dark rimmed glasses balanced on the tip of my nose, white oxford shirt buttoned all the way up to the too-tight collar, buttons straining at my bosom, sitting over my laptop, and biting my pencil searching for my angle, eyeballing my muse. A swell of electricity surged between my legs, urging me to let my movie mind run. Me – the librarian turned novelist. McKennon – the hot cowboy in the starring role.

"Yes, we're gonna start remedying that reactionary response in Faith right now."

His velveteen voice snapped me back to reality. Forcing myself to be present, I dropped the sizzling storyline, headlining this Romeo in Wranglers, playing in the background of my mind. I pressed pause with one final squeeze of my thighs and bid good day to the wanting waves writhing through me.

Go away, lusty daydream! Faith. Focus on Faith!

All the while, Faith had been waiting in the cross ties. McKennon unclipped her and returned her to her stall.

What the heck was he doing?

I had been dreaming of this, and this was not what I expected. I envisioned rounds in the arena, kicking up dust and feeling his eyes on me, his words coaching us. The only thing he seemed to have eyes for today was Faith. I put aside my desire, allowing a wave of gratitude, rather than lust, to usher in.

McKennon rummaged in the back pocket of his tight jeans and produced a plastic bag.

"We'll start small with this here plastic bag. We're gonna do this with her every day until it don't matter to her no more."

"What do you mean, 'until it doesn't matter to her anymore'?"

McKennon tied the basic white grocery store shopping bag to the snapping end of a lunge whip.

What the heck is he going to do with that?

"We'll start in her stall and then move to the round pen," he said, reaching for the cool metal hinge of her stall door and sliding it open.

Faith tipped her nose outward, sniffing the air. McKennon moved into the stall, producing his makeshift training tool. The plastic bag dragged on the aisle pavement and ever so slightly made a crunching noise as it fluttered into Faith's living quarters. Alarmed, Faith immediately eyed it, and my pulse began to accelerate. McKennon flicked the plastic bag, and it caught on the air, adding an unusual noise to the barn atmosphere.

McKennon's attention was transfixed on Faith as she leaned back on her trembling hocks, her front legs straight out ahead of her, whites of her eyes showing, and pink pulsating inside her nostrils. Then he shook the bag with aggression. Faith shot backwards like a lightning bolt and pressed her tail into the corner of her stall quivering, head swinging from side to side, searching for safety. McKennon shook the plastic bag again, and she went into a frenzied pace, traveling back and forth along the back stall wall.

"Stop it! You're scaring her!" I rang out.

"Hush now," he chided, calm inside of our frenzy. "Devon. Think how many times while at a horse show or out on the trails you might encounter a plastic bag floating by like this? Look at her – she can't even be with it. What do you think would happen if you were in the saddle right now?" He reached out and put his hand on my shoulder, preventing me from rushing to Faith's rescue.

"Just give it a moment," McKennon requested as he continued to waft the bag through the air like casting a noisy fishing line into her stall.

This was a faceoff. Faith continued to pace, alert, heightened, eyeballing the prop like it was a raging mountain lion. And McKennon continued to wave the whip, slow in arches toward the ceiling, then fast and scurried along the ground. He kept forcing bursts of noise and repeated motion. The bag was a white blur in the stall.

He was very distracting. It took effort to remain studious. I had to keep reminding myself to ignore his chiseled muscles stretching the cotton armband of his tight T-shirt as he waved the whip.

It seemed like an eternity before Faith finally stopped scurrying back and forth. Impatient, she stood in the center of her stall, pawing the ground, and snorting in angry bursts. She kept her distance, but finally focused her attention on observing the bag rather than running from it.

"There she is," McKennon said, pleased with the progress. "She is starting to accept it. Examine it. Horses are naturally curious once the fear subsides."

Faith's eyes looked less frantic. Still keeping her distance from the bag, she stretched her nose out across the stall and smelled the air. McKennon bumped the bag up against her muzzle, and her head shot up, whites of her eyes returning, but she didn't pace. He did it again, and she offered even less reaction this time. Then all at once, she released a burst of air from her flared nostrils, dropped her head, and began moving her mouth.

"See. See there," McKennon said, letting the flowing bag come to pause at her hooves. "See her lickin' her lips? Means she is accepting it. Losin' the fear. Relaxin'."

His eyes wandered from my horse to me. In them, I saw the flicker of an excited little boy.

He loved this.

I smiled back at him.

"I know this seems extreme, and it's not easy for you to watch her be so uncomfortable, Devon. But I promise you, it's for her own good. And yours. Not to mention my peace of mind. You'll see. It'll make the biggest difference. Keep you two safe. That's all I want in the world, to see you safe."

My heart expanded with his words.

Safe. He wanted me to be safe.

Those words, 'I feel like I need to watch over you,' repeated in my head. I turned to him as he held the whip taut and touched his firm cowboy forearm.

"Thank you. Thank you for wanting us to be safe."

My heart surged outward from my chest. I had an octopus heart. The writer inside couldn't help but try to define the yearning deep inside of me. I visualized eight red and purple pulsing appendages reaching out from my torso, longing to close around something, searching for a body to embrace. I wanted so badly to press my frayed self to him and have him wrap his arms around me in understanding, soothing my thirsty-for-love octopus heart. I ached to feel that kind of "safe." I didn't know what that kind of safe might even be like, but I imagined McKennon held the key to my knowing.

"Aw, shucks. It's nothin'," he said, wiggling his arm from my touch. "Now, I want you to do this to her yourself every day before you bring her out of that stall. You hear?"

I nodded.

He coiled up the cord of the lunge whip and wrapped it around the shaft of the prop, securing the plastic bag so it wouldn't make any further noise.

"It's gonna take a while, and you can expect her to react much the same the next time she experiences this, but eventually she won't be mindin' as much. We don't want to take all the reaction outta her. We just wanna take enough to take the edge off, get her to that place where when somethin' catches her eye, she goes to thinkin' rather than reactin'. We want her to stop and observe, not run and bolt. Got it?"

"Yes," I said fervently, hoping that I hadn't vocalized the hidden disappointment that he just moved away from my touch.

My emotions felt heightened with all we had gone through, Faith, McKennon and me. I knew him yet I didn't. He knew me, knew us, yet he didn't.

Again, I stood alone at the edge of the ledge, leaning forward, wanting to fall. This pining couldn't be satisfied right now. If I fell now, I knew I would be falling alone.

Patience.

McKennon backed out of the stall, easing Faith's door shut. She let out a long sigh and flung herself into the deep shavings, splaying out on her side.

McKennon chuckled at Faith's reaction as he propped the training tool up against the wall. Its work finished for the day.

"Well. Look at that ... I'd say she's had enough for today," he said, admiring my mare. Faith was clearly exhausted from the lesson, laid out on her side huffing. He adjusted his hat back on his head, scratched his refined jawline, mouth slightly ajar, and raised an eyebrow, puzzling over her.

"Think we might need to get that horse an energy drink or somethin'. Never seen an animal get so worn out so quickly. They usually fuss for some time after a learnin' like that. She's a bit unusual that way."

Momentarily taken aback, McKennon rubbed his neck and shook his bewildered head before turning his attention back to me.

"OK, listen up. This is how this is gonna go. I'm gonna teach you once a week. The rest is up to you. You're gonna be the one trainin' her, not me. I'm not your trainer. My role is to be your guide. Are you following?"

"Yes, sir. You're not my trainer. You're my guide. I'm envisioning my yoga master back in New York. Got it!" I offered him my hands pressed together and silently mouthed Namaste.

McKennon turned his head to the right, pressing his brows together, and eyed me.

"You being mouthy, Devon?" he snipped, shifting his cowboy hat lower over his turned stern eyes.

"No, sir!" I quipped, clipping my heels together, throwing my shoulders back, and saluting him with a giggle.

"Straighten up, soldier," he cautioned. "Seriously, remember start with the bag each day like I just showed you. Then I'd like you to practice in hand groundwork with her this week. If she gets jiggy, just make her stand still. Walk her all around the property, practice squaring her up and doing pivots, 180s, 360s, make her back up in between them. Keep her standing still every now and then until she relaxes. You'll know when her head comes down, and then you can move on. I'd say about 30 minutes a day. Give her some grazin' too. When you're finished, tie her up in her stall and make her stand for about 15 minutes each day before she gets her freedom. We're startin' here with some good ol' fashion horse manners. We're teachin' Faith patience. We'll start again next week. Saddle her up and meet me in the round pen same time. No riding until then. Got it?"

"No riding?" I looked down at my out-of-date boots.

"No riding, Devon. I'll let you know when it's time."

His response was firm.

"I understand," I said, masking my disappointment. I blinked up to him. "And, patience is a virtue," I sighed.

I knew I was getting just as much a lesson in patience from this man as my horse was.

"OK, then," he said, pressing his lips together in a thin line. McKennon awkwardly tipped his hat to me and backed away a few steps, studying my old school boots but for a moment, before nodding and turning to attend to his horse patiently waiting for the return of his leader.

CHAPTER THIRTY-SIX

"Hey, Devon."

"Hey, JD," I said, squinting up into the sun.

JD lifted his baseball hat off his head to run his fingers through his damp mane.

"Hot out here today, huh? How you feelin'?" JD asked, putting his cap back on then tucking the tufts of his soft blonde waves behind his ears.

"OK," I said halfheartedly, eyeing the whip with the plastic bag attached and swallowing hard at what I was about to do.

"So look. I just wanted to say that I'm really sorry about what happened at the horse show," JD said, plunging his hands deep into his pockets and rocking back on his heels, shoulders in a shrug, pink lips pursed.

"I survived," I reassured, offering a half smile and gesturing with my head toward McKennon saddling Star down the aisle. "Got us a trainer out of it too."

"Oh, good. I sure am sorry about the fall. Shoulda known you weren't ready, but I am talking about more than just that. I mean

I'm sorry about Brittany too. She used to be such a nice girl. We used to go out back when we were young. And when she was a lot thinner."

JD's usual smirk returned to his mouth. He grasped the big buckle at the front of his pants, jutting his pelvis just the slightest bit forward in an effort to attract my attention. I ignored his valiant effort.

"She never really got over me, I guess," he continued, shrugging his bulky shoulders. "She sure was pretty awful to you. Figurin' she didn't much like seeing me carin' about you, and you bein' in my trailer and all. Got a pretty nasty bruise myself from her antics."

JD raised his shirt, producing his chiseled, six-pack abs and an angry black and blue mark, surely the result of his collision with the bar furniture. The girl in purple's twisted ogre face visualized in my mind, and I shook off the memory.

"So anyway, I gave her a talkin' to. Told her that you and me are just friends. Though I wish it were otherwise," JD snickered as he tucked his shirt back in with one hand and peered at me before adjusting his manhood from inside his jeans. I half gagged at his bluntness.

Noticing my distaste, JD bumped me in the arm with his elbow, flashing his million-dollar smile.

"So anyway. You forgive me?"

"Of course. I really can't blame you for any of that. I can see how a guy like you could make a girl go crazy. In all sorts of ways," I reputed, flicking my eyes to the hand that was just in his pants.

Raising my eyebrows ready for the challenge, I reached for the plastic bag attached to the whip and began to uncoil the cord.

"What're you doin' there?" JD probed, eyeing my makeshift training tool.

"Oh, this?" I responded, hiking the whip in the air. The bag crinkled, sending Faith's head straight up inside her stall.

"Oops. Oh, just learning patience I guess. I had my first lesson with the big man. Not supposed to be doing any riding. I am just supposed to be frightening Faith with this thing."

I looked down the aisle at McKennon minding his own business and tending to his stead. As he leaned over and rummaged through a tack box, I couldn't help but let my eyes linger on his backside.

"Huh," JD huffed, jutting his chin out. I knew he noticed my distracted stare in McKennon's direction.

I reached for Faith's door and gingerly slid it open. Peering in on my horse, a pang of guilt washed over me. Taking notice of me, she lifted her delicate head from foraging for the last bits of stray alfalfa, remnants of this morning's feeding. Lone piece of hay straggling between her fuzzy lips, my eyes met her big, brown, wide ones. I swallowed hard as I stepped just inside the entrance. Not seeing that I held the whip behind my back, Faith dropped her muzzle back to the stall floor, rummaging and shifting through the shavings with her mouth, continuing the search. Looking over my shoulder at JD, I sighed and took a deep breath.

"Here goes nothing," I informed him, flicking the whip into her stall. The plastic bag fluttered in the air before landing softly atop the bedding. Faith quivered for a moment, but ultimately paid it no mind.

"Here, don't be being so gentle with it, Devon. Do it like this," JD said, slipping himself up against my backside. I could feel the cool purpose of his belt buckle on my lower back through the thin layer of my tank top's cloth. JD smoothed his hand from my shoulder, down my arm, and encompassed my hand with his. Taking grip of both the whip and me, he gave it a sharp snap. Faith's head bolted up, and she commenced the same anxious race of pacing that I had witnessed yesterday. Nervously, I pushed back into JD. Faith frightened me when she acted this way.

"Hmmm. I could get used to this," JD purred, wrapping his other arm around my waist. "I could be your trainer, you know?" His breath was warm at the base of my neck. "Wouldn't be any skin off my knee."

"What's this?" McKennon boomed from behind us.

Shoot!

I put my free hand to JD's arm around my waist and attempted to pry him off of me. I looked over my shoulder to see McKennon standing in the aisle behind us. Taking in our postures and proximity, his sapphire eyes turned to hooded slivers.

"Nothing!" I retorted, turning to JD and shoving him as hard as I could out of the stall.

Surprised, JD stumbled over the cement lip of the entry way and toppled backwards into McKennon. Swiftly, McKennon extended his gloved hands and caught JD by his broad shoulders, righting him.

"Aw. Come on, Devon! Don't be like that. I was just helpin'!" JD whined, cautiously sizing up McKennon. His presence was hard to ignore, statuesque in his eerily silent observation of me. He appeared disappointed.

Trying to ignore McKennon, I slammed Faith's door shut and stomped to JD. I was fully intent to make it clear I had no interest in him once and for all, no matter what designs he had set on me. Chucking the whip to the cement floor, I poked JD in his solid, expansive chest, eye to eye with his bull-rider stature.

"Now look here, JD. We are friends. It is nothing more than that. Do you hear me?" I said, sticking my hand out to invite his handshake. Eyeing my hand, JD looked at me in contempt.

"You got a real dainty hand there, miss. I sure do like pink nail polish on a girl."

Giving me a smug twist of his full mouth, JD leaned back against the adjacent stall, ignoring my hand still extended to him. McKennon gave us our space and just continued to observe the situation with an air of disapproval; his arms crisscrossed against his wiry yet capable frame, gripping his considerable biceps, his ocean eyes slits, mere silvery gray seams beneath the shadow of his cowboy hat.

"Friends," I repeated, sternly pumping my outstretched hand, widening my palm. Threatening him to take my invitation, I enlarged my eyes at JD. My lips pinched tight.

I can't have JD messing up this thing I've got going with McKennon. I need his training, or I'm never going to get anywhere with Faith. Or with him.

Sighing, JD pushed himself from the wall with his fingertips. "Fine! Friends."

"Let's shake on it this time, JD," I demanded. My heart hammered as I stole a glance at McKennon standing like an angry statue over us.

"You sure about this, Devon?" JD removed his ball cap, twisted the brim, and tucked it into the back pocket of his jeans. He amped up his dazzling smile and closed the distance between our faces, holding my eyes with his best sultry stare.

"We shake on it, and it's a done deal. We bull riders don't go back on our word once it's given. We shake this time, and you're not gonna get yourself any of this ... ever. Don't even know what you're missin'! Thought we'd at least go for a roll in the hay before you decided it wasn't for you," JD leered, grabbing his substantial bulge. Moving his hips in a circular motion, he cupped his manhood with one hand, giving it a few upward thrusts, and extended the other arm in the air, like a bull rider going the full eight seconds.

McKennon's disgust was audible as he groaned and dragged his gloved hand across his face, punctuating his displeasure with a roll of his eyes.

Exasperated, I shook my head and wiped my sweaty palms on my jeans before extending my hand to JD again.

"Fine," JD said, gripping my hand with a crushing force. He gave it a single pump, pulling me off balance, and toward him. "Don't know what you're missin'," he growled before flashing his perfect white teeth. Snickering to himself, JD turned to go, angrily bumping McKennon in the shoulder as he passed.

"I'll be seein' you, friend!" he bellowed as he kicked an innocent hay bale lining the aisle. His growl turned to a mutter as he jammed his hands into his front pockets and hunched his shoulders over, "Just don't want to see no one gettin' hurt again." I had to strain to hear those last words as he shot McKennon one last dagger glare.

What does that mean?

"That happen a lot?" McKennon questioned, watching JD waltz out of the barn with a chip on his shoulder. "Like I said before. Good kid. Just kinda stupid. Been hurt in the past. Thinks he's the bee's knees with the ladies. Glad to see all that charm ain't workin' on you. Figured you're smarter than that." McKennon took one long-legged step closer to me and put his hand in the small of my back.

"Don't take it personally," he whispered near my ear, a tuft of my hair fluttering on the warmth of his breath. "He'll be back to normal after his next conquest. You all right?"

"Yeah. I am fine," I breezed, bracing myself against the excitement buzzing through my body at his immediacy. It took all I had to suppress it. "JD is a total pig sometimes, but I do value his friendship. He's been pretty great to me. Except when he is hitting on me, that is."

McKennon dropped his hand.

"Yeah. I guess so. Better get yourself back to work there," he said, eyes flashing to Faith's stall.

"Yes, sir."

I retrieved the whip from where I had tossed it to the floor and reopened Faith's stall.

"Listen, Devon. I just watched what happened in there. JD was right. From here on out, you gotta stop being so ginger with her. I want you to quit being so delicate, so sensitive with Faith. Don't be so concerned with what you think her needs are. I want you to start being deliberate."

"Deliberate?" I repeated.

"Yes. Be deliberate about scaring her. No more tiptoeing with her. Eventually, if you frighten her enough, she'll get pretty darn close to ... what's that term they use for horses they try to sell for kids? Oh yeah, bombproof. Then nothin' will catch her off guard. It's people, always being so dang tiptoe. Makes 'em dangerous. You know any leaders, CEOs, presidents who tiptoe?"

"I guess not," I said, turning the whip over in my hands.

"OK, then. Remember we are teaching her that you are the alpha in the relationship. You're the leader here. She stands when you say stand. She gets in the trailer when you say get in the trailer. She works when you say work. If you are fearless, she will be too. OK?"

He gazed down on me, and my knees felt wobbly.

"OK, one fearless cowgirl coming up," I smiled a weak one his way.

"You can do it," he encouraged, taking a long-legged step backward away from me. "Go on then, cowgirl." he continued, winking at me beneath his cowboy hat.

So sexy!

I peeled myself from his presence and flung the whip into Faith's stall with gusto. She released a shriek of a whinny before bolting to the corner of the stall. I did it again, a new confidence brewing inside me and bubbling up as I swooped that bag to and fro.

A considerate smile spreading across his delectable lips, McKennon turned to go. I let him without uttering another word. Breathless from effort, I paused and caught the edge of the stall door in the palm of my hand, knuckles crooked in support of my body weight, allowing myself to lean back just in time to catch him easily swing himself into the saddle outside of the barn and cluck Star forward. His blazing blue eyes caught me watching him go from down the aisle.

CHAPTER THIRTY-SEVEN

Nodding to myself, I stood my whip and bag up against the wall. I'd been chasing Faith around her stall for a week now, and she barely flinched today. Scaring her had almost begun to feel like a game.

What will she do if I do this? What will she do if I shake that?

My guts didn't pang with guilt or horror every time there was something demanding introduction, nor did I tiptoe around her, afraid to make her afraid anymore. I knew McKennon's lesson was for her own good ... and mine.

What I once resisted (being told what to do by anyone) and where I formerly felt frustrated about being told to stay out of my own saddle (again being told what to do, peppered with a little 'I want it all now'), an unfamiliar patience bloomed.

In this first assignment, I began to learn that the racing city girl pace of my steps could be calmed, downshifted to a more leisurely gait. Feeling my feet on the earth, I actually enjoyed my walks with Faith around Green Briar.

You mean walking isn't just to get from one place to the next at the fastest rate possible?

Appreciation blossomed. Effervescent warmth stirred in me for the deliberate slow and steady of this practice – the making sure our movements were precise, rhythmical, in tune, connected. Inside my recent truce with my own zigzagging, erratic energy, Faith was clearly more peaceful.

Could McKennon tell that I was a little maniacal on the inside? Please, no.

For the first time, my horse was listening to me as her leader. Affected by my newfound presence, she would stand when I said so, rather than jigging away from the first thing to catch the corner of her eye, dragging me along with her. There was a certain power to having this thousand-pound animal, not only joined up with me on a deeper level, but complying with my commands, trusting me to show her to safety. This was something I had yet to experience in the saddle, but it sure felt good from the ground.

Plastic bag aside, I snapped the lead rope to Faith's halter and strode out of the stall for our daily tour of the grounds.

Satisfied with having put Faith through all of her groundwork without a wink of resistance, I had her perform a final 360 pivot. With Faith standing relaxed at my side, I squinted in the bright light of day and clucked her forward to begin our ascent to the top of my favorite place on the farm – the hill under the big sprawling oak tree of my first day visiting Green Briar. I hoped to catch a view of McKennon working with Star. He hadn't seemed to notice that I'd made a habit of finishing up his prescribed walks with a grazing session on the crest, perched on the picnic table watching him in wonder.

"Looking good, aren't they? The big show will be here before we know it. They'll be leaving us soon enough."

The musical singsong voice chimed in my ears and startled me upright, tearing me from my absorption with the dreamy vision circling the outdoor arena.

198

My stomach panging at the thought of his leaving again, I turned my attention to Sophia as she passed a hand beneath my horse's pearly mane. Faith continued ripping hungry mouthfuls of green blades from the land, paying Sophia's affection no mind.

Sophia idled up to me and took position on the bench seat of the table. She looked up to me with one frail, purple veined hand shading her time-lined watery eyes. I was settled on the tabletop, boots crossed over my ankles, resting next to her.

"How does he get Star to move like that? They look so effortless, so in unison?" I asked. Putting his looming departure out of mind, I propped my free hand under my chin, elbow to knee, leaning forward toward her angelic face. Faith tested the tension of her lead rope, firmly gripped in my other hand, straining for some just out-of-reach perfect patch of grass.

"Brilliant, isn't he?" Sophia purred, squinting toward the arena. Her struggle to bring McKennon into focus without her binoculars was evident as she squinted to watch him glide around the arena on the magnificent stallion. Clearly, she hadn't anticipated this visit with me atop the hill.

"I can't see him cueing Star at all. His reins are so loose. He never moves his legs. What is the secret? What am I not seeing?"

"It's called spur training, my dear."

"Spur training?"

Sophia shifted her attention back to me, gathering up the fabric of her flowing long skirt, and tucking it around her like a blanket.

"It is all about building the horse's muscles through the back so they can carry themselves in a frame. McKennon will call it the topline," Sophia paused to examine me, to make sure I was following. "When they are strong like that, there isn't any need for a fight. The rider just needs to be connected, calm, and distribute their weight, give a little bit of spur, and the animal willingly responds. The horse just offers its services, selflessly carrying his cowboy or cowgirl. It's a perfect compromise. Unity. It's a beautiful thing to watch. I'd never heard of anything like it until McKennon came around."

"Wow," I said, hanging on her words. "Where did he learn to do that?"

A smile surfaced on Sophia's peachy-glossed lips, some color sneaking up into the thin lines above her pinched, skinny mouth. She smoothed her skirt over her thighs thoughtfully.

"McKennon is a profound man," she sighed. "He is good at a lot of things other men can't do. Did you know he can make bread? His grandma taught him that."

"Bread? What kind of bread?"

Where is she going with this?

"Oh, all sorts," Sophia replied, shrugging her boney shoulders as she adjusted a wisp of white hair that caught in her feathery eyelashes. "The other thing he is good at is asking questions. He's not afraid of not knowing everything. The man will even stop for directions if he has the inkling he's lost. He spent time learning from the best trainers when he was starting out. He knew he didn't have all the answers. He even spent time working with an internationally recognized dressage trainer. He sought her out. I think his methods are a combination of the things he's gathered over the years. His method is a mixed bag of all the trainers he apprenticed under blended with his good old fashioned horse sense." She leaned back and beamed like a proud mother.

"Only broke his own rules once. Biggest lesson that man has ever learned," Sophia's musical voice trailed off, and she raised her fingertips to her lips.

My eyes wide, I opened my mouth to inquire, but she just shook her head no. Blinking uncomfortably several times, Sophia shifted herself slightly away from me.

"Not my story to tell, dear. I'm sorry."

I looked out past the tree, over the arena, and released an audible exhale as I examined the dance between man and horse happening right in front of me. I was taken with the lightness in McKennon's touch, the clouds of dust following in their wake, the copper sheen radiating off of Star's mahogany coat in the sunlight. Too far in the distance to actually see his well-proportioned face, I imagined the concentration that I was sure was fixed there. I envisioned the proud beam of his soulful blue eyes, locked, looking out over Star's arched neck and the satisfied good-natured smile of a day's hard work settled across his fine plump lips. I daydreamed of his muscles in easy ripples, dancing beneath his light cotton shirt as he rode and the sway of his hips in the saddle.

Goodness, the sway of his hips in the saddle!

My mind wandered, as it always did, to sumptuous thoughts of what that sway might be like between the sheets. Interrupting my fantasy, I felt a light touch to my knee. It brought me back to reality. Sophia peered up at me, wide-eyed.

"Oh, my dear," she breathed. Clucking her tongue, Sophia pursed her slender lips and raised her thin fingertips to her down-turned mouth. "Darling, I recognize the longing in those big brown eyes, so I must ask. Is it the horsemanship that's got you looking that way? Or is it the physical man who's driving the want I see in you, Devon?" Sophia inquired, arching a barely visible, gossamer eyebrow.

My eyes widened. *Could she see through me?*

As if sensing the tension between us, McKennon pulled Star to a halt and looked up toward our perch. He pulled his straw hat from his head, removed his right lambskin glove, and dragged his hand over his crown through his lush, dark locks before replacing the cowboy hat on his head, and tipping the brim to us. My heart skipped a beat with his gesture. I was alarmingly present to Sophia's soft eyes examining me, searching for my reaction. I revisited the promise I had made to her that day when we first met in this same place, not so long ago.

"Be careful there, dear," she said, simply. Sophia waved a be-jeweled hand to address McKennon before lifting from her seated position with a certain grace, minimal stiffness showing in her time-worn limbs. I briefly wondered if she had been a ballet danc-er in another life.

"Yes, Sophia," I replied, not meeting her gaze. "Minding my p's and q's."

Unsettled, I watched her go. My stomach in a twist, my thoughts trailing after her like the silken skirt fluttering on the breeze be-hind her.

She knew.

CHAPTER THIRTY-EIGHT

I pressed my thighs together as McKennon sauntered into the round pen. He looked hot in the tight red and black plaid shirt that sculpted to his torso, sleeves rolled up to the elbow, straw hat tipped low and over his brow to shade his alluring eyes. He had a cardboard box tucked under his arm and an awkward rolling cart bouncing along behind him.

It reminded me of the crappy navy blue one that I had used in the city to lug my dirty clothes from my barely affordable, pre-war, elevator-less apartment building to the laundry mat across the bustling street.

I was momentarily transported back to that time. In my mind, I was managing that little handcart again, shimmying between people, bracing against the honking of horns, stopping occasionally to retrieve a lone sock or stray pair of underwear that had decided to make a run for it by tumbling to the pavement, freeing itself from my heaping overflow.

I felt an instant distaste for the two-wheeler. I detested doing laundry in my early days of living in the city. I recalled saving my quarters then feeling their heft in my pocket as I struggled down five flights of stairs with a pile that I had let grow too long to shovel weeks' worth of clothes into a machine that had just serviced items which had been draped on someone else's body.

I felt a momentary glint of appreciation for my city life with Michael.

At least doing the laundry got better when I moved in with the loser.

Shaking the city and Michael from mind, I watched McKennon's cart clunk across the groove at the outer edge, trampled low like an empty riverbed by the endless circles of horses in the go-around. I waited patiently in the center, Faith saddled at my side, as it ineptly bumped along behind him, half rolling, half dragging, through the pit and falls of the hoof-printed pen.

"Mornin'," he said.

I treasured his observation of us, blue eyes slowly taking me in, then Faith, and returning to me.

"This is good. I see you can follow instructions," he added, nodding and shifting his hat back a bit so he could get a better look at us. "I like that. My kinda cowgirl." McKennon cast a shy smile, sapphire eyes smoldering, and offered me the box. An electric bolt shot through me.

I looped Faith's reins around my shoulder so I could take the carton in two hands. All of McKennon's prescribed groundwork practice had done us well. I wasn't even worried that Faith might spook at the slightest sound and take my arm off with her.

I had that going for me at least.

"What's this?" I inquired, accepting the container. McKennon seemed prepared to address that question, the expression of a skeptical journalist clearly plastered on my face.

"Don't be gettin' too excited. Didn't do any shoppin' myself or nothin', just had them lying around is all. Figured you could use a suitable pair," he explained. McKennon extended a long leg to tap the tip of his fashionable cowboy boot to the end of my round-toed, dated one. "Couldn't help but notice those antiques you've been wearin'. Size 7 ½, right?"

I lifted the lid, producing a pair of very beautiful, very expensive, square-toed, black designer cowgirl boots. I'd always wanted a pair of boots this nice. I couldn't help but flood with gratitude, a full smile extended across my lips.

"They're good for ridin'," McKennon beamed. Proud of his gift, he passed his own boot of a very similar design through the dust and tucked his fingertips into the back pockets of his jeans. "And dancin' too," he added, shyly.

Investigative mode taking hold, I flipped one of the boots over to examine the sole.

Hmm, lightly used, a little scuffed, maybe worn a few times.

I didn't care if they were used. The boots were a great replacement for my round-toed, fairly cheap, online bought, 1990s boots. I'd been embarrassed by the antiques several times and had been meaning to invest in a new pair, but never got around to it.

"Thank you," I murmured, hugging the boots to my chest. "They are really, really nice. How'd you guess my size?"

McKennon scratched his jaw, mouth in a diagonal oval, contemplating his response.

"Aw, it's not so hard to guess," he said, shrugging his shoulders, looking me up and down. "Knew someone about your stature once is all. And you're welcome. Let's get started then," McKennon ordered, nodding to the rolling cart. It was an effort to change the subject. In good student mode, I didn't probe, but something just didn't feel quite right as I slipped on the soft leather boots and cast my old ones aside.

Putting ominous thoughts of McKennon's ex-girlfriends out of my mind, I admired the boots on my feet. They were beautiful. I couldn't help but feel like a more authentic cowgirl with the designer boots on and McKennon near.

With exaggerated effort, McKennon dumped the contents of the cart in the middle of the round pen, an attempt to unnerve Faith. She stirred at the clatter, but remained sure-footed, alert, ears pricked forward, but not wild with worry as she used to be.

"That's good." McKennon nodded, rubbing his sexy, stubble-ridden chin between two gloved fingers. "Student gets an A for doing her homework."

He noticed that I'd been doing the work.

As a smile found my mouth, a flit of butterflies took flight in my stomach. I tussled the dirt beneath my new boot.

Proudly, I stroked Faith's neck and leaned in to examine the items from the overturned cart. A rope halter knotted across the noseband. A big blue tarp folded into a square. A hula-hoop. Another plastic bag tied to the end of a riding crop. A flashlight. An assortment of musical instruments. An umbrella.

What's he going to do with all of that?

"Don't mind that stuff just yet," McKennon instructed, striding toward Faith. "First, we're gonna do some slappin' with the stir-rups. Now, she's gonna wanna get away from it, but I gotta keep up with the pressure until she stops. I need you to keep with us. Just follow along and hang onto the reins. Got it?"

I nodded, tightening my grip on the leather straps that con-nected me to Faith, unsure of where this was going to go.

"OK, then. We're gonna do both sides. Each side represents a different world to a horse. Whatever you do to the right, you gotta mirror on the left. You ready?"

Putting on my best determined cowgirl face, I squared my shoulders to my mare, ready to dig in my heels. I dipped my chin once, signaling to him that I was up for the challenge.

Wordlessly, McKennon gripped the stirrup in his hands and lift-ed the leather horizontally between Faith's body and his chest. He glanced in my direction, checking my attention, and I clenched my teeth as the familiar guilt of what we were about to do to my horse crept up on me. McKennon swung the stirrup and the wide leather fender, where my leg should be resting, connected to the saddle skirt with a loud crack. Immediately, Faith's eyes went white around the edges, and her whole body convulsed. Her head shot up and yanked my arms up high, hard. I told myself to be calm as she raced sideways pulling McKennon and me along with her. The more Faith tried to escape, the more McKennon slapped the leather at her side.

"Gotta keep up a consistent pace with the slappin'! She'll eventually get that there's nothin' to fear. We just gotta rewire that flight instinct," McKennon called out to me, slightly winded.

Faith had nowhere to go inside of that pen. We chased her around, leather meeting leather over and over again.

Thwack, thwack, thwack.

My nostrils burned from inhaling the dust her skittering kicked up.

Thwack, thwack, thwack.

Faith flew sideways, ramming herself into the wooden wall of the circular pen.

Thwack, thwack, thwack.

Faith's nostrils, wide and pink, strained for extra air.

Thwack, thwack, thwack.

Stern concentration scrawled across his heavenly face, McKennon followed Faith, calm in his pace, as she tried to side-step him.

Thwack, thwack, thwack.

"You're doin' good, Devon!"

McKennon shouted encouragement as I gritted my teeth harder and held onto those reins.

After 20 minutes of chasing and leather slapping, Faith came to a halt. Head high and ear tipped toward the *thwack, thwack, thwack,* she finally heaved an enormous sigh and let her head hang low. Suddenly, my horse was oblivious to McKennon's steady drumbeat of leather to leather.

"There, see her lickin' her lips? That's good. Means she's accepting it. Relaxin'." McKennon slowed the pace of swinging the saddle attachment and stopped. "OK! We got her there. Ready to do the other side, Devon?" he asked, smirking just the slightest. He patted Faith on the rump and chuckled at me. I was winded, doubled over, holding my knees, knuckles white from grasping the reins.

This was hard work!

"This is going to occur to her as a whole new experience even though we just did it on the other side," McKennon advised, dropping a hand on my shoulder. "Come on, cowgirl. Give me some more of that try."

Bracing for the next battle, I groaned as McKennon moved to Faith's other side. He lifted the stirrup leather and brought it down relentlessly.

Thwack, thwack, thwack.

CHAPTER THIRTY-NINE

McKennon dropped the saddle leather, the stirrup thumping against Faith's side, and clapped his gloved hands together. "And that's how you do it!"

Pleased, McKennon put his hand on his hip, tilted his cowboy hat back, and mopped his brow with his forearm.

"How you holdin' up, Devon?" he asked. "Horse training ain't easy work, is it?"

"At least, I think I'm doing better than she is," I said, apologetically putting my palm to the middle of Faith's white blaze.

She was bushed. Her head hung low, big brown eyes heavy, and her breathing labored. As I stroked her face, my heart went out to my poor mare. She pressed her forehead to my palm. Exhausted from the chase myself, I scanned Faith for any bumps or bruises. While not injured, she was definitely a frothy, sweaty mess; dust once a cloud swirling around us, now clung to the dampness of her coat in a dark path of dirt, trailing from her flanks toward her barrel. She would need a bath after this for certain.

"Oh! And the rest of this stuff? What's it for?" I asked, dubiously eyeing the props.

"You'll see. Needed to get her good and tired before I start using these other things," McKennon coached, pointing to the pile at the center of the ring. "We are gonna teach her to think first, then reward her for takin' that minute to think. You know, to look at the things that frighten her, not run from them. Get her to start using the thinkin' side of her brain first and her reactionary side second. It's like rewirin' a stereo to have different sound come from the left and right speaker. Make sense?"

"With an umbrella and a hula-hoop!" I demanded.

"The method's called present and retreat. Take the pressure, in other words, a scary object to her, and, you know, *present* it. When she doesn't run, you remove it and stroke her. The retreat or removal of the scary thing is her reward. Horses naturally respond to the application of pressure and the removal of pressure. Ready to watch and learn, cowgirl?"

Slipping off Faith's bridle, McKennon effortlessly switched her into the knotted halter with a long rope lead attached. Carefully coiling the lead in his left hand, McKennon faced Faith. I watched as he arched backward, swept his hand across the round pen floor, and recovered the umbrella. Righting himself, McKennon pierced me with a long penetrating look. His eyes were deep blue like an unsettled ocean just before a storm. The expression stirred both fear and want in me. Flashing a ghost of a smile, McKennon turned back to Faith. Without warning, he burst open the once tightly tucked umbrella into its full potential right in her face. My stomach swooped like the floor had just dropped out from under me.

Faith's head shot up immediately, and she frantically thrust herself backwards. McKennon just chased her with the demon umbrella in his hand. Letting the lead uncoil until it was taut, he followed her backward flight, one long-legged step at a time.

After what felt like an eternity, Faith finally came to a halt and stretched her muzzle, nostrils flaring, out to explore the evil umbrella. Making contact, she bopped it with her nose, sniffing. Eyes wide, her head recoiled from the contact, but her body remained still.

"Goooood," McKennon purred, closing the umbrella and taking two long strides toward her. He stroked her wet neck before retreating, taking two calculated steps back. He paused, and then opened the umbrella again. This time Faith's head rose, but she remained in place. Pleased, McKennon shut the umbrella and dropped it to his side. Again, he closed the gap between them to stroke her forehead. Rhythmically, he repeated the opening and closing a series of times. Faith's reaction diminished with each repetition. On his final opening of the umbrella, Faith stood unaffected, eyes hooded with hope for slumber.

McKennon tossed the umbrella to the center of the arena and walked to Faith. He rubbed her lovingly from head to tail on each side of her body. "And that's how it's done!" he exclaimed, turning to me with the sheepish grin of an elementary school boy showing off his winning science experiment. "That'll be enough for her today. Now, your assignment for this week is to keep bringing her in here and working with the contents of this cart. Use the present and retreat method like I just taught you. Be sure to rotate through the different items in the cart. Each one will get her to experience something new. Some things she'll not mind so much, others will get her to react. Reward her for thinking and not reactin'."

"No riding?" I had to ask.

"No, Devon, no riding. Not just yet. I'll let you know when it's time," McKennon said over his shoulder as he collected the strewn about contents of the cart.

I tried not to let my disappointment show. Not being able to ride for yet another week created a sinking feeling inside of me. I felt like he had just cast an anchor overboard our ship, roped to my ankle, dragging me helplessly weighted to the bottom of my cowgirl's sea. However, I knew there was reason to his rhyme so I didn't press it. I'd keep myself afloat, drift with the tide, for now. My return to the saddle would be so sweet. I hadn't ridden her since that dreadful day of my horse show fall.

Maybe he was right, and I wasn't ready.

McKennon swung open the gate of the round pen, gesturing us back toward the barn. I gathered up my tired horse and implored myself to move, also spent. As we idled past him, his glove hand came down gently on my shoulder. I instantly tightened at this touch.

"Good work today, cowgirl," he whispered at my ear. Bashful, a smile met my lips as the heat of his sweet breath brought goose bumps to surface on my skin.

"Thanks," I breathed. I felt like my vocal cords were barely functioning. As we passed, McKennon pursed his lips and studied my face.

I was astutely aware of McKennon's presence behind us as we entered the shelter of the stable.

After depositing the training tools in the tack room, McKennon propped his back against the row of stalls as I dutifully untacked Faith, lean, muscular arms folded across his chiseled chest, eyes set in on watching me. Heightened, I set my western saddle on its horn.

Unbearably hot under his stare, I focused on a good day's work and ushered my tired horse into the wash rack. I felt fortunate to have the option to both cold and hot water.

I could use a good hosing down with some cold water right about now.

"I'm going to get her washed up," I said, an effort to lighten the mood.

"All right. Good work today. I'm going to look in after Star. See you next time."

And he was gone. Relieved to have a moment on my own again, I tied Faith and turned to adjust the water to the right temperature. I needed just enough warm to meet the cold as to not cause Faith to tense at the sudden blast of water she was about to encounter. As I twisted the tight handle, the cold water spout came loose in my hand. Astonished, I stared down at the piece of metal in my palm, and the eruption of freezing water took us over, like an icy waterfall.

Panicked, Faith strained at the lead rope tethering her to the wash stall. In her attempt to escape the temperature control gone wrong, she knocked me to the side with her hip. Slipping on the wet cement, my head crashed into the corner of a shelf that held various equine shampoos and washing tools. I was momentarily stunned. The cold water gushed into the wash rack like a fire hydrant unleashed during hot summer months in the city, images of boys playing and splaying in flooded streets danced before my eyes, water spraying all over the square enclosure.

"Easy, girl. Shh. It's OK. Please calm down," I pleaded as Faith's hooves stomped impatiently. She was a ball of nervous energy, coming even closer to my position. As the water gusted out of control, I knew I had to do something. Struck and cast to the corner, I attempted to scramble to my feet to ease Faith. Once up on my new boots, I extended my soaked T-shirt, and on impulse, I pulled the drenched piece of clothing over my head and held it to the broken spout, trying to weaken the stream. I was panicked as water billowed from the wash stall and started a river running down the main aisle of the barn.

"Someone please help us!" I called out.

Moments later, I could hear the jingling of his spurs, his gait a jog, closing the gap, and like lightening, McKennon burst into the wash stall.

"What's going on here?" he asked, eyes wild and searching. In an instant, McKennon focused in and became very aware. I was standing back to him, spread eagle, holding my T-shirt to the wall, dressed in only my prettiest red bra and jeans, wild horse beside me. Immediately, my cheeks flushed. I couldn't help but be happy I'd chosen this particular undergarment today.

"Oh! Uh, sorry? I didn't know you weren't decent," McKennon said, dropping his eyes and closing his gaping jaw.

"Come on, McKennon," I begged. "I need help here!"

"All right, I'm not lookin' or nothin'. Just hang tight," he said as he moved in to loosen Faith's tie.

I watched him lead her to the safety of the aisle. I could hear him soothing her, followed by the click of her stall door. Relief flooded me.

Seconds later, his tight torso was pressed against me, wrench in hand, working over my bare shoulders to twist the spouting water to a halt. Now, we were both soaked.

"Actually, I gotta admit, it was pretty smart thinkin' to use your shirt like that. Gotta be honest, I've been thinkin' about you wearin' those new boots all week, but didn't ever think I'd get a chance to see you like this. It's enough to make a cowboy almost blush!"

Even though the water was numbing, there was an undeniable heat between us. McKennon's wet shirt clung to his rippled muscles and stuck to my exposed skin too. The cool purpose of his belt buckle pressed against the small of my bare back. I wanted him to unsnap my bra, wrap his hand around my stomach, pull me to him, and ravage me right here in this stream of frigid water. My senses were heightened at his closeness. We hadn't been this near each other since our near kiss while I sat shotgun in his big rig on the return from the terrible horse show. As he worked his tool on the gone-rouge faucet, my body pulsated with raw desire. I licked my lips watching the tendons tense in his capable forearm as his hand twisted the tool with urgency. I clenched as his body connected with mine from behind with each turn of the wrench. My insides thrummed with his movements.

Finally, McKennon brought the stream to a stop. Relieved, I dropped my T-shirt to my thighs, blue jeans darkened and heavy with the weight of the water. I turned to face him. Arms still extended over my nude shoulders, his eyes lingered on mine. Everything in me was drawn to this man. I felt his forearms drag over my skin, and his gloved hands cupped my shoulders. He gave me a little shake.

"You OK? That water sure was cold. You sure you're not in shock?" he asked, assessing me.

I giggled and bit my lower lip. "I don't think I'm in shock. In fact, I feel kind of hot," I teased, raising an eyebrow and letting my eye's flutter up to his in my most seductive manner.

McKennon bit his own luscious lip and let his touch slide down my arm. Addressing me with his ocean eyes, he took a looksee down my neck, across my chest, and over my breasts, lingering on the lace lining of my red bra for some time.

"You like?" I asked, feeling brave.

A knowing look met McKennon's eyes. It was the kind of look that said, 'I wish, but I won't.' A half smile crossed his lips, his expression seemed almost sad. He let his gloved hand continue down my forearm. When he reached my hand, he grasped it in his and raised it to his lips.

"Been a pleasure assisting you today, cowgirl," McKennon hummed into my skin as he pressed his full, plump lips to my knuckles. My loins felt like they might erupt, hot, volcanic, love lava wanted to burst from my nether region. My heart raced as he backed away, blue steel eyes never leaving mine.

"See you soon, Devon," McKennon murmured, tucking his wrench into his back pocket. Holding me in an intense glare, McKennon ducked out of the wash rack. I was heated, despite the frigid temperature of the water that had just rushed over me. My hair in damp streams around my shoulders, I held my wet shirt to my chest to cover my brassiere, attempting to process what just happened. I was a drenched, aroused, throbbing mess.

Oh, my!

Heart hammering, I crossed my legs, clasped my thighs together, squeezed my eyes shut, leaned back against the wall, pressed my lips together, and held my breath to keep myself together.

"Here!"

His voice jerked me alert. I opened my eyes just in time to field the dry T-shirt and boxers McKennon was tossing to me.

"Figured you'd need somethin' dry to go home in. Always keep a change of clothes down here. Never know when you'll need 'em."

McKennon flashed me a playboy smile and disappeared again. Shivering, I lifted his clothing to my nose and took a deep breath of him in.

I am a woman obsessed.

CHAPTER FORTY

"OK. So, you've weather proofed her or whatever against an umbrella and all that junk in the cart. So what's next?" JD asked, rolling his pretty green eyes in punctuation, perched over the top railing of the round pen.

"I don't know, really. I am waiting for the next lesson. He said no riding though," I answered, looking dejectedly up at JD.

"Devon, you know he's just gonna be leavin' again soon, don't you? Takin' Star to the big show and all. I wouldn't be getting your hopes up that Faith's training would be complete before he goes. When it's time for him to leave, he just … leaves. Sometimes he doesn't come back for a long while. Don't matter the promises he's made to anyone," JD said, spitting the words at me in disgust.

"I know he's leaving soon, JD. Sophia politely reminded me of that fact too. Besides, I don't know what all the fuss is about. McKennon is just helping us out anyway. I'm not paying for the training, and he asked me not to call him his trainer. I'm more afraid he offered to help us because he thinks, without any guidance, I'll end up killing myself out here on Faith. I'm pretty sure he doesn't want that for Sophia or Green Briar." I paused to look up at JD. His chin was cradled in the crook of his beefy forearm, emerald eyes fixed on the cloudless sky. I wasn't even sure if he was listening to me.

"Now, worryin' about you killin' yourself with that dang horse is something I think we all got in common," JD snickered, looking down on me like a hawk, sharp talons wide open, closing in on his field mouse snack. "Sophia sure has a soft spot for you. Never seen her so willing to take a stranger in. Not since the legendary McKennon *The Savior* story anyway. Hope she upped her insurance around here, just in case you fulfill our fears."

Slightly bruised from his comment, I felt compelled to inquire about his current mindset. We were supposed to be friends after all. I was nonetheless feeling a little guilty for forcing him to shake my hand in front of McKennon.

"Are you still mad at me, JD?" I asked.

"Nah. Never been mad at you, Devon. Guess I'm just not so sure about some of your choices, is all."

JD lifted his baseball-capped head from his crossed-over arms, subtle blonde curls peeking out from behind his ears. All pretzel-like, I saw him bitterly contemplate McKennon crossing the dirt drive, leading Star toward the outdoor arena for their daily workout. Turning back to me, he shook his head, agitated. Mouth contorted into a disapproving slant, JD's wild eyes wandered all over me.

"Come on, JD," I implored. I pulled the collar of my button-down, western shirt closed in my fist so he couldn't rest his eyes on my cleavage again. Clearly annoyed at my rejection, JD flippantly pawed the air with his hand. Flexing his impressive bicep, he leaned in over the top of the round pen, arm gripping three boards down the wall.

"Aw, come on, Devon. Just havin' a little fun with ya," he whined.

"JD! We shook on this! Remember?" I hollered frustrated by his persistence.

"Fine. I remember," he muttered, chewing on the inside of his cheek. "Wait a frickin' minute!" JD dangled himself farther over the edge of the railing, slivering secret agent eyes at my feet. "See you got yourself a new pair of boots there?"

"Yes. They were a gift. A lot better than my old pair, don't you think, JD?"

Feeling proud of the new boots, I lifted my pant leg to show them off, tilting one and raising it slightly so JD could get a better look.

"Huh," JD grunted, raising an eyebrow at me. Lifting his cap and running his fingers through his golden locks, JD scratched his jaw with the others. "I'd be thinkin' *real* hard about where those boots came from if I were you, Devon."

Shame communicated through the sullen shake of his head, I stood dumbfounded, hand atop of Faith's neck as JD jumped down from the round pen's observation deck.

"What the heck is that supposed to mean, JD?" I called after him, but he just waved me off with a flip of his hand. I watched him hastily leave, ample back hunched over in anger, hands dug deep in his front pockets, huffing away.

"He knows not what he does," I whispered into Faith's muzzle, her velvet fur soft against my cheek as I led her back to the barn.

With Faith put up for the evening, I pulled my notebook from my purse to record our latest progress. I pinched the paper between my forefinger and thumb, letting the pages shuffle like a deck of cards. I had started writing down McKennon's lessons on day one, and I'd already filled half of a notepad. I didn't want to miss a moment of it.

I had to document it in case, well, just in case.

I had the sinking feeling that something this good wasn't going to last forever, so I wanted to capture it, all of it, while I could so I would remember, and before I was on my own again.

"What're you doing there?"

His voice thrummed in my ears like a favorite song, my desire tempted to turn up the volume.

"Oh ... Hi ... Um, I've been taking notes on your lessons," I said, stretching my new boots out in front of me, sitting on a hay bale. I had my notebook open in my lap, spinning my pen between my pointer finger and my thumb. "I'm a journalist. That's kind of what we do," I continued, shrugging my shoulders and offering a weak smile.

His blue eyes were as wide and warm as his grin that met them. He was luminous, and I was hot under the collar. Visions of the red bra fiasco flitted through my mind uninvited. I felt the blood flush to my cheeks.

"Huh. I've heard somewhere that good students take notes too." McKennon winked and cocked his handsome head, examining me. "Some nice boots you got there."

"Thanks, a nice cowboy gave them to me."

McKennon grinned, tipped his hat, and, with a nod of acknowledgement, moved on. I watched him stroll to Star's stall, slide the door open, fish a sugar cube from his pocket, and offer it to the stallion. I felt like a voyeur peering in on a private moment as McKennon scratched Star's ears and whispered into them.

I couldn't help but heed JD's warning.

Where had these boots actually come from? And what exactly will I do when he leaves again?

CHAPTER FORTY-ONE

"Today, you ride," he said, casually in his nonchalant, 'no big deal, I'm a cowboy, and all is well in the world,' lazy yet pretty kind of way.

Me, on the other hand, I was awakened. Excitement burst in my belly, an emotional tidal wave crashing repetitively against my insides. Blood coursed through my veins, thick and hot with anticipation like it did on the first day of school, or how I imagined it might on my wedding day when I saw my true love waiting for me at the end of the aisle.

In a moment of lost control, I found myself half hopping, half skipping toward McKennon like a little girl.

"Really? I am so excited. It feels like I haven't ridden her in an eternity. Faith is doing so well! Thank you for working with us! It is making such a big difference. I can't wait to get back in the saddle!" My words buzzing, the receiver finally picked up after the phone's gone unanswered for so long, no longer lost to a continual ring.

McKennon sighed, shifting his weight from one lengthy limb to the other, his lean legs wrapped endlessly in denim. He shoveled his hands into his back pockets, casting his knowing eyes downward, and scuffed the aisle with the toe of his boot.

"I'm sorry, Devon. Not Faith, not today anyway. Today, you'll ride Star."

My fiery hopes were extinguished with his watery words; I stopped hopping toward him, defied, midstride.

"Didn't mean to get you all riled up," he continued. "I know you are excited to get back on your mare, but I want you to know what it feels like to sit on a finished horse. This will help you understand where we are trying to take Faith. What it's like to give spur-trained cues. When you've felt that, and only then, does where we are heading become real for you and for your horse. You'll feel the real we're heading for, and there'll just be no question."

"Like magic?" I mused. "Fate even?" I couldn't help but think that my child-like, watered-down synopsis of what it would be like to ride Star must occur so elementary to him.

"Yeah. Somethin' like that, I suppose. My gut has always told me there's somethin' sorta unexplainable, mystical in the relationship between human and horse. The gut don't lie, so I don't ignore it. Too many folks do. It's the animalistic side of us. The part that links us to everythin' else in this world." In thought, he moistened his lips and pressed them together.

I could sense McKennon's attention fade from me, from any human form, as he cast his eyes, blazing blue with wisdom, toward Star's stall. A smoldering smile started across his fine, full lips, a fire clearly brewing within him. I watched like a spy as his grin reached his eyes, a considerate, friendly, sky blue squint. His expression lifted me. I felt angelic, light – a lofty, loving feeling enveloped me. For the first time, this cowboy seemed almost happy. I was witnessing the type of expression a man of his kind reserved only for those most trusted in life, a best friend, man's best friend, or the being that knows him best.

McKennon wrapped his hands around the bars of Star's stall. The stallion lifted his muzzle to greet him, a warm pulse of breath fluttering his nostrils, set wide on a charcoaled muzzle.

"Why would an animal give of themselves like this to a human? They selflessly allow us to sit upon their backs, to use them for war, to help us gather up other animals to eat. Be partners that help us live," McKennon murmured. I had to close our gap to hear his whispered words.

"It's like the universe lines up for us to bond with these animals. Don't really know why, jus' think the heavens designed it that way. It's a gift. Guess that's all I'm sure of in this world," McKennon said, a gloved hand pressed to his chest and gazing at the rafters. "Not all horses are kind. It's we humans who do it to 'em, make 'em mean, or scared or whatever. We do it to win, to be the best. We don't think of the animal. I know they are all inherently good though. That I know. I'll always trust the roots nature planted for me before the one's any man would sow for profit."

He opened Star's stall door and led the proud, broad stallion out. It was like watching royalty emerge from private quarters.

"Like you said … Fate," he nodded to me, a reassuring gesture. "Now go gather up Star's saddle and bridle. Don't bring the shanked bit that I usually ride in. Instead, bring the bridle with the snaffle on it. I'm gonna teach you a light touch. It's not in the reins, Devon."

McKennon picked up a body brush and started stroking Star's bronze coat.

"Devon?" he called after me.

"Yes?" I turned back to him, forgetting my pursuit of leather and reins, caught like a spider in his web.

"Tell me, how were you feeling riding out there, that day at the show?'

My body tensed with the weight of his question as he affection-
ately smoothed the soft bristles down the front of Star's face. My
pulse quickened as he slowed lovingly over the prominent white
mark spiraling from the center of Star's wide forehead, the mark
that dubbed his steed's name, before leaning into the grand animal's face.

"My *super* Star," McKennon hummed to his equine.

In awe, I watched his animal return the gesture, flattening
his broad, brown head reverently against his horseman's chest.
McKennon slipped his arm around Star's jaw and cast a hesitant
but seductive look in my direction, ocean-blue eyes probing for
an answer to his inquiry. A familiar flush warmed my cheeks. I
longed to press myself against the man too.

"Um, like I didn't belong. Stupid. Not good enough.
Embarrassed. I guess."

I twisted my fingers into a knot and looked away. Disgusted
with my vulnerability, I wandered off to retrieve Star's equipment,
shaking my head in reprimand, and berating myself for sharing
my ugly, secret places with him. A prickly awareness crept up that
my comments could prompt him to think less of me.

Bobbing down the aisle with Star's leather things, I hoped the
conversation was complete.

"You know you are transferring all of that anxiety to her, don't
you?" McKennon pressed.

As his observant, big blue eyes met my wide, brown, fearful
ones, I realized McKennon could read me better than anyone.

Bridle weaved over my shoulder, I tried to look unaffected,
but the truth was he had found me out. I idled up next to Star
and tossed the work pad over his awaiting withers, then heaved
McKennon's time-worn, supple work saddle up to accompany it.
Star grunted when the saddle landed on his back, aware of my effort, but nothing about the interaction seemed as fancy as I thought
it might for my first venture with a super star athlete horse.

"So does this mean that I'm not good enough to ride my own horse?" I asked, looping the cinch leathers through the girth. Chin tucked in an attempt to keep my pride intact, I pulled it tight with a series of spirited tugs.

"No, no. I'm not sayin' that at all," McKennon assured me, tipping the brim of his cowboy hat back slightly with his index finger and knitting his brow. "You're plenty good enough, Devon. You galloped with me that day in the field, didn't ya? Almost kept up with Star and me too. You dusted yourself off after the horse show, didn't ya? Wanted to get back on." He wrapped a gloved hand around the back of his neck and rubbed it for a moment. Dropping his arm, he looked up to the ceiling and shook his head, pink tongue peeking between his lips like a piece of bubble gum.

"The problem is this," he continued, pausing to raise an eyebrow. "It's you. You. Fall. Off." Poking me in the shoulder, a finger punctuated each word. "And that makes Faith nervous. Come to think of it … it makes us all nervous. That mare is a conduit of you. You know? You really are a beautiful rider, Devon. A beautiful woman, too, if you don't mind me addin'."

McKennon's eyes flashed up.

Was he trying to gauge my reaction? Perhaps. But, oh … he just called me beautiful! Wait. Is McKennon flirting with me?

I sucked in breath.

"Listen here, girl." He closed the distance between us, fast, assertive, with intention. It immediately catapulted me back to that moment of intensity in his truck.

Uh oh. I braced myself.

McKennon stood over me, a tall, inviting, hot, sexy god of a man. Gently taking me by the elbow, his eyes took me in.

I liked the way he was looking at me, as if almost through me to my soul, like I was real, like an equal, like a human trying to put a finger on life too. McKennon wasn't surveying me as a woman to conquest or a woman to endure, but as a person of interest.

This moment made me feel like merely my pulse in this world was of worth to him, like he had experienced loss as well as full self-expression, and wanted that for me as badly as he wanted it for himself.

The electricity between us had a magnetic pull. I remained still like hunter's prey, allowing his polite pondering of me.

McKennon brought a deep breath in, so deep his torso expanded with the effort, and continued, "All I think is, you just need some basic instruction. No one wants to see you hurt, 'specially not me."

My movie reel mind clicked into action, generating a new episode. In it, I would raise a forearm to forehead and fake a faint right into his strong, warm, open arms. My mouth would part just enough to welcome his mature lips. These imaginary actions would invite a kiss that would save me and startle me awake.

But this was not the time for fairytales. I put my foolish daydream aside. I had a horse to ride and something to prove.

Today, I would not fall off. Today, I'd be a cowgirl worthy of McKennon's guidance.

I slipped Star's bridle over his ears and led him out into the sunlight.

CHAPTER FORTY-TWO

"Up you go, cowgirl," McKennon commanded, intertwining his gloved fingers and nodding to them, a suggestion I leverage him for a leg up. I put my foot in his hand, and he effortlessly lifted me into the air.

Grabbing the saddle horn, I swung my leg up and over. Settling into the well-worn work saddle, I was anything but settled. A nagging anxiety washed over me.

What if I can't ride him right? What if I mess Star up? What if I fall again?

Stealing my confidence, the words bubbled up in my mind and paralyzed me, inhibiting the performance I had yet to give.

"Oh, I almost forgot! Pull your boots out of the stirrups for a minute," McKennon said as he held up a pair of gleaming silver spurs attached to a pair of floral tooled leather spur straps. "These are gonna be your new best friends. Go with those nice-looking new boots of yours. I want you wearing these everywhere you go. A true cowgirl can do anything while wearin' her spurs."

He slipped them over my boots and secured the straps.

"There. Lookin' good, Devon." He gave my foot a little shake, the spur jingling like a chime, and smiled up to me. "OK. Ready? Go on an' move him on now. You don't need a whole lot of leg or spur. Just wave your legs like the gentle flapping of a bird's wings until he moves forward."

I gathered up the reins, tight, and moved Star forward. The glee I expected to feel at riding McKennon's horse escaped me. A dark pit of gloom in my belly, I circled the ring on Star uneasily. I had barely begun riding, and my tank top was already lined with perspiration down the back. I could feel the beads sliding between my breasts in the front.

Was it that hot, or was I in a nervous sweat?

Seemingly oblivious to my discomfort, McKennon requested I pick up a lope. My whole body went tight. My breathing turned short and shallow as visions of Faith whirling around the show pen haunted me. The sound of her hooves pounded in my head, and I saw myself on my back in the dirt again. I didn't realize that fall had impacted me so much.

Had I lost my nerve?

"Devon, you gotta loosen up on him. Give him some rein. What are you so afraid of?" McKennon called out to me, my concern now obvious from his post at the center.

"That he'll go too fast. That I'll fall again," I responded through gritted teeth, embarrassed that I couldn't relax or get the feel of Star. He was bigger, different, and foreign. I felt awkward, out of control. I didn't want to go any faster. I knew Star wasn't a racehorse by any means, but something was in the saddle with me, something mental that I couldn't shake.

"Is that why you're pullin' back on the reins like that? You do that with Faith too?"

"Yes," I gasped, the reins twisted in two fists, muscles of my arms flexed, leather pulled tightly toward my chest. I could sense

Star gaping at the bit, corners of his mouth strained against the metal.

"I expected this. That's why I sent you for the snaffle. It goes easier on his mouth," McKennon explained, striding across the arena so I could hear him better. "Here's the thing, Devon. Life is fast. You can't pull it back. It's about grounding yourself. When you can do that, the world responds differently. Go *with* rather than resist. Pull him up, and come over here."

Relieved, I brought Star to a halt, pulling back on the reins hard. Reaching up to my hands, McKennon gently urged me to release my death grip.

"Look here. It's not in the reins," he coaxed, slipping the leather through my fingers, letting the reins go slack. Instantly, Star relaxed beneath me. In apology, McKennon placed a palm on Star's mahogany neck and looked into the horse's big brown eye.

"You OK, buddy?" he asked.

Grabbing my leg assertively, McKennon pierced me with his eyes. "It's here, Devon. If you want him to slow down, squeeze your calves. He'll respond." Softening, he continued, "I promise. Don't allow yourself to be your own worst enemy. Fear will eat you up if you let it. You have to let it go and choose something different. Choose to be here now. With me. With Star."

"OK," I whispered.

"Try sitting down deeper in the saddle and distribute your weight. Go on, push that weight through the balls of your feet into the stirrups like your two feet are on the ground. It'll restore your balance." McKennon demonstrated by pushing down on my thigh, through to my knee, finishing the cue with the pressure of one hand to the top of my foot, and the other pushing at my heel. Normally this kind of touch would excite me, but in this moment, I didn't feel anything. I was numbed by my fear.

"Understand?" he asked, lessening his grip and holding my boot just a little too long in the stirrup. I knitted my brow, watching, as he just stared at my boot and spur. His expression was lost, cold and faraway.

I shuddered in the saddle. Suddenly, we were in the presence of something supernatural, of a ghost. A strange combination of remorse and guilt had overtaken McKennon. It was as if he'd been transported somewhere else, remembering something about where these boots had been. JD's warning shot back at me like a bullet to my chest.

"Hey," I called down to him, wiggling my boot. "You still there?"

Regaining his senses, McKennon gave my foot a firm twist. Spooked, he looked up with his dusty blue eyes and stared into mine.

"Yeah. I'm good. Was just thinkin'. That's all." McKennon shook his head and continued, "Now, you let him know you don't fear him with your body language and by calming your mind. He'll respect your cues when you control yourself ... your thoughts. Remember it's *not* in the reins, Devon. Let him have his face. He'll do the work."

As I moved Star forward, I became light as a feather. Inside of today's instruction, the weight I'd been bearing was suddenly gone. All at once, it made sense. I realized I'd been holding back the whole time – holding back on riding my horse, on loving someone, on really living my life.

It's not in the reins.

McKennon's training was not only making me a better horsewoman, but it was teaching me a life lesson. Through him, I was learning to take my time, to sit back, to let go, and to truly believe that fate leads in the right direction. Gliding at a lope atop of his magnificent animal, my heart felt like it might explode with gratitude. The sun warm on my face, I lifted my head to the star fully and smiled.

"Life is not in holding on to the reins. It isn't in the reins, Devon. It's OK to let go," I whispered to myself, for myself, leaning forward and stroking Star's neck.

I always tried to be perfect, to control the situation, to make things right even when they were all wrong, and the puzzle pieces couldn't be forced together. I looked out to McKennon arms crossed, watching us.

All this time, I kept pulling back, but no matter how hard, I couldn't stop what wanted to go forward. It was fate that led me to this space in time, all of it, my life in the city, leaving Michael, finding Faith, ending up at Green Briar. It all forced me to go forward, and I couldn't hold it back. I wasn't strong enough to control life. I'd been living mine this whole time like a horse restrained by its rider, mouth gapping, pulling on my own reins, and blindly running through the bit. Wanting to go forward, but pulling back. McKennon was right. I was my own worst enemy.

I could be grounded. I could be here now. I could be in control even as the world around me was out of control. I could be free to be me.

"How you feelin' now?" McKennon called out.

"Amazing! Fearless! Released!" I called back. As I brought Star to a stop beside him, a current of indebtedness reached out from my chest toward him.

"All right. Now go get your mare then. You'll ride her today too. Ridin' Star was about gettin' rid of those jitters you were holdin' on to. Happy?"

I nodded, feeling the tears start to well, grateful to this man for seeing me, helping me past this roadblock. McKennon was my usher to the next level, the VIP section, with horses and in life.

"Come on down."

I swung my leg over the top of Star and felt his hands grip my hips, guiding me to the ground. Setting me down in front of him, he put his hands on my shoulders.

"You ready?"

"Yes. I'm ready. Thank you, McKennon," I said, a stifled sniffle escaping me.

"All right. I got him. You go get Faith."

McKennon dropped his hands from my shoulders. Smiling, he gathered the reins up, twisted his foot in the stirrup, and lifted himself onto Star's back. Pausing, he pointed up at the high sun, lifted his hat, and wiped his brow with the back of his forearm.

"By the way, you won't be needin' to lunge her today. It's a hot one. She'll be languid," he coached, plucking the front of his lightweight cotton shirt between two fingers and peeling it from his damp chest. I couldn't help but fantasize about him lifting it over his head.

I so wonder what would wait for me under there.

Liberated, I started toward the barn, but hesitated to look back at him. I had the sudden, empty sensation that he was going to leave. McKennon turned in the saddle, sensing me, and waved me away with that lambskin-covered hand.

"I'll be right here. Go on then."

I nodded and turned back to gather up the reason we were together in the first place. Faith was always there between us. In most ways, she was the glue that kept us together – the reason we found our way to each other to begin with. In other ways, Faith was the wall that separated us. Then again, she was the conduit for our energy, our connectedness.

As I saddled her for my first ride since the dreadful horse show, I reminisced to the many times McKennon had scratched my mare on the neck while shooting a thoughtful, almost penetrating gaze in my direction. Magnetic, he would stand close enough for me to admire, but always seemed to expertly navigate the space between us so he was safe, just out of my reach.

In return, I reflected on embracing Faith's painted muzzle, wishing it were McKennon. I intentionally placed my horse between us during particularly deep conversations on the theory of things. I did this so I had something to hold on to because every-thing in me wanted to drift to him.

As my mind recalled those early days I spent with McKennon, it became clear that he was always conscious about where he posi-tioned himself in proximity to me. He was perpetually laced with an undetermined melancholy, leaning back against his gloved hands across the barn aisle from me as we conversed. My movie mind imagined he was afraid that if he didn't pin those paws of his to the wall, he might not be able to control himself and reach out for my body.

For whose benefit did he do this ... mine or his? Who was the danger-ous one here?

Yes, Faith was our safety net. She was our rock, our reason to convene. She was our way to edge closer and closer to each other each time I led her out of that box stall in Sophia's barn – all eyes on us. We both knew I had my p's and q's to mind.

Faith was the glue that kept us together, the wall that separated us when we got too close, and the conduit for our pent up energy that had been building since that lost moment in his truck. Faith, somehow, calmed the flames of this burning desire to touch.

Selfishly, I hoped he was wrestling with it as much as I was.

CHAPTER FORTY-THREE

My saddle cried a familiar creak as I lifted onto Faith's back. She waited peacefully as I situated myself. A new trust had been established between us. I couldn't help but glow with happiness. We had crossed the finish line in a private marathon of the minds. I finally felt unconditionally at home on her back.

From the far end of the arena, McKennon's broad smile greeted me. He jogged up to us on Star.

"How's she feel, Devon?" he asked, arching his eyebrows in question.

"Like home," I answered, a shy smile meeting my lips.

"Well! That's music to my ears. Let's get ridin' then," he responded, leaning over to unlatch the riding arena gate. McKennon swung it wide open and addressed the lush fields of Green Briar beyond the entrance with an open palm.

"Yeehaw!" I hollered, confidently grabbing the saddle horn with a grind of my hips.

McKennon laughed and slapped his knee. "OK then, cowgirrrrl! Yeehaw it is. Come on."

We ponied up side by side, making our way toward the growing foals from this year's herd. As we meandered through the tall grass, it caressed our horse's chests like soft currents in Green Briar's back pastures.

I wet my lips when McKennon's eyes fell on his favorite, the Palomino-Paint filly. His gaze followed her as she wandered in a 4-foot radius around her mama, seeking the best grasses the pasture had to offer. I could tell he envisioned a show pen future for her.

"Devon?" he asked.

"Yes?" I answered.

"How you are … right now. This is how you ought to always be with Faith. I can sense that you are here with us and not in your head."

He turned his attention from the filly and held my eyes for a moment. I offered a smile to assure him he hadn't offended me.

"You need to be relaxed like you are now with her. All that stuff … I know you got *stuff* … I can see it on ya. You transfer all of that anxiety to her. Faith's got spirit, and that's a good thing. Makes 'em stand out in the show pen. She ain't one of those dead-at-the-end-of-the-bridle types. She'll never be all the way tame, just the way she's made … sorta like you, I imagine."

McKennon gave me a little wink. Flushed at his inquiry, I wondered if he was picturing me back in the wash rack wearing only my fire-engine red bra.

"You gotta work with that spirit, not against it. Any real, beautiful thing in this world shouldn't be tamed or claimed or broken. It should be allowed to be, worked with, not against, appreciated. Don't be afraid of the wild she has left. It makes her special. Work with her."

I nodded. It was all I needed to do.

McKennon nodded back. It was understood.

My mind in rewind, I realized, in a way, McKennon was always just a little more gentle with me than with any of the other people on the farm, besides Sophia, of course. He always barked orders at JD, but his eyes would soften just the slightest bit when he explained something to me.

Maybe he could sense that underneath it all, under my conjured up cowgirl confidence, the truth was I could be easily broken?

I was grateful for the fact that he never embarrassed me or made me wrong. Since I'd met him, I kept expanding in the room he granted me to figure it all out for myself.

As much as I didn't want to admit it, I did feel like I could be easily dismantled under any disapproving glare. Michael always had the power to make me feel unworthy with a mere displeased cast of his muddy brown eyes. I needed McKennon to believe in me. I needed him to believe I could be the horsewoman that I so desperately wanted to be. I needed him to believe that I could do this thing that I loved so much and that I could do it well.

McKennon had become my guide. I had begun to think of him as my hero. I silently admired him, and when I went to bed, I dreamt of him – his skill, his authority, the fact that when he said jump, people asked how high, his knowledge, his ethics, his eyes like weather, his body, his gloved hands, his mouth, all of him, even the heavy heart of his that I didn't understand.

I trusted McKennon even though I knew he had a roughness to him – a roughness I lusted after. He was free, untamable and untouchable like a wild horse. It was a spirit I could pinpoint in myself. If only we had crossed years before, before either of us had pasts to deal with. McKennon sensed my baggage. I definitely sensed his. JD wouldn't have it any other way but for me to know McKennon was damaged goods. For heaven's sake, McKennon had told me himself that he was damaged in that forbidden moment in the truck. I couldn't deny that there was still this flicker of hope we might come together even though he made himself unavailable. I did my part to stay separate from him too.

His voice woke me from my thoughts.

"Come on, girl! Let's go!"

McKennon whistled to Star. Tossing me that boyish smile I'd grown to adore so much, he took off at a gallop across our field, the first field we crossed together.

I spurred Faith on, unrestrained for the first time. The wind whipped my face as we broke into a canter to chase them, my hair flowing out behind me.

"I think you've healed me," I called out after McKennon, but I was too far behind for him to hear my cry.

I didn't need him to hear me. I felt free. I was a cowgirl chasing down my dreams, heart in my throat, reins loose, and a solitary gleeful tear careening across my hot cheek.

No, it most certainly was not in the reins.

CHAPTER FORTY-FOUR

W e dismounted in a companionable silence back at the barn, with easy smiles nested on our zen faces. I crossed in front of Faith, both of us calm, to McKennon, letting her reins bow like upside down rainbows below her low head. I hesitated for a moment before resting a hand on McKennon's solid, Adonis chest. My own pulse quickening, I felt his strong heartbeat beneath my palm. Encouraged that he didn't swat my touch away, I lifted my eyes to meet his blazing blue gaze.

"I think you've healed me," I repeated so he could hear me this time.

Tall frame hovering over me, McKennon didn't say anything, but I felt a low hum vibrate from his torso beneath my hand like the happy thrumming purr of a cat in a lap.

"What's goin' on out there?"

Interrupting the potent moment, JD emerged from the depths of the barn. Sophia in tow, he staked a position out front, leaning against an awning pole. Both of them squinting critical eyes at us.

Feeling shrouded in scandal, I dropped my hand from McKennon's heart.

Under their scrutiny, McKennon's face shifted from contented to lost, cold and faraway. Feeling the presence of that supernatural something again, I shuddered in the humid summer air. Proffering an apologetic grimace, McKennon took a series of short, quick steps backward. As he scrambled to create distance between us, a strange combination of remorse and guilt overtook him.

Conscious of Sophia's soft eyes examining the situation, I returned to Faith's side, depleted. She and JD were like high school chaperones surveying the dance floor, measuring for the appropriate spacing between the male and female partners. When it came to obstructing any slight spark of intimacy between McKennon and me, their timing was always spot on.

"Sophia ... JD," McKennon said flatly, acknowledging them with a bend to the brim of his hat. He pressed his lips into a hard line, shared a subtle disapproving shake of his head with me, and led Star swiftly past them into the dim of the stable.

I followed them, hoping to avoid contact with Sophia, but as I crossed beside her, she reached out to rest a frail, thin-skinned palm on my shoulder. Stopped in my tracks by her touch, I addressed Sophia with only my eyes, and she looked through me.

"Be careful there, dear," she said simply, a note of regret nestled in her songbird voice. "He's a gypsy soul born for leaving."

Sophia triggered a wave through me that felt vaguely like heartbreak. It snuck into my consciousness as I absorbed her words. I swallowed hard and blinked back waterworks.

"Yes, Miss Sophia," I answered, solemn.

She adjusted a loose strand of gray hair and leaned in, squaring us up eye-to-eye. Narrowing hers, she dipped her chin. It was a nonverbal agreement.

"Come along, JD. I have a few chores that could use your attending to," Sophia commanded. She exuded the effortless power of a queen. Arching her slender arm into the air, she wafted her court member forward to answer her royal beck and call.

JD, green eyes blazing, shot me one last lingering, angry look of warning, shoved his filthy hands into his jean pockets in frustration, and spun on the heels of his boots to follow Sophia who had already blazed a speedy, expectant pathway toward her farmhouse. Her gait was that of one accustomed to the trail of an entourage. Lazily, JD wandered out into the sunlight after her.

Perplexed, I turned from my contemplation of JD and Sophia back to the barn. McKennon had already stripped Star of his saddle and was leading him into his stall. I hovered in the doorway, Faith in tow, watching the pair for a moment.

"Um ... so that was sort of intense," I said, clipping Faith into the cross ties to untack her.

McKennon shook his head and flashed me a shy grin. It made my heart throb.

"They're a little overprotective, aren't they?" McKennon chuckled.

"Of what?" I asked, closing Faith in her stall and stepping to the bars of Star's to peer in at them.

"Uh ... it's a long story. Suppose no one's filled you in yet?" he asked, slipping Star's halter off and looping it over his shoulder.

"No. Not yet. Um ... you wanna tell me what that was all about?" I asked.

"Hot out there today, wasn't it?" McKennon responded. It was an evasive response to my inquiry, an obvious effort to change the subject.

Rolling my eyes in resignation, I resolved to let go of the journalistic probing I was prone to. I decided to stick to minding my p's and q's and allow Green Briar's looming secrets to continue. I felt compelled to simply agree and be content in the dark.

Complacent, I absorbed myself with watching the cowboy dream-boat before me pull at the fingers of his gloves, and strip them off his hands, one by one.

McKennon sandwiched the lambskins together and tucked them in his back pocket. As he plunged his uncovered hands into Star's water bucket, my mind danced with visions of the disrobing wash rack. I remembered the pressure of his cool, metal belt buckle to my bare back and of my illicit moment in the shower.

I moistened my lips in temptation as McKennon ran his wet fingers through his dark, thick locks, dampening his mane with the refreshing water. He tipped his head back, lips parted, just right. I was heightened seeing McKennon pleased, pleasured.

"So ..." McKennon began, continuing to slick his hair back with his right hand. He wrapped his left hand around a single stall bar and used it as an anchor to pull his muscular frame toward me.

"What should we do to cool down now?" he asked, lifting an eyebrow seductively.

My mind kicked into motion. I felt inclined to immediately drop my clothing, hop into Star's little water bucket, and ask if this smoldering bronco-buster was interested in taking a skinny dip. Thinking better of the notion, I opted to tease McKennon.

"There will be no repeating of the red under thingy show, mister!" I reprimanded, shaking a naughty index finger at his illicit, sly expression.

Oh, my goodness! This was the first time that I had ever seen him without those gloves!

Tilting my head in observation, brow furrowed in examination, I zeroed in on his hand.

Suddenly, it was as if I'd been slapped in the face. I was sucked into a time tunnel, hurling back to the present, returning from daydream. I felt like I might faint. My lungs ceased to function. I couldn't breathe.

How could I have been so blind?

I turned numb, buried beneath the icy landslide of my observation.

"*MARRIED?!?*" I gasped, clutching my throat, stumbling backwards.

His golden wedding ring burned my retinas. My eyes, gone wild, bored a hole through him. Immediately, McKennon's demeanor shifted from playful to awkward and stiff. His expression was blank. He fidgeted, trying to suppress the signals of his guilt, the shame of a man that's just been caught.

"Um ... Oh ... *this?*" he stuttered. Letting his head hang, he pondered the circle of infinity displayed on his finger. I watched him gently twist it, lips pursed.

Get a load out of this guy!

I felt the bile rise in my throat, its burn in my esophagus, as I witnessed McKennon nonchalantly switch the band from left ring finger to his right.

Right. In. Front. Of. Me.

Addressing me with those blue beauties, he actually had the audacity to smile. Compelled to vomit, my stomach turned into a churning ocean of regret. Clutching the sides of my head, I tangled my fingers in my hair, resisting the urge to tear strands from the root.

Inside, I felt like a lioness. All of my being in a rage, I wanted to bare my teeth and release a pained, broken growl from deep within. A roar that would blow his hair back and that stupid, *sexy* cowboy hat off his lying, *sexy* head before sinking my angry, exposed incisors into his adulterous, *sexy* flesh.

I am furious.

But outside, I had become a mere kitten at this realization, my heart broken, my spirit crushed, my accomplishments dampened. I went dark. The light had gone out.

I am debilitated.

"I have to get out of here," I mouthed, but no words actually came out. I was fighting a war within a breath.

Emotionless, I shrunk away as McKennon's eyes grew wider.

"Wait, please!" McKennon called out. "You don't understand."

Ugh, I can't stand the sight of him!

It happened slowly at first, one step after the other. As I recoiled from him, I was consumed with confusion. I was disoriented.

Mustering what was left of my pride, I turned and took flight down the aisle, hair flowing out behind me like it had in the field. I raced to my car. All I wanted in this world was to drive away from this place ... from him ... and *fast*.

First stop, wine store. Second and final stop, home ... indefinitely.

CHAPTER FORTY-FIVE

I slammed the bottle of red wrapped in a brown bag on the counter. Tossing my keys near it, I flung myself into a seat with a screech to rummage through my purse for the cigarettes I'd just bought. Unable to bring myself to open them, I swiveled the sealed pack across the marble and settled for repeatedly flicking my newly purchased lighter. I allowed myself to be entranced with watching the flame dance for some time before I finally dropped my weary head into my crossed arms, crestfallen.

I don't know how long I sat folded over on my barstool, broken, before I decided to pull myself together and drag my downtrodden soul to bed. I knew I'd leave the items I bought untouched in the kitchen. Just buying the deviant stuff had given me a certain vindication, a sense of defiance against humanity, or maybe just against McKennon.

"I can always have wine and a cigarette for breakfast," I called out loud snidely to no one but myself. I traced my fingertips along the long hallway wall to nowhere but the empty bedroom in my lonely, dark apartment. This was my tomb. Lying in my bed, swaddled in the blankets, and nestled deep in the body-heated sheets, I still felt cold. I was afraid to be alone with my whirling head. The thoughts had put on boxing gloves and were pummeling me like an elementary school playground bully taunting me, needling me, and backing me into a corner with nowhere to run. Sleep would elude me tonight.

I left the city because Michael was having an affair. Back then, I wondered what kind of female would actually commit such a criminal act against another woman. Distraught, I buried my head beneath a second pillow and admonished myself for having accidentally become that woman. Over and over again, I saw his ring in my mind, wrapped around that bar in Star's stall, and all I could do was bring myself to cry.

Were all of those intimate moments imagined? Even worse, were they real?

My mind was crazed; the endless stream of thoughts kept coming.

How will I ever return to Green Briar? How will I face Sophia? I had broken her rules. And JD ... how do I remedy my relationship with him? He had been right all along, trying to steer me clear of McKennon. JD was a true friend. Should I have chosen JD instead? Should I have stayed away from all of them? And Faith ... how do I find a new home for her quickly? Who will train us? Where will we go now?

The trouble, though, the real problem keeping me awake was that I'd become all fire-like inside, completely turned on, and fully alive for the first time in my life. And McKennon was the key. He was the spark that had ignited that fire, started the engine. In the short time I had spent with him, he had put ground beneath my feet when I felt like I was falling. He was the breeze beneath my fluttering wings. McKennon gave me flight and, at the same time, offered me a soft place to land.

The trio of Green Briar, McKennon and Faith had created my personal bohemia. Without all of them, I had nowhere to go. No reason to be.

How will I turn my emotions off?

Although we never crossed the physical line, our relationship was an affair of the mind. I could see now that both of us had been bridled by our past lives.

What if the cure for this longing is worse than the disease?

Sleepless, I reached for the journal in my bedside drawer. I used it for notes on stories I was developing for my editor back in the city. I kept it there because paragraphs seemed to write themselves in the night. The words called out and woke me to urgently scribble them down, or I'd risk of losing them forever.

My pen flew across the paper, the ink like a blade to an ice skating rink, just gliding. Tonight, the words became a poem forming verses for McKennon that he will never receive, that he will never see, that he will never read.

Tonight, last night, two weeks ago,
All the way back to 10 weeks past,
It all meant something –
And what it meant only belongs to me.
Right now, tonight, last night, two weeks ago,
A thousand yesterdays, and 10 years past.
It all meant something –
And what it all meant only belongs to me,
Be it in not so distant or faded memories.
To want with such fire,
Flames put out by the cool wave of commitment.
The galloping inside my chest,
The lust I bear across my breast.
A glimpse, a look, you.
Pages of a moonlight romance torn away.
Coming true as I breathe it life inside my dreams.
Magnetic. Unrealistic.
He fills me up, moves me forward.

Gives me something to fuel my passion.
I'll take what I can get, the rest I'll ration.

Tossing the pen and paper back into the open drawer, I heaved myself into the pillows, forearm across my eyes, and shook my over-whelmed head.

Seeing that ring explained so much – Sophia's warning when I arrived at Green Briar, McKennon's aloofness, JD's protective-ness, the 'this never happened' almost kiss in his truck, our ten-sion without release.

Why didn't I ever see her at Green Briar? Why wasn't there any sign of her in his house that night I spent on his couch?

"How could I have missed a *wife?*" I screamed at the ceiling. In warning, the neighbor I'd never met above me stomped on the floor. Thrusting my fists next to my body, I twisted the sheets in my hands.

CHAPTER FORTY-SIX

S hielding my puffy eyes behind big black sunglasses, I crept along the gravel drive in my little imported car. I pulled my head down between my shoulders like a turtle into its shell and used the drape of my hair to hide my face.

I surveyed the landscape looking for signs of life, signs that *he* might be on the loose, doing the two-timing prowl. As I took my chances pulling into Green Briar, his big rig truck was nowhere to be seen, neither was JD's jalopy.

Good.

My heart was in my throat as I recited a prayer to the heavens over and over in my mind that I wouldn't see him or any of them today. I just wanted to lay my hands on Faith and bury my tear-stained face in her sorrel and white patch-worked neck. I needed to feel her soft breath rustle my hair. Being separated from her because of my stupid lust for a married man was breaking me in half. Part of me wanted to run away and leave every reminder of this time in my life behind me, and the other part was drawn back to this place because of her ... because of him ... because it was irreplaceable.

I was a fool absorbed in the destructive yet undeniable force of attraction that linked all of us.

I pulled the oversized shades just low enough so I could scan my surroundings unfiltered. Finding no trace of my paramour, I slipped the glasses the rest of the way down the bridge of my nose, swallowed my heart, and flipped my long, unwashed hair over my shoulders. Tossing my makeshift disguise onto the dash, I flung open the car door.

My sneakers crunched as I made my way to the barn. The boots he gifted me were now abandoned to the back of my closet. I didn't want to look at them anymore.

How dare he give me a pair of her castaways?

Sickened at the thought of the leather pair, I squeezed my eyes shut and took a fresh, deep breath of Green Briar. The air filled my lungs with the sweet scent of green grasses, wood shavings and horses. It smelled like home. My stomach turned with the realization that it wasn't anymore.

I entered the cool barn and was quietly welcomed by the nasally vocals of soft nickering. I immediately recognized Faith's in the mix. I scurried to her stall and opened it just enough to slip my body through, clenching my teeth at the squeak of the metal latch.

Faith, her big, warm, brown, doe-eyes wide and happy, instantly approached me. I stood still, waiting, as she closed the distance between us to press her forehead to my chest. Wrapping my arms under her jowls, I felt safe. I'd been holding my breath for days. I could finally breathe, alone, here, now with Faith in my arms. Contented, we remained there for some time as I allowed the tears to pool at the corners of my eyes.

Suddenly, sensing something and without warning, Faith abruptly raised her head, pulling away from my embrace. Surprised, I wiped the wetness from my face with the back of my hand before turning to address what Faith had noticed. My lungs ceased to function. McKennon.

How long has he been there?

I stood frozen as he regarded me steadily through the bars of the stall. Shading my face with the veil of my hair, I couldn't control it ... a smile snuck across my face. It felt good to see them again, to see *him* again. Peeking at McKennon, I could see that he shared the same secret, sinister grin with me.

Taking my smile as an invitation, McKennon opened the stall door and started toward me, an almost knowing expression stenciled across his chiseled, beautiful face. He was luminous, his eyes shined bright with sincerity. He must have known that I'd been thinking of him, missing him. He licked his lips, outlined with a fine rim of stubble, and I quivered as he set those blue babies on me. Instantly, my blood began to boil beneath my skin, and I throbbed in the most heavenly places.

At that moment, I knew I would go to him. Nothing could stop me, not even if my feet had been glued to the ground. I would welcome him with everything I had. I felt awakened. I took one step then another, until I could almost feel the warmth rippling beneath his muscular frame. I reached out with my fingertips to touch McKennon. Then ...

Then ... I was awake.

My eyes flew open. With a start, I shot straight up. I was at home in my bed. Choking, I tugged my T-shirt away from my windpipe, untangled myself from the restraint of the sheets, and gritted my teeth. The back of my neck was sweaty, and my hair clung to my face.

McKennon is haunting my dreams.

Despondent, I decided to go into retreat. I wanted to disappear and jail my criminal desires to my apartment so I couldn't hurt anyone. I desperately wanted to see Faith and all of me longed for McKennon but ...

It. Is. So. Wrong. I can't go to the barn. I can't see him.

I pulled my laptop from the nightstand, powered it up, and just stared at the screen. I'd been spending my days researching a new barn, but couldn't bring myself to make the call. Zoned out, I searched the Internet for every song that had ever resonated with me about heartbreak. I drowned myself in the lyrics and blew my nose into tissue after tissue before tossing them over the side of the bed, adding to the mass accumulated on the floor. Lost deep in another paralyzing love song, I jumped a mile high when an unexpected bang came to my front door.

Who could be here now? I don't want any visitors. I hardly want to exist.

I faintly remembered missing a deadline set by my editor, but I didn't care. I knew she would never leave the city to come here for anyone. Small towns frightened her. She wouldn't even make the trek for my funeral, which could be any day now. At least I knew she'd send flowers.

I forced myself to rise, pulled a blanket from the bed over my shoulders, and navigated my way through a sea of tearstained tissues strewn about the carpet.

Scrunching my eye to look through the peephole in the door, I immediately recognized those eyes. I would know those eyes anywhere.

Again, the noise interrupted my gloomy Sunday.

Bang, bang, bang.

I debated whether to answer. I put my palm to the cool doorknob as my head rung with the sound of the one-handed, angry fist pounding on the other side.

Should I open the door?

CHAPTER FORTY-SEVEN

In the brief pause between outraged bursts of furious knocking, I peered through the hole in my door to observe my violent visitor again. He was so close to the door that all I could see were the familiar wild bursts of golden ribbon through his irises.

The banging commenced again, and I hastily pulled my greasy head away from the eyelet. The ruckus hurt my ears. I decided to answer or risk having my upstairs neighbor report me for repeated noise violations.

I really don't want to lose my second home in less than a week.

Wearing the blanket like a cape, I knew I was a hot mess. Assessing the situation, I ran my fingers through my tangled, grimy hair. Touching my cheek, I couldn't remember the last time I washed my face or even took a shower, for that matter. Looking down at my bare feet on the cool tile, I wiggled my toes, pedicure in disarray. I grimaced knowing my legs were unshaven and flushed at the sight of the cartoon character on my pajama bottoms, peeking out at me from beneath the afghan.

Catching a glimpse of myself in the mirror in the foyer, I cringed at my rosy nose and the who-knows-how-many-days-old mascara streaked across my face. My hair matted in ugly, twisted knots hung limp around my shoulders. Licking the heel of my hand, I attempted to rub the old caked makeup from my pale cheeks to no avail. Shaking my head, I simply flung the blanket over the top of my dirty locks, Little Red Riding Hood style. Pulling the soft cloak tight around my chin, I boldly went where no woman should ever go and cracked the door. Inching it open, he appeared in the sliver between the molding and deadbolt, eyes widening at the sight of me. He physically took a step backward.

Was he repulsed or startled by my appearance?

I couldn't tell which, perhaps it was both.

Oh goodness. Am I that frightening?

It hadn't occurred to me that I might actually carry an odor from being in this unkempt state. At least, he was chivalrous enough not to pinch his nostrils closed and waft the air. Gauging his reaction, I knew I looked atrocious, and there wasn't any hiding from it. I just didn't care anymore so I swung the door wide open.

Eyebrows furrowed, muscular arms protectively crossed in front of his broad chest, he leaned over me to view into my disheveled apartment. He eyed the unopened wine bottle and cigarette pack on the counter. A few stray tissues had attached themselves to the tail of my blanket and left a trail down the hall like breadcrumbs back to my bedroom lair. Concern was written on his face.

"You OK, Devon?" he asked.

"I guess I am just feeling a little cuckoo these days," I grunted, flipping the blanket off of me and onto the floor so the zillion little yellow cartoon birdies printed on my pajamas could come out from hiding and be fully appreciated by my taken aback guest.

"I'm not gonna be here long. Just wanted you to know that he'll be gone today, Devon. You can get back out to the barn, see your mare. She's been missin' you."

"Where did he go?" I couldn't help but ask and silently shamed myself for being so quick to inquire.

"To the big show. I'll be heading out today too."

"Oh. That's right," I said, biting my lip.

"Can't stay locked up in there forever, Devon. You need to get out, put on your big girl boots and deal with your business."

Adjusting his ball cap low over his brow, JD tucked a stray soft blonde curl behind his ear, flashed me a sad smile, and turned to go.

Pausing for a moment, he turned back again, examining me from head to toe with his bright green and golden flecked eyes. I could see the regret behind his dark eyelashes.

"Knew this was gonna happen," he said, shaking his somber head.

"Why didn't you ever tell me, JD?"

"Can't say why, but I'm sorry, Devon."

In thought, JD chewed the side of his cheek and swatted his thigh, incredulous.

"Me too, JD. Me too. I am sorry for so many things. Thanks for coming here and checking on me." The words weren't coming out right. I had so much to say, but I didn't have the energy.

"Is this good-bye, JD?" I asked, wondering after him.

"Don't know, Devon," JD said, shrugging his hefty shoulders as he plunged his hands into his front pockets. "You ought to go take a shower now, cowgirl."

With a cavalier nod, JD turned to go, leaving me standing in my doorway.

I needed to take care of my business. JD was right. I decided to take his advice. I closed the door behind me and leaned against it for a moment. Pushing off, I began stripping my clothing from my body, leaving a trail of castoff garments, long overdue for a launder, in my wake.

The shower felt good. I pretended to cleanse away my sins, but deep down, I knew it wasn't going to be that easy to wash away the dark days behind me. I tipped my head back into the blast, feeling the rush pulse against the back of my head. I let my hair dangle in the arch of my back near my tailbone as I fought off the memories of McKennon pressed against me in the wash stall's renegade water stream.

"Stop it, Devon!" I said into the echo of the barren white ceramic tiled bathroom. "You will not visualize McKennon as that man ever again … ever!"

I lied to myself.

Presenting the front of my body to the warm water, I paused the violent scrubbing to let my hands explore my tummy then my breasts. I tried to imagine a day when I might be able to fantasize about the touch of a man without envisioning him.

Luckily, I had time to work on that because McKennon was gone. JD, my champion, gave me the all clear. I would go to Green Briar. I would reconnect with Faith. I would apologize to Sophia. I would gather my things and what was left of my sanity. I would find us a new place to call home before he returned.

We'd become ghosts. It would be like we were never there. It would be like McKennon never happened.

I lied to myself.

CHAPTER FORTY-EIGHT

I t had been weeks without a lesson, without a glimpse of his strikingly handsome tan face, without seeing the gently weathered corners of his eyes soften when Faith and I entered his gaze, without the comfortable, pregnant with want, silences we shared while searching for stories to tell in an effort to prolong the leaving and to occupy each other's space, without the awareness of feeling his baby blue's study me from afar. I would miss how my heart fluttered with possibility as I drove my car to where his horses were.

As I pulled into Green Briar's driveway, I knew I would never feel the sheer joy of just looking to see if his truck would be parked ahead again. Alone in the empty barn, staring at Star's empty stall, the end was real. McKennon had left for the show. Faith and I would be long gone before he returned. I felt left behind.

This place had become home, given me purpose, a family. Now so much was left incomplete because of this enduring link between McKennon and me.

I needed to see Sophia to right the wrong I'd done her and fix the plague I had brought to the farm. I needed to fill the void.

"It's good to see you, dear," Sophia cooed as her wobbling, frail hand guided the screen door open with a squeak. I admired her short manicured nails, primly painted a pale pink.

"It's good to see you too, Sophia. I've missed you. I've missed Green Briar."

"Would you like some sweet tea, dear?" she asked.

'That would be nice," I answered.

Sophia held up a crooked index finger, signaling me to wait at the door as she paddled barefooted, back into the belly of the aged farmhouse.

"Come. Sit," Sophia said as she reappeared, toting a tray with two tall glasses and a pitcher of sun tea. I followed her across the porch, listening to the jingle of the ice cubes. Setting the beverages on a wicker table, she motioned me toward a pair of big white rocking chairs.

The old-fashioned things seemed trapped here at Green Briar, but it all appealed to me. The simplicity, the remedies, the garden berries, the passed-down bread baking of grandparents, the golden rules that were adhered to and still used, the satisfaction of knowing that problems could be solved inside a conversation over a glass of sweet tea. The "old West" still seemed to be alive through her eyes and muted the digital world I was fleeing from. If only I hadn't ruined it all by branding myself with the badge of an almost adulterer.

"Sophia. I am so sorry. I've ruined things. I didn't follow your rules. You were clear when I arrived here."

I couldn't bring myself to look at her.

Sophia clucked her tongue, handed me my glass, and grinned giddily at me.

"Sheesh! That's all water under the bridge now, dear," Sophia giggled and pulled her bare feet up into her rocker, folding them snug under the hem of her long floral skirt. A slow smile crossed her lips, and she bounced a few times in her seat like a blissful, excited little girl on Christmas morning faced with multiple brightly wrapped packages, Santa's work tucked neatly under a Douglas fir tree awaiting her.

"I have an opportunity for you, my dear," she beamed, before coyly taking a sip from her glass.

I opened my mouth to inquire, but before I could speak, she interrupted me.

"Sometimes you just have to reach out and grab what you want, my dear, even when everything seems to be telling you not to."

"What's this about, Sophia? What happened with McKennon ..." I blurted out, utterly confused.

"Not my story to tell anymore, dear. It's yours now."

CHAPTER FORTY-NINE

It had been a little over three weeks since Sophia watched his eight-horse trailer pass her by, and disappear down the dusty dirt road, heading north to that million-dollar horse heaven on land. She told me about how JD's rig trailed behind, all rattle and clunk, to participate in the bull riding event that ran in tandem with the renowned show. She recollected on the last gossamer wave she had given them, and then they were gone. My heart sank with her recreation of the event.

But now, here I was, settled behind the steering wheel after weeks of radio silence and complete solitary to embark on a journey, not arranged by me. I didn't know what McKennon was thinking.

I certainly hadn't spoken to him since he left, but Sophia assured me that he was comfortable with me visiting the show to take video and pictures for her given she had become too fragile to make the trip. Sophia had even gone so far to contact Sallie Mae. Sallie Mae had a relationship with the local horse journal, and they were interested in taking a story from me on the show. I agreed to the write up because I could use the income after missing the last assignment from my editor. Not to mention, it was my first opportunity to catch a glimpse of a championship horse show.

My heart skipped beats in anticipation of feeling the energy and documenting the royal vibe. I had jammed my laptop into its case and checked for a full charge on my camera. Ever since I was a child, I had dreamed of having a horse of my own that would be good enough to compete at a show of this caliber, at a show that would be named something like "Congress." Under McKennon's guidance, it finally seemed like it could be possible, but it wasn't possible anymore. Not with McKennon anyway. I would find a way to get there with Faith one day, but at the moment, more than anything, I just longed to be in his presence again, to feel that electric jolt through my body when McKennon merely walked by, to feel the rush down below when he'd catch my eye.

Just this one last time.

McKennon was my drug, my muse, my addiction. Today, I was a woman consumed by wanderlust. I buckled myself in and took a deep breath.

OK, ready, set … GO.

I consoled myself that it would be a great, long road trip – 10 hours north to think, to drive, to listen to my favorite songs, to contemplate where my life has taken me, to daydream about a man I could never call my own.

In the isolated hours behind the wheel, my lips pursed, twitched, pouted, smiled, and frowned. I gripped my lower lip time and time again with my front teeth as my mind ebbed and flowed, replaying our story like a movie through my mind. I envisioned all the ways this imaginary story of ours could go.

Was this trip our sequel?

I realized over the past months, I had been living in my daydreams rather than in reality. The real reality was that I up and left my previous life and my fiancé. I tried to coax myself back to some realistic ground. I'd had crushes before. I'd even been in lust with untouchable people before.

Why couldn't I turn off my heated emotions this time?

I'd never gone so far with this heavy of a yearning in my chest, nor ever had I felt this sort of connection. I shook my head in the midst of it all and suddenly turned cool with foolishness.

What was I thinking?

I forced myself out of la-la land and sat up straight in my seat. I clutched the steering wheel now officially driving again, alert, aware.

"I am on assignment. I am a writer. I am bringing back a story. I am documenting this for Sophia and for a publication. I am a professional," I said into the emptiness of the car.

I adjusted the radio to a heavy metal song, blasting the last romantic slow song out of my ear drums. I rolled down the window to allow a burst of cool air to rush my face. I pinched myself as a reminder to push this pulsating desire down deep, away from him, away from her, so far away that no one could see it.

I stole another deep breath, pushed my face to the open window, and in a hurried swallow, decidedly buried my feelings below, inside, behind a cool exterior.

"Friendly, but aloof!" I said, jutting my index finger toward the ceiling of my car, emphasizing the point to no one but myself. This was going to be my chosen stance when it came time to confront him.

Friendly, but aloof.
Friendly, but aloof.
I would be friendly, but aloof.

CHAPTER FIFTY

Suddenly, I saw it – the sign for his exit. I was merely 20 minutes from the show grounds, from McKennon, and from having to bury my emotions. Soon, we'd be face to face.

Where had those nine hours and 40 minutes north gone? Had I really been so inside my head, or was it my heart, that all that time had passed without my knowledge? Was I even living in the here and now, or was my life becoming better in my fantasies?

My car crawled along the fairground's thoroughfare. I weaved between fancy horse trailers and big diesel rigs. All the fenders were lettered with the names of important horse trainers and their chosen place to practice in the United States. As I screened the scenery for his outfit, my heart pumped blood through my veins at a rate my doctor would scorn.

It was on the later side when I rolled in, so I wondered if everyone had turned in already from a long day, rather a long month, of showing. I shook my hair at the thought.

No way! This is Congress.

I recalled the stomach-turning moment when JD said, "If you can't get laid at Congress, then you're doing something wrong."

"Classy," I said. I overturned the desire to vomit in my own mouth as my mind roared in again.

Wouldn't that line from JD's lips mean, in layman's terms, that late nights and partying would be the norm? McKennon wasn't really that old yet, and he liked to sip some whiskey now and again.

I rounded a turn, my front tires crackling on the unpaved driveway rocks, and there, glowing in the beam of my headlights, was his trailer.

His name in lights just for me.

My heart jumped rope inside my chest.

Was he in there? Should I knock on his living quarters? What if his wife was in there with him?

I parked my car, tiptoed to the trailer door like a private investigator, and leaned my ear against the cool metal portal to his world. I really didn't want to get caught at his door.

Why? I hadn't actually done anything wrong, nor would I.

I took a step back and tried to convince myself. "I am his student," I said firmly, dipping my chin in self-assurance.

A strong breeze whipped the October air around me, fluttering leaves at my ankles and burying my old school cowgirl boots in rich autumn hues. I still couldn't bring myself to touch the gifted ones. I wiggled my toes, which slid the leaves off to the side. I tipped my head back. I had always found fall refreshing after the dog days of summer had passed by. My skin felt warm as the cool air burned my still summer-sunned cheeks. I drew in a deep cleansing breath of fresh air and raised my hand to knock, but something caught my attention before my knuckles could meet the aluminum.

A piece of paper fluttered on the back of a breeze. It was haphazardly tucked under the windshield wiper of his truck. I lunged toward it.

A message! Should I read it? Maybe it was meant for me? Could he be expecting me? Was he thinking of me then?

I parted the folded note. It read,

'At Broncs. Celebrating. Come on down!!!'

Puzzled, I dropped my hands, clutching the dubious note against the top of my thighs. It was generic with not one but three exclamation points.

Was it for me?

It could have been for anyone, male or female, wife or lover, student or fellow trainer.

Broncs could only be another bar of the horse show lifestyle. I could only assume a Silver Spur variety.

Did he win big?

Come on down, I repeated in my head. *Did that apply to anyone?*

Dazed, I left my car next to his trailer and started walking toward the horse barns where Star was sure to be stabled. The grounds were a ghost town. I was praying to cross just one soul that could point the way to Broncs.

I passed from the RV parking lot into an open area and spotted a man driving a golf cart at breakneck speed across the wide-open space in front of the stabling buildings. I waved my arm, pumping steadily, hoping to flag him down before he ran me down. Luckily, he saw me and slammed on the brakes. I just blinked at him for a few moments in disbelief. I couldn't believe that a golf cart could make such a screeching, squealing sound with its tires.

"What can I do for you, little lady?" the stubble-ridden gentlemen cheerfully slurred from his chariot.

This man was more than a little drunk. If his garbled words hadn't given it away, the enormous half-finished bottle of whiskey lodged between his legs certainly did.

"I am looking for Broncs. Do you know where it is?" I asked.

I examined the random placement of his facial hair patches, wondering if he had just attempted an inebriated shave.

"Sure I do, miss! Hop in. I'll take you there! I was jusssst leavin' the party, but if I walk in with the likes of you, everyone will want to talk to me all over again!"

Oh boy.

I was so desperate to see a certain someone who is attached to someone else and doesn't even know I am here that I would accept a ride from the only person around – a drunken guy in a golf cart with lines as terrible as the best soap opera. I hesitated for a moment before climbing into the electric devil on four wheels. I decided to take my chances in order to get closer to Broncs and to *him.*

"The name's Gerald," he yelled in my general direction.

I clutched the roof of the cart with one hand and shouted, "Nice to meet you, Gerald! Let's g –"

My head snapped back as the drunken cowboy slammed on the pedal and took off before I could finish. Gerald hit every pothole in a half-mile radius by the time we crossed the interstate and came to a sliding stop in front of a neon sign with a cowboy digging his spurs into a flashing red, green and yellow bucking horse in motion. We had obviously arrived at Broncs.

When I dismounted his buggy, I felt like I had been riding a Standardbred trotter for days. I thanked Gerald. He barely finished tipping the bent brim of his hat before he tipped over into the passenger seat. I wiggled his shoulder.

"Gerald?"

Not responding, he rolled to his back, threw his leg over the seat, and scratched his belly swell as a brownish-clear whiskey bubble grew between his lips. Gerald was out cold.

I shrugged my shoulders.

I guess Congress is as crazy as they say.

I turned from my intoxicated chauffeur to the front of Broncs. I shook my head at the thought of entering. I didn't know what I was doing.

Was I creating all of this drama in my mind?

I was just his student with a pretty good horse. He probably didn't even feel, know or sense anything. I had counted the weeks, days, hours, minutes, miles until I'd lay my eyes on McKennon again.

I mustered my confidence, walked through the bar doors, and passed into a completely different world.

CHAPTER FIFTY-ONE

A faint memory of The Silver Spur flickered through my thoughts as I crossed through the doors of Broncs. I was overwhelmed by the stale smell of years of spilt beer and smoked tobacco. The scent immediately thrust me back into my early years in the city when that smell on my clothes was a permeating morning reminder of the late bar nights of my young adulthood.

Feeling my oats, I sauntered over to the bar like a fresh filly out to pasture for the first time in the spring after a long, cold, hard winter. Broncs was rowdy, and I could feel that my moves had caught the attention of some admiring cowboy eyes. I hadn't looked around too much though, for fear I'd actually see *him*.

I didn't want anyone to think I had come here for him.

I recited my mantra internally. *Friendly, but aloof. I am on assignment. I am a writer. I am bringing back a story. I am documenting this for Sophia and for a publication. I am a professional.*

I'd only leaned on the bar for but a second in attempt to get the female bartender's attention when I felt pressure at my rear.

I turned abruptly to find a handsome cowboy at my service and clearly looking to score.

"Howdy, my little bombshell. What'll you be having this evening?" A wry grin crossed his lovely mouth.

I was momentarily disappointed, but grateful not to be alone.

"Thank you, kind sir. I'll have a cosmo," I said, taking a page from our attempt at a night out dancing.

JD's eyes widened as I knocked him in the shoulder and giggled.

"I am just kidding, JD. I'll have a beer. Anything light will do."

"No mind eraser?" he kidded back, batting those devilish big, beautiful green rock star eyes.

JD tipped his hat to me then whistled to the busty female bartender. Under a black felt hat, she wore two auburn braids over each shoulder, sported a sparkly red tube top and had the shortest shorts I'd ever seen glued to her curves beneath black chaps. Almost instantly, a light pint of beer appeared, and the bartender poured a shooter for JD. I couldn't help but think that JD had surely done her before.

"The shot's on the house, baby," she purred. She glared at me before bouncing off to the next customer of her choosing.

"I guess so," I said under my breath.

"What?" JD questioned.

"Nothing. I was just talking to myself. Thank you for the drink. You are too kind."

"Nothing to it, pretty lady. See, I am here celebrating a big win for our buddy over there."

My heart stopped as JD leaned back against the bar, sucked down his drink, and pointed his finger across the room. My eyes followed the length of his arm right down to the end of his dirty fingernail where it landed on a round table at the center of another dance floor.

I gasped and clutched my chest. There, *he* was point and center in the middle of Broncs, bottle of whiskey to his left, his *wife* to his right, and a rowdy group of people chanting some slurred sort of congratulations in his general direction.

Why was she here now? Why hadn't she accompanied McKennon to the last show? Was their relationship on the rocks? Were they trying to work it out here? Now?

"Come on," JD said, grabbing my hand.

I was lunged forward with the force of his pull as JD proceeded to drag me to the table in the round as a song about a big city woman gone country blasted through the jukebox. I couldn't help but think it could have been written about me. I had only moved from the city a short while ago, and now I was a patron to places like The Silver Spur and Broncs. JD continued tugging me along like a steamboat through heavy waters, crashing me into waves of people, until suddenly we halted in front of McKennon's table.

"Lookie what I found," JD said, raising an eyebrow at McKennon. "Found this pretty little lady all by herself at the bar trying to get a drink from Trixie. Guessin' she didn't know Trixie don't serve chicks, just us cowboys. All I had to do was buy this one a beer, and she came over here with me. Go figure."

Playfully, JD popped a pretend punch into my shoulder as the red began rising to my cheeks.

All the unfamiliar men at the table whooped. They clinked their drink glasses together as their eyes walked all over me. I felt like I wasn't but a piece of meat up for auction.

"Great job, JD," said a guy introduced to me as Tex. "She's a looker!"

McKennon's wife rolled her eyes, sighed, and crossed her slender arms over her ample chest.

"Yeah. Way to go," slurred another cowboy as his bug-like eyes zeroed in on my smaller chest. He formed an 'O' with his lips and gave a long, low whistle. A series of yips and yeehaws proceeded. I was obviously not as drunk as this table. I kept my eyes on my old school boots through the crazy introductions.

Or was it a hazing?

I just kept staring down, afraid to look up, to see *him.* I felt stupid for coming all this way. My mind was muddied with thought. Suddenly, I was whipped back into the present as I felt a hand carefully slip beneath my chin and lift it.

And there he was, beautiful, blue eyes beaming.

McKennon leaned to me and whispered next to my ear, "I won today ..." His breath was hot and laced with liquor, and my blood was boiling.

My eyes widened in his pause as he pulled back and locked his stare on me.

"I won *big* today. Star ... he was ... *perfect.*"

I was silent, meeting him with my frame and my eyes, but not my voice. *Well, there goes my story line.*

He continued. "Seventy-five *thousand* dollars big!"

I touched my fingers to my lips.

"Oh! My gosh ... Congrats ... Um ... That's an unbelievable amount of money."

Gently, he grabbed my upper arms, and I went limp like a ragdoll.

What is his wife to think about this?

McKennon gave me one quick jolting shake, moved his hands to sandwich my cheeks, and towed my face toward his.

"Devon ... Devon. Don't you see? I've made it!" His smile was wide, broad, brilliant, and reminded me of a proud little boy showing off a new completed project to a parent. "This is what I've been working for."

Were there tears beginning to form in his whiskey-soaked eyes?

McKennon gave a quick shake of his head and cleared his throat. He dropped his gentle cradle of my face.

"Moving on then," he said, softly. "Moving on," he said again.

I sensed he was embarrassed to have let me look that far into his emotional state.

He shifted gears, "That young buckaroo there may have bought you your first drink, but I'm gonna buy you 10 more!" McKennon gestured toward JD and teetered briefly on his heels.

I couldn't help but raise my eyebrows, knit them together, and give him a half-assed smile. I put my hand on my hip.

"You are three sheets to the wind! Aren't you, Mr. Kelly?"

McKennon snickered, wobbled again on the back of his boots, slapped the round table, and sat down hard next to his *wife*! Like taking a jump kick to the forehead from a black belted karate king, I was yanked back to reality.

Friendly, but aloof. I am a professional. I am here to cover a story. Why? Why did I want this man so much? What was it that made me dream of him? Was I really that unsatisfied with my life? No, not really. I did lack in the romance department ... maybe that was it.

I shook my head. I had to stop this.

Friendly, but aloof. Just this one beer, and I'll go.

Anxious, I sat down next to JD, took a slug of my beer, and started up mindless conversation with the guy named Tex to distract myself. I couldn't stop peering over at McKennon and his wife. I looked for his ring. It was there.

I kept watching them out of the corner of my eye. I felt her watching me too. I swallowed hard, wishing myself small as she assessed me, looked through me.

I knew McKennon's wife would be pretty, but she didn't look quite like what I'd imagined. Actually, her looks surprised me. She seemed more fairy than cowgirl. She wore her hair very short. It was ebony, sleek and shiny. Her eyes were big, blue and icy. Their color matched McKennon's except hers were far fiercer when they settled on me. Her nose was straight as an arrow, slender and small. Her lips were two plush pillows, the perfect shade of pink with a simple swipe of clear gloss accenting them. Her cheeks were high and rosy. She looked very healthy, fit, toned. She glowed beside him. She was striking, could have been a supermodel, but I assumed her petite stature made that unlikely.

What was I thinking? How could McKennon ever feel anything for the likes of me with someone like that beside him?

Jealousy surged inside. Reaping the benefits of voyeurism, I watched while she whispered in his ear, sprinkling her intoxicating pixie dust all over him. When he laughed at her words, my heart clenched in my chest. I wanted to look away, but I couldn't. My eyes were locked on them. Staring me down, his wife pursed her perfect lips and tucked an untamed lock of McKennon's dark hair behind his perfect ear. Inside, I crumbled.

Silly girl. How could I have possibly thought I'd be his type?

My head whirled with images of McKennon effortlessly lifting up her diminutive frame and pressing her to the wall of the bar as she wrapped her athletic legs around his waist. My mind whipped up images of a satisfied McKennon cupping her perfect breasts and licking his lips — a page from my own fantasies about him, except in this one, his wife took her rightful place. She was now center stage in my warped dreams about her hot cowboy husband. As she twisted her manicured fingertips in the fringe at the base of his neck, my cheeks flushed thinking about his hands in her short tresses, their clothes falling to the floor of his trailer. I wished it could be me instead.

McKennon ordered another drink and draped his arm across her back.

"I think you've had enough, McKennon," she said annoyed, rising from the table. I watched her scoot out of the pleather booth, her ample bosom pushing forward in her V-neck T-shirt.

McKennon rose too.

Always the gentleman.

"Excuse me," she said, addressing the table.

She looked at me, raised an eyebrow then dismissed me with a flick of her petite hand, on it a massive stone. Catching McKennon by the chin, she pulled him towards her.

"I'll be seeing you later. You're drunk," she spat.

McKennon smiled in her grip, didn't say a word, and shrugged his shoulders. She shook her head and dropped his beautiful chin.

"I'm going now. You've earned this celebration, but watch yourself, McKennon," she said, giving me one last eyeball.

He nodded and dropped back down in the booth, beside me, hard.

What just happened?

My stomach pitted out as McKennon's misses dismissed herself. I eyed the pockets of her designer jeans as she made her way through the smoke screen of the bar to the double doors.

Even her ass is perfect!

When she disappeared through the exit, my insides sank again.

Good! It's clear she knows he's my trainer. I am not a threat. She's not on to us 'cause there is no us!

After watching her go, my senses returned to the ongoing at the table. As JD slipped out of the booth to covet another drink and the bartender, I felt it like hot knives through my skin. *His* fingertips were at the base of my spine.

Oh no! Friendly, but aloof. Friendly, but aloof. Friendly, but aloof.

CHAPTER FIFTY-TWO

At his touch, I shifted in my seat and scooted a millimeter away, feeling hot rush my face. My reaction caused him to remove his fingertips. McKennon looked bruised like a puppy that I'd just punished with a rolled up newspaper. I met his eyes and lifted my chin gesturing toward the door his wife had just exited.

"Aw, never mind her. Here," McKennon slurred, sliding a shot glass toward me. He pinched his between two fingertips, golden band gleaming at me in damnation, and gave me a sultry look of challenge.

Oh well.

It was nice to see him. I figured a little liquid nerve numbing certainly wouldn't do me any harm given the strange turn of events swirling around me.

So, we proceeded to drink. And we talked and drank and talked. At his inquisition, I began sharing details of my life. I told him things I never shared with anyone, not even Michael. I felt like he was doing the same as if we were kindred spirits, friends even, from another lifetime. For the first time, it wasn't awkward between us as we sat there in a round booth, celebration all around us. He opened himself to me, me to him, and the whole time I knew it was wrong.

Did he?

I couldn't bring myself to do anything about it. I felt a joyful numbness, a youthful flirtation. I wasn't really absorbing it all, just basking in it. It seemed like a dream.

Oh, the rumors that would spread because of our proximity!

No one bothered with us for a long time. I couldn't help but wonder why no one intervened.

What is everyone on tonight? Doesn't anyone else see what is wrong with this picture? Why is this god-like cowboy sitting here with me and not chasing after his angry wife?

HE IS MARRIED!

I lowered my eyes to the faded finish of the tabletop. It was painted with wet beer rings, spilt salt and ashes. Again, he touched my chin.

"I won big today," he said, a garbled whisper.

I blinked, acknowledged him with a weak smile, and forced myself to look away. McKennon shifted toward me and extended his well-muscled arm across the back of my position in the booth. I thought he might inquire if I was OK, but before he could speak we were interrupted by JD armed with another tray full of tequila shots. JD bumped the edge of the table, spilling tequila on my shoulder, but I was too blurred to care.

What's one more anyway?

McKennon, JD and I raised one in hand and tossed them down the hatch.

Him, her, me – all a blur.

"Come on, Dev! Let's cut a rug!" JD bellowed, catching my hand after I replaced my drained shot glass on the tray.

I hesitated, hoping McKennon would object, but before he could, JD tugged me to my feet. JD led me to the dance floor just as a boot scootin' boogie was coming to a close and, of course, the jukebox kicked over to a slow song. I didn't have it in me to fight the booze, or JD, so I just surrendered. I put my head on his shoulder, all the while, wishing it were McKennon's instead. Halfway through the dance, McKennon interrupted us.

"Can I have this dance, Devon?" he asked, bowing to me.

It felt almost cliché. And JD just backed away, winking at me.

Winking at me? What is it that everyone seems to know that I don't know?

At all of my 5'4", I felt so small as McKennon wrapped his arms around me. Gently, he pulled me to his tall, slender, rippled stature. I knew I should resist, but I let myself give way in the same surrender that led my head to JD's plaid shoulder.

"Doesn't anyone else see this as all wrong?" I mustered.

"Come on, Devon. We are just dancin'," McKennon murmured into my hair.

As much as I loved being in his arms, so close that I could feel his heartbeat, my better side had to say what I was thinking.

"But you are *married*! What will people think tomorrow?" It just fell right out of my mouth.

"You don't have everything figured out. Do you, Devon?" he said plainly, not letting go as I writhed in the span of his arms like a wild animal scooped up in a blanket.

I didn't understand. In my state, I just let him hold me and guide me about the dance floor. I just gave in, gave up, swaying against his frame.

As our song came to a close, the clock hit 1:45 a.m., and Trixie rang the last call bell. A final round was ordered, and we all joined in. Eyeing me, JD tossed back his thick slick of liquor and stepped between us.

"I'll take her back," McKennon said before JD could even open his mouth.

JD nodded, tipped his hat, turned on his heels and was gone.

I couldn't help but worry inside of myself.
I can't do this! Where is JD going?
JD always got me out of these situations.
How could he leave me now?
Then we were alone in that empty Broncs bar.
"Let's go," McKennon urged.
I followed.

CHAPTER FIFTY-THREE

It was as if his big win had invited a blank page for us – no introductions, no before, no after, just us, he and I, me and him, McKennon in celebration and me in elation over being with him again. We were away from home, away from the barn, away from wherever his wife had retired to.

We walked in the crisp October after bar morning air.

To where?

The alcohol buzz had my thoughts swirling and flushed; my cheeks several shades deeper than usual. My mind was a tornado of one-way conversation with myself as we walked on silently through the horse trailer laden parking area, apart yet together. In our stupor, we brushed against each other haphazardly.

In the dim light, I lost my balance. My body was an uncoordinated tangle of limbs. I swung to the right. Embarrassed by my sloppiness, I reached out toward McKennon, but he wobbled to the left. I heard him laugh to himself.

One foot in front of the other! Come on, Devon.

On the next round of imbalance, we collided. We both laughed out loud. Finally, he broke the heaviness in the air.

"I guess we did some celebratin', didn't we, Devon?"

"I think so," I managed. I was nodding my head a little more than necessary, and my mind told me that I should stop. My body responded what felt like minutes later.

"I am glad you came to my barn," he said, appraising me warmly, matching my slower stride.

"I am too," I said shyly, appreciating that he had tempered his long-legged gait.

"I must be nuts," McKennon muttered out loud, but it sounded like it was meant for only him. He shifted his cowboy hat on his head.

"What?" I said, stopping and facing him abruptly. McKennon stood stone cold, facing forward, not acknowledging me. "Nuts about what?" I asked again.

Without warning, McKennon turned and faced me. Taken aback, I felt like I could collapse at any moment under his intense gaze. I reached behind me to stabilize myself. I felt the cool aluminum rim of a horse trailer's wheel well. Before I could start sounding words, he had his hands on my hips and lifted me up above the tires. He sat me down gently on the lip of the wheel well. My heart was beating through my chest. I felt dizzy.

Speechless, we just looked into each other's eyes, his vast like oceans. We were quiet for some time. Then he started to move toward me, closing the gap between our mouths.

God, I wanted this so badly.

I bit my lip, assembling the strength to protest.

"Why don't we get our horse, err, my horse that we've been working on so hard to a big show like this before we go doing something that could separate us?" I blurted out. I brought Faith and my dreams back to the foreground

Remember the horse, the glue, the wall, the conduit.

"Please just let me kiss you, Devon," he moaned.

"I can't."

"Please, I've been dying to since we first met that day on the hill. I wasn't sure how to feel about that inclination at the time, but then I got to know you, and I just knew that my instinct was right. You know?"

"Really?" I breathed.

McKennon was so beautiful. It almost hurt to look at him. His revelation made my toes curl inside my cowgirl boots, and my heart started beating off its chain in my chest. And then, like an alien had inhabited my body, in my warped sense of being, I heard myself cave.

I could always blame it on the alcohol.

"OK, but you have to promise to talk to me tomorrow like nothing happened. Like this was just a catch in time because we drank too much. Like nothing happened, McKennon! Do you hear? Promise me that no one will ever know. Not ever!"

"I promise," he whispered softly next to my ear. There was a hint of confusion hinged in his response as he continued, "What do you want me to be for you, Devon?"

"Nothing. I like you as you are. Please just be you. But don't tell her."

McKennon's hand fell from my shoulder and slipped down my arm, leaving hot blazes across my skin where his touch had been. Blue eyes smoldering intensely, he cupped my elbow.

"Devon ... my wife ... she –," his voice cracked.

He paused to catch his breath and put his hands on his hips. Pressing his lips together in a fine line, McKennon looked up and addressed the starry sky.

"My wife," he continued, putting his left hand over his heart. "She died two years ago, and I've been at a real loss ever since." He sighed dropping his head, chin to chest. "It was always our dream to find the one that could win at the Congress."

It was starting to make sense now. The tornado in my mind stirred again, whipping up windy thoughts of McKennon's constant melancholy, JD's words of warning, the ghostly presence lingering at Green Briar, Sophia's request to mind my p's and q's, and his gift ... the boots.

Goodness! The boots! Had I really been wearing his deceased wife's designer boots?

"I ... I don't know what to say," I gasped, feeling nauseous.

Buckling from the wheel well, I found myself on my knees. This was too much to process ... this combination of too much cocktail, mixed with too much information, and a new wave of emotion. I was overwhelmed, that much I knew. McKennon dropped beside me on his knees too. He touched my thigh. "Who ... who ... was that woman back there then? The one who was with you tonight?" I asked, recalling the pretty fairy.

"Just another trainer. A friend is all. Known each other for a long time. She was friends with my wife," he said, twisting himself beneath me so he could see my face. "Hey, I thought you knew about my wife and all that. Was sure Sophia would've told you about all of this before you headed for the show. I told her it was all right to tell you."

The look of shock I felt sprawl across my face was enough to tell him that no, I hadn't known all that. I pursed my lips to speak, to ask what had happened, how it happened, but McKennon shook his head and put a finger to his lips.

"Shhh. Not now ... another time ..."

Then McKennon, my cowboy god, leaned into me with a force I'd never known. It was all passion, lust and desire. I felt an animalistic fire rise up in me. His face was so close, so real, so the essence of what I thought a man should be.

All I could do was look at him, caught in his beautiful gaze. It was finally a gaze for me. Finally, I knew, like I never knew before, that this dance had been real. It wasn't a figment of my imagination after all.

"I think I am psychic, you know?" he said, leaning in closer. "That'd make some people laugh, but I know it's true. Just like I knew it with my wife, and now I know it with you." He reached up with both hands, gloveless, and placed his warm palms on either side of my face. Cupping my cheeks, I saw the longing in his mystical blue eyes, a happiness reflected there.

"It's been so long since I've touched a woman," McKennon groaned near my ear, breath hot on my neck as he ran his fingers through my hair.

I let him take me, and he softly tasted my lower lip.

"Mmmm ..." he hummed.

I don't know if I am ready for this!

I dipped away from his mouth and collapsed in the span of his warm arms. My head was spinning. I was a confused, nervous, drunk cowgirl. Losing myself in his embrace, I distracted myself with the way he smelled. I throbbed from head to toe.

McKennon eased his fingertips beneath my chin and lifted my flushed face to him. I felt like a deer in headlights. I was overwhelmed with his beauty. Unable to resist any longer, we met in the middle, both lunging toward the other, leaning in. He kissed me slow. I returned his kiss eagerly, twisting my fingers in the hair at the base of his neck. His stubble scrapped my hot cheeks, but I didn't care. Moving my hands over his body, my nails dug into his muscle-rippled back just a little too hard, but he didn't seem to care.

As he took my lower lip between his and sucked gently, I reached up, and removed his cowboy hat so I could run my fingers through his thick, dark mane of hair. I wanted to possess every inch of McKennon, touch every strand on his lovely head. I felt like a beast, wild, crazed, consumed by desire. McKennon pulled away and looked me in the eye with his blue lances. I let my arms drop on his shoulders.

"You taste even sweeter than I thought you would, Devon," he said through his smile.

I licked my pulsating lips. I could taste the liquor on his breath. It was sweet and kind of salty. McKennon moved in again. This time he kissed me with such savage passion that I felt like the world around us might erupt. He took my bottom lip into his teeth, lifted me from my knees, and pressed my back against the cool aluminum of the trailer so I could feel all of him. McKennon didn't even need to be inside of me to make this feel complete. Kissing me hard and then soft again, he moved his hand up my leg and grazed his fingertips gently over my jeans.

He almost touched me there!

I moaned into his open mouth, receiving his tongue, as his bare hand slid over my belt loops and across my stomach. He paused for a moment over my belly button, kissing my earlobe then nibbling my neck. Quivering at his touch, I could see him watching me out of the corner of his eye, pleasured.

"Is this OK?" he murmured softly against my neck

"Don't stop," I whimpered. "Please ..."

I sucked in breath as he moved his warm hand further up my ribs just beneath my bra. His touch was hungry, urgent, but at the same time gentle, polite, respectful. Different. McKennon extended his other arm across my bare lower back clutching me to him, his mouth fully on mine. I could feel his big, silver belt buckle cool on my tummy. And, something even more substantial, solid, pressing against me beneath it. I couldn't help but smile and press my lips together as those all too familiar butterflies took flight, swooping straight down ... *there* ...

"Devon," he whispered.

I could only purr and pant in return as his palm glided over my bra and cupped my breast. My heart pumped wildly beneath his hand, and my breathing grew even more ragged. My blood molten, hot lava in my veins.

"Pinch me," I gasped, breaking from his mouth.

"Why?" he asked into my hair.

"Because … I think I might be dreaming."

"Better pinch me too then, cowgirl," he responded into the crook of my neck.

I pressed my thighs together as McKennon pinched my rear.

I couldn't believe this cowboy Adonis thought he might be dreaming too … because of me … because of my kiss, my lips. I felt curious about what was next. I was nervous to do more. I was afraid I might do, say, be the wrong thing and scare him away.

But then, McKennon pulled me even closer, and my nerves evaporated. I'd never felt this way. Adored. Lusted after. Appreciated. I could feel the want in his kiss … the healing that might be occurring there.

Stop thinking, Devon. Enjoy this! It's real.

So I let go of the reins and pulled McKennon to me.

I knew now that life is not in holding back. It just isn't in the reins.

MCKENNON EPILOGUE

Devon didn't know that I had worked it all out with Sophia. I wanted her to arrive after I'd shown Star so she could be there to support me whether we had won or not. I remember how it felt. I felt warm and happy for the first time in such a long while when I told Sophia that I realized I needed Devon to be there no matter what happened.

But, that was then …

Now I just sit here idle, been this way for a while, rearview mirror adjusted, so I can watch her go round and round in the pen on that painted pony. I know she knows I am watching her.

Boy, had they gotten good! Because of me, they got good because of me. Devon and Faith reminded me that I still had something left to give, a will to train again.

Looking away from Devon's image spinning in the mirror's reflection, I splay my gloved hand out in front of me. I rest it on the steering wheel while my truck vibrates and chugs diesel beneath me. Slowly, I ease off my soft lambskin glove, one finger at a time. And I just stare at it, that left hand golden band. It still means everything to me, but now it also means nothing.

I glance up again to make sure she is still going around and around. I wiggle the wedding ring off my finger and expose a calloused white ridge where it had always been. Running my thumb over the raised groove it left on my skin, I hesitate at my ring finger's tip. I feel my pulse accelerate as I think about its loss, at no longer having it be a part of me.

The past and future hover together and collide in this single decision. I turn the ring over and over in the palm of my hand, rub the calloused ridge with my thumb again, and with a sigh, force the ring back to its rightful place. I just can't take it off.

Lifting my hat, I run my fingers through my hair and shake my head. I see JD saunter up to Devon in the rearview. He takes the place at the rail that I should be occupying right now.

JD tosses his arms across the top railing and rests his head on them. Disgust, jealousy, indecision, and questions of loyalty blaze through my veins. Too many emotions are blinding me, confusing me. I have to get out of here.

Ramming the truck into drive, I jam my boot to the gas pedal and speed off, kicking gravel up behind me. I know I am making a scene. I flee down Green Briar's drive, heading for the easy choice. I realize I am taking the easy exit. When the going actually got going or tough, I always got going myself.

Squeezing the steering wheel, my knuckles white, I look up and see the beautiful pair minimizing. Devon and Faith are no longer in harmonious motion, now they are merely a stopped speck, watching me go again. I feel sick. I know that JD is telling Devon, "I told you so," and reaffirming to her that I am broken, that I won't ever get over it. Maybe I am ... and maybe I won't.

My heart races when I think about being with Devon, but at the same time, my heart is broken being without a different "her."

I am to blame. I pushed that damn animal too hard. It was all spurs, battles and pinned ears with the horse because of my wanting to win so bad. I rushed it all. I had forgotten my roots, everything I'd learned. How could I have put her on top? I risked and lost everything with that decision.

My eyes begin to blur, hot tears building, ready for rupture, under the excruciating memory of her pinned under that damn horse, JD shrieking for an ambulance, those last words ...

"Ken, I love you."

Ken. She was the only one who ever called me Ken.

PLEASE ENJOY A SEQUEL PREVIEW:

MCKENNON AND DEVON'S STORY CONTINUES

CHAPTER ONE

I've been living my life like I've been shot out of a gun since she died. What is the point? Being on my own is the only thing that's made sense since she's been gone. But when Devon showed up on the farm, I realized that I was still breathing, still lusting for something. I felt blood, warm, in my veins again.

Yeah ... cool, composed McKennon – that's how I was supposed to be. That's who I was for them. I always left Green Briar when I felt a bender coming on – our wedding anniversary, the anniversary of her death, all the moments in between. It could be anything. Something small, a single memory, would set me off, and I was no longer a man in control.

I didn't want anyone to see me like that, not Sophia, certainly not Devon. JD was the only one I'd call if I got really bad – a fist-fight, an unpaid tab, waking up not knowing where I was. He was her brother after all. We were family. Family is all you can count on in times like those.

The whiskey bottle tumbled out of my grip, startling me awake. I was alone on top of some crude, red velour bedspread, all velvety and crusty, in this dive hotel room.

Hazy, I watched the ceiling fan rotate slowly above me and thought about the kiss with Devon. Devon was the real deal. I didn't think a man could find two of those in a lifetime. I liked how I would walk into the barn, see Devon, and the dynamic would immediately change. Was it curiosity, energy, a common spirit, her innocence, or the newness that began our relationship?

My heart pounds as I recounted my fingers tangled in her auburn hair, her breath sweet, and her lips hungry. All of that pent up want surging between us finally let loose after months and all at once. I tossed my arm over my eyes, headache blazing fire in my mind. Devon's warm, big, and beautiful doe eyes fade. I saw my wife again. She's pinned under that damn animal.

I need help. I know that. I am stuck, and I can't move forward. JD is mad at me for thinking of moving on with Devon. The boots may have been a mistake, but it's been years now.

I should be able to move on. Shouldn't I?

The problem is I can't.

ABOUT THE AUTHOR

Carly Kade is an Arizona-based author and enjoys competitively showing her registered Paint Horse. In her free time, Carly works on her next novel, reads voraciously, spends time with her husband and two adopted dogs, and loves exploring the great outdoors.

Feeling Social? Join the herd and connect with Carly Kade Creative on Facebook, Instagram, YouTube or Twitter.

Can't wait to find out what happens next for McKennon and Devon? Visit Carly's blog at carlykadecreative.com for sequel sneak peeks, updates, and release info.

Reviews are golden! If you enjoyed this book, please leave a review on Amazon or Goodreads. Your readership and support is greatly appreciated!

ACKNOWLEDGEMENTS

In the Reins is dedicated to all the horses and humans, past and present, who joined my journey as I learned to ride.

To the sport of horse(wo)manship. When I am riding, I am the best me, the peaceful me, and free. The barn is my true happy place.

To my husband, my cowboy, my first editor, my business partner, my one and only, without your endless faith in my writing, this book would never have been finished. You kept me going when I was stopped.

To Gpa for relentlessly driving me to my riding lessons, strapping me into my helmet, and teaching me to draw horses.

To my parents for taking the leap and gifting me that purple halter (and so much more) on my 10th birthday.

To my first horse, Missy, never a day lame and the best life coach a young woman could ever ask for.

To my current horse, Sissy, you are the one I have always dreamed of owning.

To my editor, Ann, you made this book better and became an irreplaceable friend in the process. Thank you.

Made in the USA
San Bernardino, CA
13 July 2016